A WOMAN'S PLACE

A WOMAN'S PLACE

Linda Grant

CHARLES SCRIBNER'S SONS
NEW YORK

Maxwell Macmillan Canada
Toronto

Maxwell Macmillan International
New York Oxford Singapore Sydney

Charles Scribner's Sons
Macmillan Publishing Company
866 Third Avenue
New York, NY 10022

Maxwell Macmillan Canada, Inc.
1200 Eglinton Avenue East
Suite 200
Don Mills, Ontario M3C 3N1

Macmillan Publishing Company is part of the Maxwell Communication Group of Companies.

Library of Congress Cataloging-in-Publication Data
Grant, Linda, 1942–
A woman's place : a Catherine Sayler mystery/Linda Grant.
p.   cm.
ISBN 0-684-19631-X
1. Sayler, Catherine (Fictitious character)—Fiction.   2. Sexual harass-ment of women—California—San Francisco—Fiction.   3. Private investi-gators—California—San Francisco—Fiction.   4. Women detectives—California—San Francisco—Fiction.   5. San Francisco (Calif.)—Fiction.   I. Title.
PS3573.I44975W66   1994
813'.54—dc20   93-39191
CIP

Macmillan books are available at special discounts for bulk purchases for sales promotions, premiums, fund-raising, or educational use. For details, contact:

Special Sales Director
Macmillan Publishing Company
866 Third Avenue
New York, NY 10022

10   9   8   7   6   5   4   3   2   1

Printed in the United States of America

To Susan Dunlap
As fine a friend as she is a writer

Acknowledgments

My thanks to the many women who shared their stories of sexual harassment and intimidation with me. Many of the incidents in this book are drawn from their experiences.

I also want to thank Michael Young, whose feral imagination once again helped birth a book; Michael J. Prodan of the California Department of Justice, who educated me about criminal profiling; and Elizabeth Lynn, Sensei, Eastshore Aikikai.

I am indebted to the following people for generously sharing their expertise: Alison Luzar of Integral, Dr. James Breivis of Kaiser-Permanente San Francisco Medical Center, Anthony Chavez of Mechanics Bank, Inspector Earl Sanders of the San Francisco Police Department, Gary Fenstermacher of Mach One Alarm, Gerald Hatley of Comdisco, Virginia Meyer of DHL Systems Inc., and Maureen O'Boyle, Edie Heillman, Susan Miller, Karen Klimas, Eileen Easterbrook, and Jane Evans for background on corporate culture in general and the computer industry in particular.

Finally, I want to thank Susan Dunlap, Marilyn Wallace, Barbara Dean, Anne Jensen, and Andrew Williams for their sensitive and perceptive comments on the manuscript, and Erin and Megan for keeping Molly on track. With all this help, any errors that remain are strictly my own.

A WOMAN'S PLACE

Prologue

I don't dwell on the past. No point in that.

But I still can't stay in the same room with a man wearing Paco cologne. And there are times when a ringing phone makes my heart race. I read the newspapers, but I skip certain stories.

The nightmares come less often.

Chapter

1

"You'll love this case," Jesse said. "It's so perfect we ought to pay them to let us do it."

His dark eyes danced, and his grin—broad and wicked—should have warned me off. Instead, I said, "Tell me about it." My mistake.

"Sexual harassment," he said. "They want to hire us to catch a guy who's harassing women."

"Lots of guys harass women," I said. "Some of them are on our client list." Normally, I'd have jumped at the case. Normally, I wasn't planning to spend two weeks in Mexico.

"Right. That's why you ought to love this. How many times have you complained about some jerk putting the move on you? Or had to smile when you wanted to smack some guy? Well, this time you get to do it."

"I'm going to Mexico next week," I said. "And, why are you so anxious to take this particular case? What's in it for you?"

"The harasser is a hacker," Jesse said. "He's done some interesting stuff. I'd like to go after him."

Two fantasies for the price of one. I got to smack around a chauvinist and Jesse got to play hide-and-seek in someone else's computer. "A hacker's duel," I said. "Just like the old West."

Jesse has a theory that the computer revolution created a new frontier. He likes to compare today's entrepreneurs, software geniuses, and venture capitalists to the gamblers, gunslingers, and prospectors of long ago.

I'm less than enthusiastic about this metaphor. When you're in the corporate security business and your clients include high-tech companies, it's unnerving to realize that your partner thinks he's working at the OK Corral. "And just who are you—Wyatt Earp or Doc Holliday?" I asked.

"Just Wyatt Earp's trusty sidekick," he said in a phony accent with a mocking grin.

I tried to imagine Wyatt Earp in high heels with a black sidekick carrying a laptop and a six-gun and couldn't suppress my laughter. Jesse joined me.

"So you're telling me our client is who? Jesse James?"

"Our client is the mayor of an honest, hard-working community that has just acquired a band of roving gamblers and is trying to teach them to sing in the church choir," he said. He could tell by my expression that he'd pressed his metaphor too far. "Actually, the company is Systech Financial Applications, headquartered here in San Francisco. They deal in banking applications software. Clients are small to medium banks, and the software covers most of what a bank needs to operate—accounting, checking, savings, lending, ATMs. They've got programs for everything from minicomputers through mainframes."

"Another software company," I said. Jesse loved anything connected with computers, and since I'd made him my partner last January, our client list had become increasingly high-tech. A better person would have been pleased and grateful. I wasn't. It's not that I'm intimidated by technology; it's just that Jesse is always several steps ahead of me in that area, and I hate playing catch up, even with my own partner.

Jesse tilted his head and raised an eyebrow, his "So?" look.

Before I could say anything, an ambulance came tearing down the street, siren screaming. We both paused to let it go by. This only happens about twenty times a day. It's the down side of being several blocks from a major hospital. I don't know if there is an up side. To the hospital, I mean.

But the neighborhood has advantages that more than compensate for its proximity to Mount Zion Hospital. The first is the gracious Victorian that houses my offices. High ceilings, tall windows, lots of light, and nice neighbors. You don't get a view of the Golden Gate on this side of the hill, but the rent's cheaper, and my office is only a few blocks from my flat so I can walk to work. That's the second big advantage. The third is the array of ethnic eateries just down the hill. In San Francisco, war and famine abroad mean a new cuisine down the block.

The ethnic eateries were calling me. I put them on hold and turned my attention back to Jesse. "And who's the band of roving gamblers?"

"KeeGo, a start-up out of Texas. Well, they were a bit beyond a start-up, but not a lot. Anyway, KeeGo makes client-server software."

"How about you do this in standard English," I said. I was with him so far, but it's easy for Jesse to get carried away and slip into technobabble.

"Okay. Take your standard mid-sized bank. They've got a whole slew of personal computers sitting on desks and back at the central office they have a big mainframe that does the heavy lifting. Or maybe they have a mid-sized computer and they're thinking of moving up to a mainframe. KeeGo comes along and says, 'Wait a minute. You've got a hundred-fifty PCs; put them all together and you get more computing power than a mainframe at a fraction of the cost. We can sell you the software to hook those babies up through local and wide area networks and get them to do all the stuff a mainframe does.'"

"Pretty appealing," I said.

"It's the direction the industry is going," Jesse said. "Systech could read the writing on the wall. They wanted in. Buying KeeGo gives them that. Allen Leggett, the president and CEO of Systech, figures it puts them at least a year ahead of the competition."

A year isn't much time in most fields, but in the computer industry where things change every week, being a year ahead is a big jump. "And where does the harassment come in?" I asked.

"Well, whenever one company absorbs another, there are strains. Some folks move up, some down. Systech and KeeGo are very different companies. Systech people work with banks; they've got a reputation to protect, so they're fairly conservative. KeeGo's younger, flashier, heavily male. It's not an easy fit."

"That's not harassment," I said.

"No, but let's just say that the standards of behavior at the companies were somewhat different," Jesse said. "A number of the KeeGo guys aren't real popular with the Systech women. Human resources has been dealing with that. But about a week ago, pinups appeared on the bulletin board and a number of women got raunchy messages on their electronic mail. Yesterday, someone put epoxy in the women's room door."

"Jeez," I said, "software companies don't exactly conform to the business practices of banks and law firms, but that's a bit much even for them. Why not just fire a couple of guys?"

"They've got to catch them first," Jesse said. "And they'd like to avoid firing any key people, if you know what I mean."

I knew exactly what he meant. Systech had bought KeeGo to get its product, but what the company really wanted wasn't printed in the manual. It was inside the new employees' heads—their knowledge, experience, everything they'd learned as they created and marketed the software. And the KeeGo guys knew that, which was why they figured they could be as outrageous as they wished.

"So what do they want from us?" I asked.

"To catch one guy—and it has to be a salesman, not a programmer—so they can make an example of him and put the fear of God in the rest of them.

"Leggett wants to get on this fast, and he wants us to do it. He called yesterday and I told him you were in Denver, but he wanted to see me anyway. He's hoping to meet with you today."

I considered the situation. Jesse played his ace.

"Anxious as he is, he'll pay real well," he said. "Enough so you and Peter could go to Mexico at Christmas and take Molly with you."

He had me. My lover, Peter, and I had planned our escape to Mexico six months ago, before my fourteen-year-old niece decided to run away from home, come to San Francisco, and move in with us. Now we were hostage to school schedules, and a vacation in October required so much work that it had lost much of its appeal.

I don't know a lot about this parenting business—okay, I don't know anything about it—but it seemed to me that the kid could use some stability about now, and even though my secretary, Amy, had agreed to move into my flat and serve as stand-in parent, I'd had a lot of second thoughts about this vacation.

If I put the vacation off, I could stop worrying, at least about that. And I could stay here and get paid to do a job I'd enjoy immensely. It isn't often in life that someone pays you to act out your fantasies. After years of pretending to ignore insulting moves by jerks with more power than brains, hassling the harassers could be fun.

I'm an investigator, specializing in corporate work. That means everything from playing the "dumb blond" secretary to pouring over ledgers. I keep an eye on employees who are too

poring

chummy with the competition, figure out where the money
went when a company comes up short, and dig up information
that clients, prospective employees, and other executives would
prefer not to divulge.

Because I'm a woman in a man's field, I have to put up with
a certain amount of poor behavior. But I'm my own boss, so I
don't put up with a whole lot. Like most women my age, I have
some scars. Which was why this job appealed to me so much.
And why I shouldn't have been so quick to take it. Scar tissue
can dim the vision.

Chapter

2

It's hard to carry on a conversation with a man who's staring at your breasts. Harder when there are three—men, not breasts.

I resisted the temptation to check my blouse for a broken button or large catsup stain. This was round two at the OK Corral, and I wasn't about to blink.

I'd taken round one the day before when a big guy with a Texas accent had patted me on the behind. I'd reached over and returned the compliment, commenting, "Not bad. A little time at the gym would tone that right up." Everyone had laughed, but not everyone thought it was funny.

Now, a muffled snicker behind me revealed that we had an audience. Ten-thirty was prime time at the coffee machine. I made an elaborate show of looking down at my shirt, then back up and announced in a loud voice, "Those are breasts, gentlemen. Women have them. Hadn't you noticed?"

A giggle and a louder guffaw from the wings. Three pairs of eyes jumped up to meet mine. Patches of red dotted the cheeks below them, then each of the faces composed itself into a nasty frown.

"Ms. Wainwright would like the supplemental survey sheets from everyone in the minicomputer division by five o'clock," I said pleasantly. The tallest of the three, Tex, lowered his eyebrows so far I wasn't sure he could see, and the guy next to him went all squinty and looked like an angry terrier.

I turned to go, then looked back, "Oh, and keep working on that eye contact. You'll get it down yet."

As I walked away grins and glowers identified the factions in the office as clearly as if they'd been wearing team uniforms. The women in the room, and about half the guys, were smiling; the rest looked as if they'd happily strangle me.

As Jesse had promised, I was enjoying this case. And his analogy to the OK Corral wasn't so wide of the mark. The KeeGo guys conducted themselves with an arrogance reminiscent of cowboys in town at the end of a long cattle drive. I couldn't figure out why they'd risk getting fired until I realized that they must believe that they were simply too valuable to be canned.

To a large extent they were right. Systech had paid plenty for KeeGo and was committed to making the client-server product line its big producer. While to the user, the client-server system would appear much simpler than the mainframe it replaced, there was nothing simple about the software that connected all those PCs together and made it possible to route and retrieve information. Systech wasn't about to let go of its KeeGo brain power.

But the salesmen who thought they were indispensable had miscalculated. If they were hostile to women, I'd give them a woman they could really hate. I'd be in their faces at every opportunity until one of them made the stupid mistake that got him fired.

I had been introduced as a telecommunications consultant redesigning the voice-mail system that routed and recorded telephone messages, you know, "Press one if you want X, press two if you want Y, press twenty-seven if you want to throttle the attendant." My cover gave me an excuse to interview every member of the company about their voice-mail needs. It was a chance to watch the way they reacted to me, to push a bit here and there and to see who pushed back.

The questions were all standard—How many calls do you make in a week? How many messages do you get? What kind of messages would you like to leave for callers?—that sort of stuff. But the way I asked those questions, and how I responded to the answers, depended on my sense of the interviewee. I could do that interview all the way from anxious-to-please subservience to hostile challenge.

I'd only interviewed a few Systech guys so far, and they were all pleasant and professional. Their counterparts from KeeGo were a less polished bunch. Most of them treated voice mail as a remnant of the dark ages and me as just a step above village idiot. Two of them had actually called me "darlin'" or "honey." Systech's human resources office had its work cut out for it.

I was on my way out of the lounge when a tall blond woman with a broad smile gave me the thumbs-up sign and beckoned me to join her across the room. Sheila Wainwright, Systech's first and only woman regional manager, made no effort to hide her enjoyment of the scene I'd just played out.

Sheila was built like an athlete, thin but solid, with a longish face dominated by intelligent gray eyes. Today she wore a deep blue dress accented with a red belt and scarf. More interesting than pretty, she was the kind of woman you wouldn't notice in a crowd but couldn't miss in a smaller gathering.

"Have you heard the one about the firm that was looking for a new director of marketing?" I shook my head. "They had three candidates, all women. One woman had an M.B.A. from Stanford and ten years' experience, the second had an M.B.A. from Wharton and was the youngest vice-president at Proctor and Gamble, and the third had a Ph.D. from Harvard. Do you know which one they picked?" She paused for effect. "The one with the big boobs, of course."

We both laughed, and several heads turned our way. Sheila ignored them the way an actor ignores the audience. "It's funny how the guys who love to dish it out just can't stand to be on the other end," she said.

I laughed and nodded, as aware of our audience as she. The smell of smoldering egos lay heavy on the air.

The men had abundant reason to resent Sheila. Just three weeks ago she had been promoted to regional manager of the minicomputer sales division. Since that division would handle the new client-server products, it provided the straightest shot at a spot in national for an ambitious manager. The KeeGo guys were furious because they'd assumed the job would go to one of them. And the Systech salespeople were certainly not immune to jealousy. It was hard to say who resented Sheila the most—her former colleagues or the KeeGo boys.

Having won round two, I beat a strategic retreat to my temporary office. I wasn't in a big hurry to find out what was on tap for round three.

I'd been on the job less than a week and I was still getting a feel for the players. I liked Allen Leggett, Systech's CEO and our new client. He was a low-key, serious guy who looked more like a college professor than an executive. He'd founded Systech and designed its first program, an accounting package. The company was his baby.

Leggett seemed genuinely distressed that women were being harassed, and not just because it could cause him legal trouble. He talked about "our people" as if they were family, and he seemed to mean it. Yet, I felt that the connection was more abstract than emotional. He was a shy man, probably more at ease with things and ideas than with people.

He'd provided me with an organization chart and company roster, and I'd spent the last few days studying them and putting names to faces. I like this part of an investigation for the same reason that as a kid I loved jigsaw puzzles. At the very beginning, before you've figured out the pattern, each piece is its own little world. Then slowly, you see how those worlds fit together and patterns begin to emerge.

Now the pieces are people and bits of information. I enjoy these first meetings when I know nothing about them, and I love the moment when I sense the pattern.

The only pattern I had so far was the one on the organizational chart. Systech's sales, marketing, and development divisions were divided into three areas to match the three types of computers their products served, and status and salary reflected a clear hierarchy. At the top were the divisions dealing with the mainframe applications, designed for the biggest, most complex computers. Next came the applications for midrange computers, and at the bottom were those for minicomputers and the LANs and WANs, local or wide-area networks, that linked them together.

But that corporate hierarchy was in the process of being turned on its head. With the decision to acquire KeeGo and commit to software for client-server systems, Systech had shifted power from the mainframe to the minicomputer division. The big bucks, and the excitement of being out in front, now belonged to a division that not so long ago had been at the bottom of the heap. It must be very sweet for Sheila and her minicomputer colleagues.

As I was going over notes I'd taken the day before, there was a knock at my door, and a voice I recognized as Jesse's said, "Ms. Sayler, tech support."

"Come in," I called.

Jesse was wearing a green-and-navy rugby shirt, jeans, and running shoes. Tall and lanky, he looked to be in his early twenties, though he'd turned thirty last month.

He'd started at Systech a week ago. I'd followed a few days later. He was working as one of the guys charged with the care and feeding of the internal computer network. A good place to catch the prankster when he left messages on electronic mail. Also a good place to pick up gossip. Techies are virtually invisible, often being regarded as an extension of the machines that they service. Jesse maintains that being black and a techie is the next best thing to being a fly on the wall.

"You must be the lady with the breasts," he said as he sat down opposite me.

"Watch your mouth," I warned.

"You better watch your back. One guy made a joke about burning bitches at the stake, and the rest pulled out their matches. You sure do have a way with the opposite sex."

"Jeez, some guys just can't take a joke," I said. "I hope you're enjoying this as much as I am."

"*No one* is enjoying this as much as you are," Jesse said with a grin. "But I'm having a good time. I'm still learning my way around the system. Be easier if their internal programs were standard, but lots of stuff they made up as they went along."

"Like what?"

"Mostly the systems programs. Some stuff they wrote themselves, some they bought. Lots of it has been put together to meet needs as the company grew. So instead of a set of coordinated programs, you have dozens of little programs that interact with other little programs. No manuals or documentation for lots of stuff, just notes from one guy to another. All those little programs can mean lots of unlocked doors. That's the problem."

"Have you figured out where the E-mail messages came from?"

He shook his head. "How. Not where. Someone changed the log-in program last week to capture the employee passwords, then a couple of days later he changed it back. The security manager missed it. I'd never have caught it if I hadn't checked the backups. Until we change the passwords, he can sign on as anyone he wants."

If our prankster could change the log-in program, he'd figured out how to get super-user privileges. That meant he could play god with the computer. With super-user privileges, the prankster could read anyone's files and make changes to those files or even to the system itself. Only someone with a lot of programming experience could have done that. Either one of the salesmen had skills we didn't know about or one of the programmers was involved.

"You going to suggest they change the passwords?"

"Yeah, I told Jenkins, the security manager, about it. He's issuing a directive telling everyone to choose new passwords."

"You don't think it'll make the prankster more cautious?" I asked.

"No," Jesse shook his head. "He's got to expect it. Even if we didn't know how he'd done it, the E-mail messages prove there's unauthorized use of the system. Once the passwords are changed, he's got to come back in again. That's when I get a chance to catch him." I could see Jesse enjoyed the prospect of the hunt as much as I was enjoying bugging the office chauvinists.

"So, heard any useful gossip?" I asked as he got up to leave.

"Useful, no. Colorful, yes. Mostly about you, and none you'd want to hear."

Chapter

3

Is your enemy's enemy your friend? It seemed that way for the women at Systech. They adopted me with enthusiasm, forgave me for asking a million questions and watched my antics with relish.

Just before noon a dark-haired woman in a tan-and-green print dress stepped into my office. "We're going to lunch. Would you like to join us?" It was Elaine Burskin, the only saleswoman in mainframe accounts, and now that Sheila Wainwright had been promoted, the second-highest-ranking woman in the sales division.

"Or did you bring your lunch?" she asked. Bring lunch? Not likely. Not since Molly moved in and began a systematic assault on my refrigerator. Everything but vegetables seems to leap straight from the grocery bag into her stomach. This morning's trip to the larder had yielded eight moldy heels of bread, a mushy banana, and not much else. Definitely not lunch.

"I'd love to join you," I said.

"Do you know Tonia Decena from downstairs?" Elaine asked as we walked to the elevator. She moved with considerable grace for someone wearing spike heels just short of stilts. Damned good thing, one misstep and she'd break an ankle.

"I don't think so."

"She works in development. She's one of our best programmers."

"Did she come over from KeeGo?" I asked.

"God no. I don't think they had women at KeeGo. No, Tonia's been here for a couple of years."

Development was the division that created, maintained, and constantly tinkered with the programs that were Systech's life blood. It was located on the second floor of the three-story converted warehouse that housed Systech. The ground floor was devoted to production, shipping and receiving and the third floor to corporate and western regional offices.

Management had spent plenty to convert the third floor of the brick warehouse into offices. The company had thrown up walls to create private office space, installed ceilings, and covered the rough plank floors with carpeting. Only the older brick walls with their tall windows bore witness to the building's previous incarnation. Those and the elevator. It grumbled like an ad for Alka Seltzer.

In the lobby we met a young woman who reminded me for a moment of my niece, Molly—same slight build, almost-olive skin, and short, curly black hair. Even the same mischievous grin, but with a few years to take a bit of the attitude out of it. She wore a navy cotton skirt with a light blue blouse and low-heeled sandals, giving her a more casual look than the women upstairs.

Elaine introduced us. Tonia had a firm, confident handshake. She said, "I've heard a lot about you, Catherine. The story of you patting Bob Kingsley's butt was a big hit on the second floor. Of course," she added in a lower voice, "they'd go ballistic if you did it to one of them."

We stepped out the front door and were momentarily blinded by the sunlight. It was not only bright but hot, a relatively rare event in San Francisco. All that sunny-California hype refers to Southern California, where the weather, like the inhabitants, tends to manic excess. San Francisco is another story.

July and August are cold here, as many an unwary tourist has learned. The heat in the central valley draws the fog through the Golden Gate, blanketing the city in chilly damp-ness morning and night. In September the valley cools, the fog withdraws beyond the Gate, and summer arrives at last. But this kind of heat in October was unusual.

"Mama's Café?" Elaine asked, squinting in the bright light. We all nodded and set off down the street.

Systech's offices were on Townsend Street, not far from the old train station. The wide street was almost deserted, lined on one side by the high fence that ran along the railroad tracks and on the other by warehouses that provided only a skinny line of shade at this time of day. I savored the dry warmth of the sun on my skin.

"Isn't it great?" Tonia said exuberantly. "I want to go to the beach."

"Ah, but not the beach here, the beach in Mexico," I said.

"Or Hawaii," Elaine suggested.

We all laughed, feeling a little tipsy on sunshine.

"So how is development?" I asked Tonia as we walked.

"Terrific. I love it," she said. "'Course you have to be into computers. And crazy people. We techie's are a weird breed."

"Are there many other women in development?"

"Oh yeah. Actually, it's a pretty good place for a woman. None of the games that go on upstairs. I mean, programmers are judged on what they do. The program works or it doesn't. Not like sales or marketing, where past performance doesn't count and if you make the wrong enemies it can screw up your career."

"You're lucky to be downstairs," Elaine said. "It's been a zoo since they brought the KeeGo guys in. It's bad enough just having to put up with them, then they pull these stupid practical jokes."

"What's with the jokes?" I asked. "I've never seen anything like it."

"They're pissed because Sheila was put in charge of the minicomputer sales. These guys think they're such hot shit, it really galls them to have to work for a woman, especially Sheila."

So Sheila's promotion was the event that precipitated the pranks. Allen Leggett, Systech's CEO, hadn't suggested a connection, but the timing fit. The first prank was only days after her promotion was announced.

"I still don't get the jokes," I said. "It's more like being back in high school than in a business."

"You haven't worked in a start-up company," Elaine said. "They have the corporate mentality of a fifteen-year-old boy—or a thirteen-year-old girl." Tonia laughed and Elaine explained, "I have a teenage daughter. I know whereof I speak.

"Anyway, start-ups are corporate teenagers. They know it *all*. They are cooler and smarter than anyone, and no one can tell them anything. They're pulling these tricks to let us know that just because they've joined the company doesn't mean they're going to play by the rules."

"So you figure the KeeGo guys are behind the pranks," I said. "Any idea which one?"

"John DeMarco or Bob Kingsley, maybe both of them. That'd be my guess," Elaine replied.

Mine too, though I wasn't exactly sure why. "What makes you pick them?" I asked.

"I don't know," Elaine said. "Nothing specific, really. It's just their attitude. Neither one of them thinks a woman's good for anything but the bedroom or the kitchen."

"That's not quite fair," Tonia objected. "Maybe it's true of DeMarco. He's always putting somebody down and it's usually a woman. But Bob Kingsley's a pretty nice guy. He always asks about my mom, and he's real polite."

"He asks about your mom and my daughter, but he never

asks the guys about their families," Elaine said. "It's just his way of dealing with you as a woman rather than a colleague. And he's only polite so long as you're deferential. Listen to him talk about Sheila sometime; you'd think Bitch was her first name."

We turned the corner and saw the red-and-white awning of Mama's in the next block. The pavement radiated back the heat of the sun. I felt a trickle of sweat run down between my breasts and wished I was wearing a cotton T-shirt instead of a silk suit.

"I don't mind the tricks," I said, "but the personal stuff is pretty gross." Gross was a tame description for the pornographic analysis of my anatomy and the creative suppositions about my sex life that had greeted me this morning when I turned on the computer and called up my messages. Even though I'd expected something of the sort, I was still unsettled and even embarrassed by it. I'd printed it out, but I understood why other women might have just erased the ugly words and tried to push them from their minds.

"You mean the trash on the E-mail? We've all been getting that," Elaine said. "Just erase the damn things. Don't let the bastards see that they bother you." Her voice had taken on a sharp edge.

"You should save them," I said. "Take them to human resources. Get them to nail this guy."

Elaine made a sharp sound, more like a bark than a laugh. "And what are they going to do? The jerk who's doing this got around the security manager. You can't fire a phantom. Besides, I'd bet Leggett isn't too anxious to catch the creep. He doesn't want to lose anyone from KeeGo at this point, not when we're not even sure how their damn applications work. He may act shocked and appalled, but business is business."

"Besides, there's no proof it is the KeeGo jerks," Tonia said. It could just as easily be someone from our side."

"Really?" I said.

Elaine shook her head. "Not likely. There are probably some who think this whole thing is a hoot, but I can't see them risking getting fired."

"So has everyone been getting these messages?" I asked.

"Most of us on the third floor," Elaine replied. "Some of the secretaries haven't, at least they claim they haven't. But everyone who's in sales or marketing has. And you've gotten them down in development, haven't you?"

"Oh, yeah," Tonia said. But that was all. She studied the pavement and crimson patches sat on her cheekbones. She wasn't as tough as she pretended to be.

We reached the welcome patch of shade under the awning at Mama's and stepped inside. The café was clean but spartan. In a few years, someone would come along and cover the walls with wood and mirrors, put in track lighting, and double the prices. For now, it was an honest working-persons' restaurant, right down to the smell of onions on the grill.

It was a salad-type day, but not here. Mama's salads were a pile of iceberg lettuce with some tired tomatoes tossed on top. Fifties salads, with orange French dressing. We ordered sandwiches.

As we waited for them I asked, "Why are these guys in such a lather about Sheila's promotion?"

"Because she's smarter than they are and she doesn't take any nonsense from them," Tonia put in.

"Sales guys hate to report to a woman," Elaine said. "It isn't just that they think women are inferior, though most of the ones from KeeGo do. A woman changes the rules. They know how to get along with another guy. They can talk sports, go out drinking, do whatever it is men do when there aren't women around. They buddy up and figure that the other guy'll cover their butt. They can't do that with a woman."

I could hear the resentment in Elaine's voice. I didn't think

I'd like to be a guy reporting to her and I didn't expect that Sheila's attitude would be any more charitable.

"It's not just the KeeGo guys," Tonia said. "I heard Frank McFadden complaining that Sheila only got the nod because she's a woman and Leggett's worried about the feds."

"Oh, yeah. And I heard him tell one of the other guys that she slept her way to the promotion," Elaine said. "McFadden's one of ours, transferred in from the Chicago office. He's just pissed because he came here thinking he'd make regional manager. He's in the minicomputer division, but he didn't even get in the client-server subgroup."

"Funny how it's always merit when a white male is promoted and sex or quotas when anyone else gets the nod," I said.

Both women laughed knowingly. "Did you hear the joke about the guy who took a year's leave and went to live in Europe?" I asked.

They shook their heads.

"Well," I said, "he had a big party when he came home, and his friends were surprised to discover that he'd had a sex-change operation. During the party a friend said, 'It must have been painful to have your balls cut off.'

"'Yes, it was,' he said, 'but that wasn't the worst thing.'

"After a couple of more drinks the friend said, 'It must have been really painful having your dick cut off.'

"'Yes, it was,' he said, 'but that wasn't the worst thing.'

"Another couple of drinks and the friend asked, 'So what was the worst thing?'

"'Coming home and finding my salary cut by thirty-nine percent.'"

Both women howled. I don't usually remember jokes, but this one had stuck in my memory. I'd gotten it from my lover, Peter, whose affinity for the oppressed makes him a strong feminist.

Our sandwiches arrived as I was telling the joke. The waiter hovered in the background waiting for the punchline. He probably didn't find it quite as funny as we did.

"You know, the KeeGo guys are jerks and McFadden is sour grapes, but lots of the guys in programming are mad at Sheila for legitimate reasons," Tonia said as she extracted a hefty slice of onion from her sandwich.

"Like?" Elaine asked.

"She's out of line," Tonia said. "I really like Sheila, and I've tried to tell her, but she just doesn't listen. Now that she's in sales, she can't come down to development and meddle with the programs. She even wants to read code. That's not her job. And it really upsets people when she does that."

Elaine nodded. "I know. Sheila doesn't understand some real basic stuff about how business works. She's been doing the same with the marketing people. Paul Nye says it's because she never played Little League, so she never learned about teamwork."

Tonia nodded. "Paul's the one with the great blue eyes?" she asked.

"And the cute tush," Elaine said with a broad smile.

"God," Tonia said. "If the guys heard that, they'd accuse *us* of harassment."

"Noticing is not harassment," Elaine informed her with a wink. "Discreet noticing." We all chuckled.

The waiter came by to refill our water glasses. Probably hoping for another joke. He was out of luck.

All that was left of Elaine's sandwich was the crust. She put it down on her plate and finished her iced tea. "Well, I don't envy Sheila being back under Jorgensen's thumb again," she said.

"Jorgensen?" I asked.

"VP of sales," Elaine replied. "Sheila and I worked for him years ago when he was regional manager of PC sales. Talk about jerks!

"You had to submit sales reports every week, which was more often than anyone else demanded. And when you got called to his office, there'd always be two chairs side by side and while you went over your report, he'd put his hand on your thigh. All the time he was talking about sales figures and promotions and bonuses, his hand'd slowly move up under your skirt."

Elaine's voice had become hard. Time and pressure can create diamonds or oil, but there's nothing beautiful or useful about the aging of anger. I felt something knot up in my own stomach in response to her story.

"I don't even think it was a sexual thing with him," she continued. "It was power, pure power. Put your hand on his to stop him, and he'd start talking about how he was considering reassigning territories, meaning you could end up with Outer Mongolia.

"And he never looked down. He had his eyes on your face the whole time. Just watching you squirm and letting you know who was in charge."

"And now he's Sheila's boss again," I said.

Elaine nodded.

"Does he still pull the same stuff?" I asked.

"Not likely, things have tightened up a lot in the last couple of years. He wouldn't risk that today," she said. "But even without the hand on the thigh routine, I'll bet he still finds ways to drive Sheila crazy. He hates assertive women."

"He probably loves the stuff the prankster's pulling," I said.

Elaine shrugged. "Who knows? He doesn't spend much time with us peons. Too busy buddying up to the boss and buttering up the board. Sheila's damn naive if she thinks she's got a shot at moving into corporate as long as Jorgensen has his foot on the glass ceiling."

Chapter

4

I lost round three that afternoon.

I came back from lunch, walked into my office at Systech and sat down at my desk. I knew almost at once something was wrong. It was like sitting on a sponge.

I jumped up and put my hand on the back of my skirt. Definitely wet. The palm of my hand was a bright red. "Shit," I said as I realized what the back of my gray skirt must look like. The red stuff on my hand was probably red ink, almost certainly permanent.

I'd bought my gray silk suit less than a month ago, and it had taken a whole Saturday to find something I liked. I wasn't sure which galled me more, the cost of replacing it or the fact that I'd have to go shopping again.

And somewhere outside my door was a guy waiting to see me walk out with a huge red stain across my butt. And a bunch of other guys who'd get a great laugh out of the situation. I wanted to break something. No, someone.

• • •

I unclenched my teeth, no point in increasing my contribution
to my dentist's retirement fund, and walked to the door to see
if anyone on the platform was watching for my reaction.

The regional sales division occupied one end of the third
floor and its offices were arranged around a central platform
that was divided into cubicles with shoulder-high partitions.
Salesmen from the minicomputer division had offices around
the platform. Elaine's prime suspects, DeMarco and Kingsley,
just happened to be standing across the room.

When I first met them, I'd thought of the two as Tweedle-
dum and Tweedledee even though they were quite different
physically. One was dark and lean, the other blond and built
like a refrigerator. But both wore the same style expensive suit,
the obligatory Rolex and gold jewelry, and soft Italian leather
shoes. I'd bet their shorts had designer labels.

John DeMarco was tall, dark, and not quite handsome; he
had an almost ascetic quality. His lips were too thin, his movements tightly controlled. Even his laughter seemed rationed.

I'm sure he was suave and charming with his clients, but
around the office DeMarco was a master of the verbal put
down. He would have argued that he ripped into men and
women with equal vigor, but his jibes at women were particularly derisive and often included insulting sexual suggestions.
He was the first to tell a story that put someone in a bad light
and the quickest to recognize weakness in a colleague.

And that wasn't even the worst thing about him. The worst
thing was his temper. The day before, I'd watched as he stalked
up to one of the women in marketing and began yelling about
the schedule for the next release of the program. He'd
slammed a manual on the desk so hard that the cup nearby fell
to the floor and broke. She'd backed away from him in fear
and he'd just kept coming until he'd actually backed her into a
wall. From what Elaine told me, it wasn't the first time. The
men didn't think it was a big deal, but many of the women
were afraid of him.

The blond was named Bob Kingsley. He had a pale, reddish complexion, looked like he'd probably burn in direct sunlight. His hair was a nondescript light brown but expensively cut to give him that blow-dried casual look. I don't know how genuine his Texas accent was, but he played the "good ole boy" role for all it was worth.

He was friendly to the point of being overly familiar, smiled and joked a lot. I could see why Tonia thought he was nicer than DeMarco, but there was a patronizing quality to his banter. I'd heard one woman complain that he'd responded to a request for information with, "Now don't you worry your pretty head over that."

And I agreed with Elaine that there was another side to his personality. When I'd interviewed him about the communication system, he'd been congenial, almost courtly. After I returned his pat on the butt, I'd suddenly become invisible. I could see him as the one suggesting burning bitches at the stake, or pouring red dye on my chair.

The only other man I could see on the platform was Frank McFadden, who was talking with one of the secretaries. I remembered Elaine's comment that McFadden resented being denied a place in the client-server group. Might he, I wondered, figure that a series of childish pranks would be blamed on his rivals from KeeGo? If one of them were fired, the slot he'd wanted so badly might just open up.

McFadden was a small man in a big man's body. He wasn't awkward, but he didn't seem completely at ease in his body. He was nice-looking in a sort of bland way and he was friendly and outgoing, but I didn't really trust him. Maybe because he always smiled. That alone was enough to make me suspicious.

He'd been in San Francisco less than six months, having transferred in from the Chicago office, but women like Elaine already had his number. "He's a real Don Juan," she said, "with women who are younger and subordinate. He barely speaks to those of us who are at his level, and he heads the other way when he sees Sheila coming."

No one on the platform gave me a glance, so I backed up and closed my door. They might be playing it cool, but someone out there was waiting for my entrance, and I wasn't about to give him any satisfaction.

I called Jesse in tech support and told him what had happened. "Find an excuse to be on the floor," I said. "Get as close to DeMarco and Kingsley as you can. Maybe one of them will get careless and shoot off his mouth. You might keep an eye on McFadden, too."

"On my way," he said.

The best revenge would have been to get a duplicate of the skirt I'd just ruined. However, the suit had been the last of its kind a month ago, so that was out.

I waited until I thought Jesse'd be on the floor, then called Elaine. She was out, so I tried Tonia. "Would you please come to my office," I said. "I need help with something."

Tonia was shocked, then furious. I was surprised by the depth and ferocity of her anger. At lunch she'd seemed more embarrassed than angry at the prankster's tricks.

"He's just such a shit," she said. "Look at your skirt. That'll never come out. And of course it's red, just to remind you, just to humiliate you. All they can think about is sex. If they didn't keep their flies zipped, their brains'd leak out."

I couldn't help laughing at the last image, and that broke the tension so that Tonia smiled sheepishly. "I'm sorry," she said. "I just get so tired of this stuff, of always having to watch what I wear, and what I say, and if I smile too much. I feel like a canary at a cat convention."

"I thought it was better downstairs," I said.

"It is, and Systech is a pretty great place, but before I came here I was the only woman at a start-up like KeeGo. I guess I haven't quite gotten over that yet."

I nodded. Sometimes things that don't seem very important to anyone else can take a long time to get over. I can still remember with embarrassing clarity being refused a place on the sixth-grade baseball team because "real teams don't have girls on them." I'd bloodied the nose of the little creep who delivered that judgment, but I still didn't get to play on the team.

With her experience at a company like KeeGo, Tonia might be helpful. "Do you know many of the salesmen?" I asked.

"Only slightly. Sales and development don't mix much except when they're screaming at us to get a product out faster. How can I help you with this skirt thing?"

The quick change of subject might have meant nothing, but something subtle had shifted in Tonia's manner when I asked about the men in sales, and I was curious to know why.

"I don't want to give this guy the satisfaction of walking through the office with this all over me," I said. "Do you think you could slip away and get me another skirt?"

"Sure, I'm ahead of schedule right now. What do you want me to do?"

"Just go downtown to one of the stores and get me a black straight skirt, size ten."

"No problem."

I gave her all the money in my wallet, enough for a decent skirt, but a lot less than I'd paid for the one I was wearing.

Chapter

5

Two hours is a long time to stand around in a wet skirt. I piled a stack of time sheets on my chair so I could at least sit down, but I didn't get much work done. I did have some stunning revenge fantasies.

I was in the middle of a particularly satisfying one when Tonia got back with the skirt. She had nice taste in clothes. The skirt she'd bought would be a welcome addition to my wardrobe. I was glad it wasn't one of those tight minis. Maybe it's because I've had to defend myself in a couple of difficult situations, but high heels and tight skirts make me uncomfortable. They're almost as effective as binding a woman's feet for making her vulnerable to attack.

Tonia was a sharp kid. She'd even brought a plastic sack so I could put my skirt in my briefcase without messing up the inside. I switched clothes and we walked from my office to the elevator as if nothing had happened. I didn't spot anyone obviously eye-balling my door when I came out. I hoped Jesse had seen something I missed.

I had to stop by my real office to take care of odds and ends

30

on a couple of other cases. As I drove across town, I realized that the messy sludge of anger in my stomach was about more than the skirt. Since lunch, part of my mind had been stewing over Elaine's tale of Jorgensen's fondling. It brought up painful memories from long ago, memories I thought I'd put behind me. Maybe what I thought of as scar tissue was only a scab.

By the time I got home I was tired, hungry, and grouchy. I opened the door and was blasted with the Dead's "Casey Jones" at full volume, supplemented by a deep baritone from the kitchen. Loud music has become a fact of life since Molly moved in several months ago. At least Peter has managed to convert her to sixties rock, so we get to listen to stuff we enjoy. But on nights like this one, I long for the old days when my only social interaction involved opening a can of cat food.

Peter was in the kitchen peeling garlic and tossing it into the food processor with handfuls of deep green basil. The air was sweet with the pungent odor of the two herbs. The half-empty bottle of wine told me he'd been waiting for me for a while.

He turned and winked, the kind of wink that might have been a prelude to a delayed dinner in our pre-Molly days.

"I need a shower," I announced before he could wrap me in his arms.

"Something wrong?"

"Don't ask. I'll tell you after I shower."

I'd spent the entire afternoon with the unpleasant sensation of ink caking on my skin, and I couldn't wait a minute longer to try to scrub it off. Of course, it didn't come off. Not entirely, at least. I might have had better luck if years of drought hadn't forced me to install one of those low-flow shower heads that converted a highly sensuous experience into Chinese water torture.

Peter had obviously warned Molly; the stereo was down to less than ear-shattering volume by the time I emerged from the bathroom and both looked mildly apprehensive when I came into the kitchen.

"What happened?" Peter asked as he handed me a glass of wine.

I sank into a chair and gave them the high and low points of my day. "I cannot tell you how annoying it is to stand around in wet clothes with ink all over you for two hours," I said. "I would happily strangle this guy if I could get my hands on him."

"Guys can be such jerks," Molly said, then looked at Peter and added, "Present company excepted, of course."

"Oh, I can probably be a jerk, too," Peter said. "Got any idea who it might be?"

"Probably, but I can't be sure. Is there time to call Jesse before dinner?"

"Sure," Peter said. "I'll start the pasta now if you think it's going to be a short call."

It was a short call. Jesse'd kept an eye on Kingsley, DeMarco, and McFadden, and all three had stuck around the office until after I left, but none of them had done anything to give himself away.

During dinner I asked Molly how things were going at school. She was starting her freshman year at Headlands, a private high school in San Francisco. She'd been a freshman at Palo Alto High last year, but she'd spent most of that year in open warfare with her mother and the school authorities, and we all thought it better for her to get a new start.

She hadn't been a lot more enthusiastic about school this year than she had been last, until a boy named Craig caught her eye and the hormone dance kicked into high gear. I was rooting for her friend Jason, who seemed like a nice kid, but

Molly dismissed him as "just a friend." Jason was sweet; Craig had an earring, dressed in black, and was saving for a motorcycle.

Molly didn't have much to say about school, and she was far more interested in discussing my adventures at Systech than she was in talking about algebra or English. I was telling her about Jorgensen's hand games when she interrupted with, "I hate guys like that."

"Oh?" I said, trying to keep my voice casual. "Something like this happen to you?"

"No big deal," she said. "Just this jerk in algebra who put his hand on my butt."

"And?"

"I told him to get the hell away from me."

"Good. And was that the end of it?"

"Yeah. He moved his hand. Me and my friends sit way over on the other side of the classroom now."

Times like this I wish I'd had a bit more preparation for this parenting business. It didn't sound like a big deal, and Molly had handled it well, but even at Headlands, where I expected that there was a low tolerance for sexual harassment, it was the girls who adjusted. The boy might be out of line, but Molly and her friends were the ones who moved.

After dinner I got Molly started on the dishes. She still quoted child labor law whenever confronted with household chores, but her protests had evolved from open rebellion to good-natured joking. The irony was that she'd done more than her share of chores when she lived with her mother. I wasn't about to let my sister accuse me of being a soft touch.

Peter suggested a walk to the ice cream store and I readily accepted.

Daylight saving time had a week to go, and at eight o'clock

at night the sky was an electric blue and the air still held some of the day's warmth. The gray fog that had squatted on the city throughout much of the summer lay out beyond the Golden Gate, and tonight San Francisco actually looked like it was in California.

The sidewalks were full of people. San Franciscans don't get a lot of chances to go strolling without their jackets, and everyone was in a festive mood. I waved at my neighbor Ruth from up the street. At eighty-eight, she's still one of the most lively people on the block. The man she was walking with was at least ten years her junior. I hope someone looks at me that way when I'm eighty-eight.

"So what do you think of Molly's new boyfriend?" Peter asked.

"I didn't know things had progressed that far. Do you know something I don't?"

"Only that she spent almost an hour on the phone and every fourth word was 'Craig.'"

"Terrific. Just what we need. She finally stops hanging out with the runaways on the street, and now we have Craig, the would-be biker."

"It's probably just a pose," Peter suggested.

"I'd still rather she were interested in Jason. Why did she have to pick the toughest kid in the class when there are plenty of perfectly nice guys?"

"Because you women always like the bad boys," Peter said with a leer as he slid his arm around my waist and pulled me closer.

"No groping on the streets," I said. "And I didn't fall for you because you were a 'bad boy.'"

"I'll bet your parents wouldn't believe that. Here you leave your highly respected cop husband and end up with a thoroughly disreputable private eye. I think they'd second my theory on bad boys."

He was right, of course, about what my parents thought. They'd never understood why I divorced Dan Walker. He was smart, attractive, and successful. For my dad, himself a cop, a homicide inspector with the SFPD was the ideal son-in-law. Add to that that, Dan and my parents shared the opinion that I ought to find another, less dangerous line of work, and they all got along just great.

I was the odd woman out. And I didn't take it well when Dan, who claimed to be enchanted by my independent nature, kept pressuring me to find another job. We were well matched in stubbornness, Dan and I. We could probably have kept on fighting for years, but I got tired of that routine.

I looked up at Peter, definitely the bad boy as far as my parents were concerned. He'd been a hippie radical in the sixties, and while his hair was shorter and his red beard was better trimmed, his politics and distrust of authority hadn't changed. The fact that he was a private investigator who frequently worked criminal defense was the final straw. No way was this man son-in-law material.

Not that I cared. Having tried marriage once, I wasn't anxious to do it again. Peter and I were both independent enough to understand each other's need for space, and while he hated to see me in danger, he accepted my right to run my own life.

"So why *did* you fall for me?" Peter asked.

"I fell for you because you are the only man I know who can recite most of 'Fern Hill' after drinking enough ouzo to put a Greek under the table."

"That's because I am Greek at heart, Greek and Welsh, of course."

"It didn't hurt that you have the bluest eyes I've ever seen, and a great laugh," I added. "What attracted you to me?"

"Sex," Peter whispered in my ear.

"Oh, thanks a lot."

"I liked the way you moved, like you knew where you were going and you were comfortable in your body. And I liked your sense of humor, humor's important. And . . ." he leaned over to nuzzle my neck, "you turned me on."

"Hold that thought," I said, snuggling closer to him and thinking how very nice it was after spending a day with a bunch of jerks to come home to a man who didn't confuse aggression with masculinity.

Chapter

6

It was just past dawn when I awoke. The mob of birds outside my window sounded pleased with themselves; they were probably taunting Touchstone, my overweight and underquick tomcat. I snuggled closer to Peter. He automatically put his arm around me, and I moved in a little closer. I detected signs that he was waking up. After all, I'm not a detective for nothing.

His hand found my breast. He's a detective, too. Doesn't miss much, even early in the morning. "Breakfast in bed?" he whispered in my ear.

I rolled over and ran my hand down his body. "Since you're already awake," I said.

At Systech that morning, I made a point of greeting each of the men I suspected and watched their reactions. No smirks or telltale grins, no subtle references to my change of clothes. The chair had disappeared from my office, and been replaced with a clean one. No one in janitorial could tell me who had ordered the switch. Another dead end.

But the prankster's move had given me an opening I needed. Now that I was a victim, I had a great excuse for suggesting to other women in the office that we band together to catch the guy or guys who were driving us crazy.

Elaine was my first recruit. She stopped by my office as she came in. "I just heard what happened. Those guys are such jerks. I'm really sorry."

"Revenge is so much more satisfying than regret," I said. "You want to help me catch them?"

"You better believe it."

"We're both fairly sure it's Kingsley or DeMarco. What we need is proof. If we organized our people, both women and men, to keep an eye on them, it'd only be a matter of time before we caught one. You game?"

"Count me in," Elaine said. "But I wouldn't limit it to the KeeGo guys. I can add two or three of the old-timers who might easily be involved."

"Do it. Then talk to the other women and the men you trust."

"My pleasure. We won't have any trouble rounding up a posse. Or a lynch mob."

I spent the rest of the morning interviewing the marketing department about voice mail and met Paul Nye of the blue eyes and nice tush. Elaine and Tonia were right, he was cute. I'd bet a lot of women were disappointed to notice the ring on his left hand.

Paul was not a fan of voice mail. He argued for E-mail; I defended voice mail. I don't think I won him over.

As I finished the interview, I sensed he was uncomfortable about something. Finally, he cleared his throat and said, "I heard about what happened to your skirt yesterday. I'm really sorry. I just want you to know that there are a lot of guys here

I listened with a certain fascination. Sheila and I were about the same age. We both liked to win. I've been told it isn't my most appealing trait. I'll bet Sheila'd heard the same thing.

"What about the pranks?" I asked. "You think it's the KeeGo guys?"

"Absolutely. But the beauty of their scheme is that they won't be alone for long. Every practical joker in the office has been aching to pull a number of his own. Someone may already have done it. If he hasn't yet, he will soon."

"Do you have any proof it's the KeeGo guys?" I asked.

"No, and I don't care. I don't give a damn about the jokes. I'm out for bigger game."

"Like?"

Sheila took a mental step back from me. She was suddenly less animated, more wary. "Oh, nothing really. I'm just more concerned with getting the new applications moving than worrying about an adolescent prankster."

"Nothing really"—alarm-bell words. Words to pay attention to. I wondered what bigger game Sheila was after and why.

Two women in marketing and one in sales encountered white mice when they opened their desk drawers that morning. The first two were cool; they just closed the drawer and called maintenance. The third screamed and jumped around as if she were auditioning for a cartoon. Everyone laughed, and most of us felt a bit guilty about it. Elaine scored several new recruits for her posse.

After lunch she called with our first break. "You should talk to Tonia," she said. "She thinks she knows who's responsible for the stuff on the E-mail."

"I'll go right down," I said.

I was glad for a chance to visit the second floor. It was a bit like a parallel universe, so different was it from the polished offices upstairs. The second floor was warehouse chic. The floors were carpeted, but the beamed ceiling had been painted white and all the exposed pipes and vents done in primary colors that converted them to design elements.

It was an open environment, offices around the outside, partitioned cubicles in the middle. And each cubicle was a colorful portrait of its occupant. In some, every square inch was covered with pictures, cartoons, various objects pinned to the wall. Others were sterile and austere, as if bodies occupied the space but minds were elsewhere.

Tonia's space was less cluttered than most and the snapshots and pictures on the walls had been arranged rather than just slapped up. It looked as though she came from a large family, and the white frame house that appeared in several pictures was probably somewhere in the Midwest. A teddy bear sat on the shelf above her monitor along with a tiny Buddha, a delicate vase with a single dried flower, and a Mexican ceramic owl.

Today, Tonia wore tan slacks and a navy tank top. She didn't look much older than a high school student. Her eyes danced with excitement and her voice was conspiratorial as she said, "Let's go to the conference room.

"I started thinking after lunch yesterday, and I realized it can only be one guy," she said almost as soon as she'd closed the door. "I mean, I haven't seen him do anything so I don't know for sure, but it's got to be him."

"Why?"

"Well, there are four guys from KeeGo in programming. You'd have to know them to understand, but Clark Phillips is the only one that fits. I mean, Larry Lau is so far out in his own world that he only touches down once a week or so. He forgets to eat lots of times. Steve Mar is such a purist that he's offended when anyone puts jokes—any kind of jokes—on the E-mail. And Arnie Smith would probably do something like this, but he's so totally involved in a project that's due next Tuesday that I think he's given up sleeping."

She paused to catch her breath. Her face was flushed with excitement. "The thrill of the chase," my first boss, Keith Stone, used to call it. It's addictive, that feeling—the clarity and intensity when your mind puts you one step ahead of the guy you're after. I love that feeling; it's exhilarating. It can also be dangerous.

"Clark has the time and he'd love it," Tonia continued. "Picture your average fourteen-year-old—all lust and longing and no idea of how to relate to a woman. Put that in a short, plump, twenty-seven-year-old body and you've got Clark. *And* he's been hanging out with Kingsley and DeMarco lately. He thinks they're the coolest guys in the world. He'd probably do anything for them."

"Sounds like our man, all right," I said. "You're sure it wouldn't be one of the Systech programmers?"

Tonia shook her head emphatically. "No way. I know those guys. They'd never do stuff like this. It's Clark."

"Okay," I said. "We could go to the security manager and maybe catch Phillips in the act, but I don't think he's the only one involved, and I'd sure like to catch the jerk who ruined my skirt. Will you keep an eye on Clark and let me know if you see anything that might help us nail one of the guys upstairs?"

"Sure thing," Tonia said with enthusiasm. "It's so weird seeing him sitting over there and knowing he's thinking that stuff. Makes me real uncomfortable."

"I know," I said. "We can't stop what he's thinking, but we can sure as hell make him keep it to himself."

● ● ●

I called Jesse as soon as I got back upstairs. "I know who the hacker is," I said. I tried not to sound smug.

"Clark Phillips," Jesse said. "I caught him this morning when he tried for super-user privileges." Smug didn't begin to describe his tone of voice.

"Damn. Just this once I thought I was ahead of you," I said. He laughed. "What next?" I asked.

"He doesn't know I was watching. He's created a new account named Satyr, so that's where the next batch of E-mail stuff will come from."

"I can hardly wait," I said.

We had a culprit, just not the right culprit. Allen Leggett had told both Jesse and me that he did not want to fire a programmer. He wanted a salesman. That was fine by me. I was really looking forward to nabbing the jerk who ruined my skirt.

I wrote up a brief report on Phillips, ran it out on the printer, and headed for the corporate offices at the east end of the building.

Corporate and western region were on the same floor, but they were worlds apart. In corporate, carpets were thicker, offices bigger, and secretaries prettier. In fact, there wasn't a secretary in corporate who was over thirty or weighed more than one-twenty. It was eerie, a bit as though they ordered them from the same place they got the pastel art work on the walls.

The guys in corporate were mostly over thirty and a long way over one-twenty. They looked like older versions of the guys in the rest of the company, which in fact they were.

I gave Leggett's secretary my report, and as I turned to go, a male voice said, "Ms. Sayler?"

I turned to face a man in his late thirties with a tan that screamed Hawaii. Prematurely white hair, thick and full, blue eyes so light they were almost silver, and a smile that was broader on the left than the right. He was just under six feet, solidly built, moved like an athlete. A hunk, definitely, a hunk.

"I'm Scott Jorgensen, VP of sales," he said, extending a large hand. I could feel callouses as we shook hands. "Could I speak with you for a minute?"

As we walked to his office I had only a moment to reflect on how different he was from what I expected. From Elaine's story of his hand-on-the-thigh moves I'd imagined—what? A slimy guy who looked like a toad? Hardly. But I also hadn't expected him to be so attractive. Got to watch those unconscious assumptions.

Jorgensen's office had that sure symbol of importance, a good view. It looked out on the Bay Bridge and the East Bay hills beyond. The other warehouses in the foreground weren't so great, but when you sat down you didn't notice them.

The source of the carcinogenic tan was evident in the decor of the room. Nautical devices were strategically placed like bits of sculpture, and the wall behind the desk displayed several large photographs of a sailboat. Smaller photos showed groups of men on the boat. Leggett appeared in most of them. There was only one photo of a woman, a pretty brunette with two pre-teen boys.

The desk top was beyond neat. Even the edges of the papers in the outbasket were aligned. I wondered if such tidiness came from living on a boat or whether he wasn't more than a tad compulsive.

"Allen tells me you're working on the harassment problem," he said as he ushered me to a chair. I wondered who else "Allen" had told.

"Do you have information that could help me?" I asked.

"Not beyond what you already know," he said. "I was hoping you could tell me more about what's going on. It appears this is coming from someone in sales, so, of course, I'm very concerned about it."

I wondered how he really felt. Did he identify with the

prankster? Or was he annoyed because the pranks were a challenge to his authority? Was he worried that too much attention to the issue of sexual harassment could lead to scrutiny of his own behavior?

There was absolutely no reason to poke at this guy. He had nothing to do with the reason I'd been hired. But I poked, anyway. Putting on a perfectly bland expression, I asked, "What can you tell me about larger patterns of harassment in Systech?"

"I beg your pardon?" He didn't gasp or look guilty. They rarely do.

"I'm trying to be as thorough as I can," I said. "Harassment can take many forms."

The silver-blue eyes became flinty. The muscle in his jaw tightened. "I believe the pranks are the problem here," he said.

"Oh, definitely," I said, letting my voice not quite match my words. I kept my eyes on his face and let a silence stretch.

Jorgensen watched me in return, not breaking the silence. Just as the hand on the thigh wasn't about sex, this wasn't about the prankster. It was about power, pure and simple. Seeing who would blink first.

Neither of us blinked, but after a long, tense silence, I said, "Well, I have to get back to catching the prankster. Sexual harassment is a serious matter these days."

He was gracious as he showed me out of his office, gracious and unconcerned. I hate guys like Jorgensen. So safe and so self-satisfied. He could get away with damn near whatever he wanted, and he knew it. The boss and the board were his friends. The woman who complained about him would only destroy her own career.

It's a very short jump from impotence to rage for me, and I made it as I walked back to my office. My whole body clenched up like a fist, and I felt a wave of heat that had nothing to do with the weather outside. I kept my head down to hide my expression and to discourage any attempts at casual conversation, walked quickly, and made it to my office without meeting anyone. I managed to shut my door only a shade harder than usual.

The last delivery of office mail was at four-thirty, three manila envelopes with a column of names scratched out and mine added at the bottom. One was from Sheila, one from the manager of marketing, and one with the sender line left blank and my name typed.

I opened that envelope carefully, wary of another prank. Six color photos slid out onto my desk. Four showed naked women being tortured and sexually abused. Every woman's nightmare in garish color.

But it was the other two that made me catch my breath. In one a blond woman was bound spread-eagle on a table; in the other a dark-haired woman was tied to a chair. The wounds on their bodies were shocking, but it was their eyes that disturbed me most. They stared out in glassy emptiness. They were not the eyes of the living.

Chapter

7

My stomach knotted. My mouth was so dry it was hard to swallow. I stared down at the photographs in disbelief. They were too horrible to be real and too convincing not to be.

What the hell was going on?

I took a couple of deep breaths. My stomach still felt like it was full of rocks.

I lined the pictures up on my desk and looked more closely at each one. They were all photographs and the men and women were different in each picture. I studied the faces; none of them were from Systech.

The photos didn't appear staged. The women seemed genuinely terrorized, and their wounds looked all to real. I kept coming back to the last two. To the eyes that stared without seeing.

I told myself the women were probably only unconcious. I wasn't convinced. Staged or real, this was ugly stuff, and the guys who got turned on by it were scary. No one you'd want working in the next office. Or even down the hall.

I wondered if Elaine or Tonia had gotten similar photos. If

they had and I called them, I'd be drawn into their reactions and the powerful emotions the images evoked.

I spent the next twenty minutes trying to figure out if there was any way to trace the photos. I was fairly sure they weren't available on the racks of even the most hard-core porn shops. The folks who distributed this kind of stuff didn't advertise.

It was almost five when I left Systech, and the streets were clogged with rush hour traffic. As I inched my way along and sat in endless lines behind endless red lights, I realized that it wasn't just the pictures that were bothering me.

I was still raw from the meeting with Jorgensen. At one level I'd enjoyed our confrontation. But it had also stirred painful memories and all the ugly emotions I'd packed away with them. Jorgensen, with his power and assurance, reminded me of a professor I'd had in college. I knew how it felt to sit in that chair next to a man who could promote or destroy your career and to feel yourself completely powerless.

The memory of it still filled me with humiliation and rage. God, I'd been young then. I hadn't had a clue about what was going on. I was so proud to be his star pupil, to have him show interest in my papers and invite me to his office to discuss his research. When I'd felt his thigh against mine, I'd thought it was an accident, and had just moved away. He didn't even seem aware of putting his hand on my knee.

The memory was so sharp that my stomach still knotted just as it had then. I was furious at myself for letting it get to me. It hadn't even been a big thing. I was not seduced or raped. So why the hell was I still carrying it around?

Driving usually helps me sort things out. I guess I didn't drive far enough. New York might have been far enough. Divisadero Street wasn't.

I parked two blocks from my office and walked uphill past the mixture of dusty antique stores and slick new boutiques that mark a neighborhood in transition. A year ago the boutiques were winning, now they're struggling to hang on. I hated them when they arrived, and I'm sorry to see them fail. Doesn't make much sense. Feelings rarely do.

I was a bit out of breath and still caught between old emotions and new worries when I reached the office. The rest of the staff had left, and the big white Victorian was still and empty. Not even cold coffee left in the pot.

Jesse arrived about twenty minutes later. If he'd known my mood, he'd probably have stayed away. I handed him the envelope as soon as he walked in. "I got something in the office mail."

Jesse shook the pictures out onto my desk and stared at them thoughtfully. When he turned to me, his face was grave. "Pretty ugly stuff," he said.

I nodded. "Very," I said. "Makes me worry about what's going on here."

"What do you mean?"

"This is a long ways from pinups and beaver shots, even from garden-variety bondage. I wonder if our man is coming unglued."

Jesse sucked on his lower lip. "I don't know. It's offensive, but I don't know that it means anything."

"Oh, really," I said, my voice rising. "And if those were pictures of black males being tortured and killed, would you feel the same way?"

Jesse looked startled. He started to protest, then looked down at the pictures. "No," he said. "I don't think so. Because there're guys out there with sheets and guns."

"And there are guys out there who rape and murder women. So how's it different?"

Jesse stared out the window for a moment. "I don't know. But sex is, well, it's complicated. I looked at a lot of this stuff for a first amendment project in college. It was pretty shocking, but it was all made by consenting adults."

"I don't think those two women who look dead were consenting," I said. "And I'm not convinced about the others, either. Guys who go for pictures like that scare me."

Jesse grimaced. "Guys have all kinds of fantasies, doesn't mean they ever do anything about them." He looked back at me. His face was troubled. "Doesn't even mean they'd want to. It's probably hard for a woman to understand."

I looked down at the pictures then back at Jesse. "You think this is about sex?" I said. "I think it's about the same thing the Klan's about. It's just a different set of victims."

We kicked it around, not exactly arguing but not agreeing, either. Jesse claimed he saw my point, but that didn't mean he understood it. On the other hand, I could never really understand how he felt as a black man. I could be outraged and appalled by racial hate crimes, but I didn't live with the subtle and not-so-subtle racism that could turn ugly at any time.

Tuesday night is one of my aikido nights. As I hurried home to pick up my clothes I realized how much I needed to go to the dojo. I started studying martial arts as a means to defend myself—and it's saved my life more than once—but the urgency I felt tonight had nothing to do with fear. I craved the peace and clarity that class could bring.

The white emptiness of the dojo always calms me. It is a space that creates its own psychic equivalent. White mats, white walls, tall windows, no adornment other than a small shrine to Morihei Uyeshiba, the founder of aikido.

Gina Lori teaches on Tuesday nights, and I always look forward to her class. She's deeply serious about the art, and she does it with such obvious joy that it infects everyone in class. Even the macho guys who get there by mistake, having confused aikido with kung fu, are captivated by her gentle good humor. You can see them relax as they realize you don't have to kick someone's teeth out to defend yourself.

I changed clothes and joined the others on the mat to do some stretches before class began. Every muscle in my body seemed to have tightened up during the day; I felt like an overstrung violin.

The first half of class, my mind chattered and my reactions were a bit slow. Then at some point, the soup of messy emotions began to settle. Like sand in a pool of water, the anger and the fear that lay below it, the frustration and the confusion drifted down until the surface was clear again.

Toward the end of class, Gina clapped and we knelt on the mat. "Most of you are doing the throw well, but you're not paying enough attention to the *ukemi*." Ukemi is the act of receiving the throw, taking the fall.

"Uke's role is to attack; usually that means being thrown. That doesn't mean you give up and space out. When you take the throw, you must be present. You protect yourself and be ready to attack if you get another chance. To do that, you have to stay connected to your partner.

"Catherine," she said, bowing to me.

I bowed in return and moved forward to act as her partner. She extended her right arm to signal that she wanted me to attack. She slid her foot forward a bit then pivoted sharply and brought her hand to her right shoulder, drawing me around so that I faced her with my elbow raised in front of my face.

"What happens if Catherine loses the connection here and lets go?" she asked.

I let go and she feigned a punch at my face. "See, that connection protects you. It tells you what your partner is doing. Lose it and you're vulnerable. Watch again."

This time, when she had me facing her, she brought her right hand up under my elbow and rotated it toward me forcing me down toward the mat. She stepped in so that her leg pressed against my body and pushed.

I let myself fall but kept my eyes on Gina and held myself in a position that would allow me to come up if she released the pressure on my elbow.

She froze the throw at that point. "See how she's keeping that connection? She's down, but she isn't giving up. She's ready to counter if I get careless." Gina released the pressure on my elbow and I rose from the mat, bringing my fist up to strike her.

"That's right," Gina said. "Always be ready, even as you're thrown, keep that connection and watch for a chance to counter. Okay, try it again, and pay attention to the connection."

By the time I headed home, I felt calmer than I had all week. I thought about Gina's admonition to pay attention to the connection. That'd be harder than usual in this case. The ugliness of the snuff photos repelled me. A lot of this job is understanding your quarry, getting inside his head. But I didn't want to be anyplace near this guy. Managing my emotions could be as tough as catching the prankster.

Dinner was not the warm family scene I'd hoped for. Molly communicated in monosyllables and even that seemed to require enormous effort. Peter had picked up Thai takeout and she spent dinner isolating each ingredient and pushing it around her plate. Her major contribution to the conversation was an occasional dark comment on the possible origins of the unidentifiable items she wasn't eating.

Peter tried to make jokes and proved immediately that he was capable of grossing out even a fourteen year old. I made a couple of unsuccessful tries at conversation; Molly responded with shrugs and grunts. I felt like I was dining with a black hole.

I watched her and tried to figure out whether her silence was just normal teenage moodiness or if it might signal a deeper problem. This parenting business is damn hard. Like finding yourself in the middle of another culture where you understand only a small part of the language and almost none of the nuance.

And it hurts. Nobody ever told me that. It hurt just to sit across from Molly and feel locked out. I spend much of my life getting information from people, tough people, sometimes dishonest people. But that's easy compared with getting a fourteen year old to tell you what's bothering her.

Peter got another Tsing Tao from the refrigerator and poured us each some. "I ran into Bill McCoy today. He's the guy who helped me on the Valposi case, that girl I was hired to find just after we met."

"The one who ran away with the Hell's Angel?" I said.

"He wasn't really a Hell's Angel, just an unkempt biker. Her parents assumed any guy on a Harley was a Hell's Angel."

"He wasn't such a prize as I remember," I said. "He beat her up a couple of times."

"It turned out her dad had also beat her up, so she figured it was all part of a relationship."

"That's sick," Molly said.

Peter turned to look at her. "Yeah, it is. But I don't know how much you can blame the boy. His dad used to beat him up every Saturday night. He probably thought that's what a man did."

"What happened to the girl?" Molly asked.

Peter took a drink of beer and began the saga of Mia Valposi. I watched with a certain fascination as he drew Molly into his story. The scowl melted to just the hint of a frown, a sign she was concentrating on his words, and she put her elbows on the table and leaned forward as she listened.

"So you sent her back to a father who beat her?" she asked when Peter reached the end.

"The family went into counseling," Peter said. "And her

grandmother got involved, so there was someone she could go to if things got bad at home."

"Was she okay then?"

"I don't know," Peter said. "I hope so."

Molly looked troubled. She wanted a happy ending. "But the biker could have come back. She could have run away again."

"Yeah," Peter said. "Life doesn't come with guarantees. Her grandmother'll help her if she asks, but she's got to be willing to go to her. I don't know if she'll do that. She had a lot of trouble asking for help."

Molly nodded, still frowning. "I guess I should do my algebra," she said. "Can I do the dishes after I finish it?"

"Sure," I said. "I'll even dry, if you ask me."

She smiled for the first time. "Okay, thanks."

"Very nice," I said after Molly left the room. "You did a masterly job of drawing her out."

"I've had a lot of practice with skittery kids, some of them are almost like wild animals. You have to ease up from the side. Catch them off guard."

"I wish I could figure out what's going on with her," I said. "Do you have any idea?"

Peter shook his head. "Not a clue. We'll just have to wait till she wants to talk about it."

The snuff photos forced their way to the front of my mind again. The women had been so young. And someplace in San Francisco men were buying photos like the ones I'd received. They might even have been taken here.

"I need an opinion on something," I said. I brought the envelope into the kitchen, closed the door and dumped the pictures on the table.

Peter studied them. His face was grave. "These from Systech?"

"The office mail," I said. "Jesse doesn't think they mean anything. They worry me."

"I can see why," Peter said. "They're scary. At the very least, you're dealing with someone with a twisted sense of humor and a lot of hostility toward women."

"And at the most?"

Peter shook his head. "Trouble, real trouble."

Chapter

8

I dreamt of women with eyes like the slick surface of slightly stagnant pools. One woman beckoned me to her, and as I approached, she took out her eyes and held them in her palm like two blue-and-white marbles. Her eye sockets were empty.

The dreams didn't scare me, but they weren't pleasant and it annoyed the hell out of me that my subconscious was running wild. I couldn't get the snuff photos out of my head. They looked so damn real. I don't know that they've ever nailed anyone for killing a woman in a snuff film, but I know cops who suspect it happens. When I thought of the photos and of all the throwaway women—the runaway girls, prostitutes, drug users—who could disappear without anyone looking too hard, it seemed all too possible.

And even if the photos were merely cleverly created illusion, what of the dark fantasies that made them valuable? The men who bought or traded these pictures wanted to believe that they were real. That alone was enough to disturb my sleep.

• • •

The last time I looked at the clock it was just before three, and I was too deep for dreaming when the alarm woke me at seven. It took two cups of coffee to get my eyes open.

Elaine was waiting for me when I arrived at Systech. She'd gotten a package similar to mine and so had Tonia. "I'll bet Sheila got one, too," she said grimly. "But she's been in a meeting, so I couldn't talk to her. No one else seems to have gotten anything like it."

I called Tonia and asked her to join us, and we compared notes. The photos we'd gotten were similar but not identical. All had come through the office mail, and none contained any clue to their sender.

Elaine was furious. "I'm taking mine straight to human resources," she said. "Not that they've been able to do anything so far."

"Do you think these came from Clark?" Tonia asked me.

"I don't know," I said. "But they feel real different from the E-mail. I think it's someone else."

Tonia nodded. "Yeah, me too. But I'm still going to tell human resources that I think Clark's behind the E-mail messages." She tried to pretend she wasn't worried, but her voice had a tight, thin quality and there were circles under her eyes. She reminded me of myself at her age, desperately trying to hide her vulnerability. Like me, she was probably more afraid of appearing weak than of the things she had reason to fear.

Elaine must have noticed the same things I had. "You okay?" she asked Tonia.

"Sure," Tonia said. "It's no big deal." But I knew it was, and my heart went out to her.

She got out of my office as fast as she could, and Elaine followed her. As she left, the older woman said, "Oh, be sure to check your E-mail."

I turned on the computer and called up my E-mail with some trepidation. There was a message from Satyr, and it included a file containing a scanned image of some guy's genitals. Combine the powers of computer and copier and what do you get? Some guy's privates.

After yesterday's photos, there was something almost innocent about the fuzzy scanned image. It reminded me of years ago when bored office workers first discovered that copy machines could photograph more than memos. Offices were flooded with grainy records first of people's faces, then of other parts of their anatomy. A few people went a bit far, and not everyone found it as amusing as I did, but it was all done in fun.

The scanned image had the same adolescent quality as the earlier X-rated copies. So did the pranks. But not the snuff photos. Sheila had suggested that the pranks might inspire others to join in. If she was right, my job had just gotten harder.

I got a call from Sheila about an hour later. "Can you come to my office?" she asked tensely. I told her I'd be right there.

"Elaine says you got pictures," she said as soon as she'd shut the door.

"Yes. You, too?"

She nodded and perched on the edge of her desk. "Some charming guys out there. Look, I don't want you to worry. This isn't about you. They're doing this to get me to back off."

"Back off from what?" I asked.

"From a bunch of things," she said vaguely. "Yesterday, I requested that Tonia be put on the development team for the client-server applications. The KeeGo programmers are pissed about that. I also informed everyone in this division that they'll have to serve as final managers for their accounts. That means that they're responsible for making sure clients get answers to questions and solutions to problems. Kingsley and DeMarco just about went through the roof. It'll really cramp their style to have to arrange service for their accounts."

Sheila said it with a smile, and I smiled back appreciatively.

The discomfort she was causing the KeeGo guys must be very satisfying, but she wasn't after revenge. Both moves would give her valuable information about Systech's new product. Forcing Kingsley and DeMarco to deal with and report on their clients' problems would tell her how the product was actually performing. Meanwhile, Tonia would be studying the program and picking the KeeGo programmers' brains.

"No wonder they're upset," I said. "And no wonder Leggett put you in charge of minicomputers."

"Allen gave me this job because he figured these guys would think I was just a dumb broad and they'd open up more with me than with a guy," she said frankly. "He's probably right. And I plan to give him not only what he wanted but a lot more as well."

As I left her office I wondered about Sheila's "a lot more." That's one drawback of this job; you're always looking for what's beneath the surface. Doesn't make for an open and trusting nature.

I was startled out of my thoughts by two salesmen from the midrange division who nearly ran me down as they headed for the lounge. I tagged along behind to see what had them moving so fast. Maybe someone had brought doughnuts.

Someone had brought doughnuts, and that someone was none other than Jerry Keegan, the founder of KeeGo. Keegan wasn't a large man, about five seven or eight and fairly thin, but he occupied a lot of space. He radiated energy and he drew people to him like a magnet. He stood in the middle of a group of salesmen, gesturing and laughing, talking faster than most people think. Everyone in the room was focused on him, and I could sense them slowly inching forward, wanting to get closer to him.

It's fascinating to watch that kind of charisma. It lights a spark in the people it touches, makes them feel a bit more alive. Keegan was talking about the new client-server applications and all around him heads nodded and people smiled. Excitement crackled in the air. I wondered how Allen Leggett, the low-key CEO of Systech, felt about his dynamic new associate. Keegan wasn't a man to stay in second place for long.

I wasn't as taken with Jerry Keegan as the salesmen were. He reminded me of a junk bond salesman or a corporate raider, long on charisma and short on ethics. Kingsley and DeMarco's attitudes were probably strongly influenced by their boss. If my hunch was right, they were all of the rape-and-plunder school of corporate conduct. The sooner I gave Leggett an excuse to smack them down, the better.

I left Jerry Keegan to his adoring crowd and walked back to my office. I needed a way to get to Kingsley and DeMarco. My original approach of trying to provoke them had only cost me my skirt; and when it came to applying pressure, Sheila was doing a much better job than I ever could. Time to try another tack.

These guys were so impressed with themselves, I figured they might fall for a bit of ego polishing. Now, any intelligent man would have been instantly suspicious of the unlikely transformation from in-your-face to under-your-thumb, but I was counting on Kingsley and DeMarco to be too self-absorbed to think too deeply about a bit player like me.

Acting submissive had another advantage. If one of the men had sent the snuff photos, he'd assume he'd succeeded in scaring me into better behavior. That ought to please him, and possibly tempt him to carelessness.

Kingsley, the tall Texan, was out with a potential client, but a call confirmed that DeMarco was in. I took an interview sheet and headed for his office. My ostensible goal was to gather further information on his voice-mail needs. We'd already done this once with me being assertive and sarcastic. Now we'd try sweet and admiring.

DeMarco was wearing more in accessories than many men

pay for a suit. His blue-and-mauve silk tie was like an impressionist painting, and the leather of his shoes looked soft enough for gloves. His dark hair lay smoothly and perfectly in place, and not a flake of dandruff dotted his dark jacket.

DeMarco hadn't forgotten my previous poor behavior, but it only took a few comments on his obvious superiority as a salesman to earn his forgiveness. I thought I might be laying it on a little thick. That wasn't a danger.

He began telling me how they'd done things at KeeGo. "Jerry Keegan understood that you've got to spend to make a buck," he said. "You've got to wine and dine these guys. You don't do seminars in St. Louis, for chrissake. You do seminars in Bermuda. Wine, women, song, the whole thing. Give them a good time before you pitch the product."

"It's clear that you're just much more high-powered than the salespeople here at Systech," I said.

"You better believe it. I can't believe they put a woman in charge of sales," he said, apparently unaware that he was speaking to a woman. "Women are great at support, but not at sales. For sales you need the drive, the competitive spirit, a killer instinct.

"You know Bob Kingsley, hell of a guy. Now, Bob is a natural salesman. He'd wrestle alligators to make a sale. Last year at the company picnic, Bob sprained his ankle playing touch football. You think he stopped? Hell, no. He taped it up and played the rest of the game on it. That's the kind of guy Bob is. A real competitor."

A real idiot, I thought. But what do I know? I'm a woman. I kept an admiring smile plastered on my face and made the matching sounds. DeMarco regaled me with stories of lavish entertaining and sales seminars in exotic places, with an emphasis on prices, brand names, and amounts of alcohol consumed.

When he paused for breath and just before my eyes glazed over, I said, "And you guys have such a sense of humor. I guess that's part of being a great salesman, too."

That prompted stories of a series of practical jokes at KeeGo that made me think Systech had gotten off lightly so far. I laughed appreciatively at each joke, and when the time seemed right, I said lightly, "Not too hard to guess where the mice in the drawers came from."

DeMarco's smile vanished and he frowned. "What the hell are you suggesting?"

I looked shocked. "Nothing," I said. "It's just that most of the folks here seem so kind of dull, I figured the prankster must be someone with a bit more—I don't know—pizzazz." I tried to sound admiring, even flirtatious. Like a woman who got turned on by domination.

DeMarco's gaze was still angry. His dark brows were pulled down so far they almost met over his eyes. "You're not going to pin those jokes on me," he said.

"Hey, the jokes aren't my business," I said. "I'm only here for a few weeks. I'm just enjoying the show."

DeMarco's reactions were not those of a man who was playing sexual cat-and-mouse. He'd been defensive and quick to deny any role in the pranks, but if he was turned on by submissiveness, I'd seen no sign of it. If he was the source of the snuff photos, their purpose was more likely tied to business than a twisted kind of pleasure.

And that brought me back to Jerry Keegan. Why was he schmoozing with the regional sales staff? His office was in the corporate wing. I wondered if the pranks could be part of a calculated move by Keegan to create dissension. I couldn't see what purpose they might serve for him, but that didn't mean there wasn't one.

I stared at the blank wall at the end of my office and tried to figure out what he might be up to. I wasn't making any progress when the telephone startled me out of my musings. It was Jesse. "I've been monitoring Clark Phillips's, the KeeGo programmer's, computer activity," he said. "He's spent a lot of time browsing through the system today."

"Any idea what he's up to?"

"Nope, but I think it's time to bell the cat," Jesse said. "I'll talk to Jenkins, the security manager, and bring him in on what we're doing. He and I can monitor the system so that we'll know whenever Phillips goes for super-user privileges."

"Good idea. There may be more going on here than we thought." I told Jesse of Keegan's surprise visit to the employees' lounge. "It's just a hunch, but we sure as hell don't want to take any risks with the computer system. In fact, you should probably monitor all four of the KeeGo programmers. Can you do that without tipping them that we're watching?"

"They won't have a clue. Jenkins and I will see to that." I could hear the excitement in Jesse's voice. Things were starting to get interesting.

Chapter

9

Thursday morning I woke to sun for the fourth day in a row.

It's nice to get up to a warm house. Nice but distracting. Makes me think of vacation, makes Peter think of vacation, too. Makes us both late for work. Or it used to before Molly moved in.

The morning's E-mail messages were as raunchy as usual, but the author seemed to have reached the limits of his imagination. He'd begun to repeat himself. Maybe anonymous exhibitionism was losing its thrill.

The more I thought about Sheila's reactions to the pranks, the more curious I became. I wondered what "bigger game" she was after and how it might relate to the snuff photos that bothered everyone but her. Maybe if I could get her away from the office, she'd talk more freely. I called to see if she wanted to go for lunch.

"I can't," she said regretfully. "I'm up to my ass in alligators. No time to eat."

"Want me to get you a sandwich when I go out?" I asked.

"That'd be great," she said. "Anything but ham. And no onions. And a Diet Coke if you can."

Systech's brick building had been quite comfortable, so I was surprised by the heat when I walked outside. The air was absolutely still and a bit stale. Sunny weather tarnishes quickly in the city. It's only bright and sparkly for the first couple of days, then the effluent of city life builds up and slowly becomes visible in the air. Each day the sky is a little less blue, and the brown smudge at the horizon grows darker.

There weren't any delis right near Systech. I decided to drive down to a place on China Basin. It wasn't the closest place but it had great pastrami sandwiches.

China Basin is across one of the channels dug from the bay to allow boats access to the low-lying land south of the Bay Bridge. The old mechanical drawbridges are still in use, but they look like creatures from an earlier age, social realist sculptures glorifying a kind of commerce and industry that is increasingly deserting the city.

The China Basin Building sits like a great beached ship in the middle of the basin. Two blocks long and only a few stories high, it dwarfs everything around it. The Basin Deli is in a considerably less grand building across the street. The line at the counter mixed guys in coveralls with yuppies in various business attire.

It occurred to me as I made that judgment that I didn't look any different from the women I'd classified as yuppies. Not a comforting thought.

I drove back to Systech with the rich smell of pastrami tantalizing me. If I hadn't needed to see Sheila, I'd have looked for a sunny spot near the water for an urban picnic.

I carried my aromatic sack to her office, opened it, and

passed it under her nose. "Breathe deeply," I said. "The smell is almost as good as the taste. You want company or are you too busy for that?"

"Sure, I'd like company. My doctor says that the combination of food and sales reports produces ulcers. You can save me from myself."

As regional sales manager, Sheila got a table as well as a desk. A good thing since the desk was covered with piles of papers. The table was only half-covered.

Sheila seemed never to do less than two things at a time. She brought a pad and pen to the table so she could take notes as we talked. I was hoping for the kind of chatty conversation that borders on gossip and provides all sorts of useful information. Sheila wanted answers to the questions she'd asked at our last meeting.

Fortunately, I'd had my assistant, Chris, take care of that research so I had some answers. But delivering a report on voice-mail systems put a real dent in my enjoyment of my China Basin pastrami.

Sheila looked tired, but she was even more animated than usual, agitated even. When she put the pad down and massaged her temples, I asked, "Is something wrong?"

"Nothing really," she said, but her manner contradicted her words.

"More pictures?" I asked.

She shook her head, put her sandwich down, picked it up again. "Kingsley and DeMarco are tougher players than I figured," she said. "And smarter.

"Last night they got into the computer of one of my saleswomen and changed a number in her fax file. She came in early this morning to send a fax to a company in Los Angeles, where we have a big sale pending. It had to reach them for a meeting at nine. It never got there. Now she's in trouble, and that means I'm in trouble."

"Couldn't she have mistyped the number?"

"That's what Jorgensen says, that she screwed up; but the woman says she selected it from her file. She did the same thing yesterday to send another fax and it worked fine. This morning, it didn't."

"You're sure it happened after hours?" I asked.

"I can't prove it, but I'm sure. I know because someone was also in my office last night."

I put my sandwich down. "How do you know?" I asked.

Sheila popped up and began to pace. "You won't believe it, but this isn't the disorganized jumble it appears," she said. "I know where everything is, not just which pile, but where in the pile."

I nodded and tried not to look incredulous. Sheila was a piler, stacks of paper sat on every available surface. There was even a pile on the floor next to her desk. Hard to believe she could keep track of it all.

"As far as I can tell, nothing is missing," she said, perching on her desk, "but two of the piles were switched, and in one, some papers that were on the bottom moved to the middle."

I turned and looked at the door. "Wasn't your office locked?"

"Sure, but you can open it with a credit card. Six months ago one of the guys bet another he could open any office door in this place. He won. It was always a joke, until now." She jumped up and walked to the window then back again, picked up a folder, put it down. Played with a pencil. Finally, sat down again in her chair.

"You're sure, absolutely sure, that someone was here after hours?" I asked.

Sheila nodded forcefully. "I'm sure. But of course there's no way to prove it."

"Maybe there is," I said. "You use electronic keys. Are they coded for each person?" While office doors at Systech had conventional locks, access to the different areas in the building was controlled with electronic keys, little plastic cards that looked like credit cards but acted like keys. You put one into the electronic lock and if the codes matched up, it let you in.

Behind that electronic lock is a computer, which can capture information and store it. While many businesses just give everyone the same key, some high-tech firms issue individual keys with unique codes, and the system records the time and place that each key is used. It's really like an automatic time clock, tells you who was where when. I've caught more than one in-house thief who didn't realize he was signing in when he carted off inventory.

"I don't know about the keys," Sheila said. "But even if we know who it was, it won't do any good. He'll just say he was working late, and we won't have proof to the contrary."

We wouldn't have enough proof for a jury, but we might well have enough for Leggett. "At least you'd know who to look out for," I said.

Sheila's mouth set in a hard line. "I know who to look out for," she said. "It's either Kingsley or DeMarco, maybe both. And if I don't get them soon, they're going to get me."

Sheila was in a tough situation. It wasn't only the KeeGo guys she had to worry about. There was a good chance Jorgensen was just looking for an excuse to demote her, and she was surrounded by people anxious to help him.

When I got back to my office, I called Jesse. "Are the electronic keys individually coded?" I asked.

"I don't know," he said. "But give me a minute and I can find out. The data from the locks is on the network."

I waited and listened to the soft click of computer keys in the background. A couple of minutes later, he was back.

"The keys are coded by individual. Every time someone uses one, the information is captured and stored in a locked file on the network. What more do you want to know?"

"I want to know everyone who came into the regional sales

and marketing area last night after Sheila Wainwright left. She thinks that was about nine o'clock."

"I'll have it for you in a half an hour," he said.

The keys could be just the break we needed. My stomach got that light, floating feeling from too much excitement. I tried to concentrate on other work, but I knew I wasn't going to be good for anything until I got Jesse's call.

That call was mercifully quick in coming but damnably frustrating. He'd checked the files twice and found that no one had entered the sales area between nine last night and six this morning. Not even the cleaning crew had been on that part of the third floor.

"Someone must have been there," I insisted. "Could Clark Phillips or someone else have altered the files to erase a name?"

"Not since yesterday at seven. That's when Jenkins and I finished up. The system is now set up so that Jenkins's computer beeps and records all the keystrokes whenever anyone tries for super-user privileges. That means that when Phillips or anyone else tries to get into places he isn't supposed to be, we'll know exactly what he was doing."

"And no one was here after nine?"

"No one," he said. "Either Wainwright is confused or your prankster can walk through walls."

It's poor form to snarl at your partner, so I bit back my frustration until I was off the phone. Damn. We'd seemed so close. And Sheila had been so sure. I was still half-convinced she was right though I couldn't think of any way she could be. And why would someone break into her office, go through her papers, yet not take any of them? I had to admit, Sheila's story just didn't make sense.

I waited until my frustration level had dropped below simmer and went back to the old game plan. I reached for the phone to see if Bob Kingsley was in. It rang before I picked it up.

"Ms. Sayler, Mr. Jorgensen would like to see you," a smooth female voice announced. "Would it be possible for you to come to his office now?"

I wished I had a good reason why it wasn't possible, almost anything, even a root canal, but I agreed to come. I was too curious not to.

Jorgensen kept me waiting for ten minutes. I practiced my breathing and watched the waves of irritation and even less admirable emotions that his little display of power inspired. I was getting ready to tell his secretary that she could call me at my office when he was ready to see me, when the intercom buzzed and she told me to go in.

Jorgensen was sitting behind his desk. He didn't rise when I entered. Instead, he very slowly and very obviously let his eyes move down my body and back up. There was nothing subtle or furtive about it, and his smile said that he enjoyed immensely any discomfort that it caused.

I was shocked, I didn't think guys did that anymore, not guys in jobs like Jorgensen's. Then I was furious, because he could do it and get away with it. What was I going to do, run to the boss and complain that his buddy Scott had *looked* at me. Leggett was a decent guy; I doubt that he'd have understood the games a man like Jorgensen played with women.

I swallowed my irritation, sat down and said, "You had something you wanted to talk to me about?"

"I was wondering how much longer it's going to take to catch the guy who's pulling these pranks. It's very disruptive to office morale." He said it with his eyes on my legs.

"Do you have any suggestions?"

"I rather thought that was what we hired you for," he said, finally looking me in the eye.

"You didn't hire me. Allen Leggett did," I said. "I report to him, everything I find." I put the emphasis on "everything," then I stood up and walked to the door. "Unless you have something germane to the investigation, I'll be getting back to work."

Jorgensen just leaned back in his chair and smiled his superior smile. "By all means," he said.

I steamed all the way back to my office. It's clear to me at moments like this why I didn't become a cop and why I'll never be part of a large corporation. I can tolerate a lot of stuff that other people think is hard. I've spent hours in a cold car on a dark street watching a door to see who comes out, gone undercover as a cleaning lady and a drug dealer, been threatened and even shot at. What I can't take is the stuff that gets dished out every day in offices all over the world.

As I calmed down I began to wonder why Jorgensen would risk such behavior. He knew who I was and why I was there. Surely he wasn't stupid enough to believe that he could intimidate me into leaving. I found that thought even more insulting than the way he'd treated me in his office.

I gave my office door a harder slam than I'd intended, checked my chair, plopped down, and picked up the afternoon mail. At the bottom of the stack was a brown envelope with a typed address and no return on it. I had a sick feeling in my stomach as I held it in my hand.

Four photos—four women in different forms of bondage, all with ugly wounds. One with haunting glassy eyes. They weren't as shocking the second time, but they were no less disturbing.

A fifth photo stuck at the edge of the envelope. I pulled it out and gasped. A naked woman hung suspended by her wrists, red welts across her body. Where her face should have been, a photograph of my own gazed back at me.

Chapter

10

I took a couple of deep breaths and forced my mind to focus.

I studied the photo. It didn't look familiar, though it was clearly me. It had been cut so that there wasn't much background. A patch of red behind my right ear, a larger green area that could be foliage but could also be a building or a car. Nothing to tell me where it had been taken.

My stomach felt as if it were full of rocks, and my heart had not only speeded up but seemed to have grown larger. Where the hell had that picture been taken? Had he followed me? Did he know where I lived? Who I lived with? Did he know I wasn't who I pretended to be?

Leggett was supposed to be the only one at Systech who knew Jesse's and my identities. He'd told Jorgensen, but he swore he'd told no one else. Not even his director of human resources.

I'd used a phony address for my personnel file, and even Leggett didn't know my home address, so the only way someone at Systech could know where I lived was to have followed me home.

The rocks in my stomach grew heavier as I realized that I hadn't bothered to check for tails when I left work at Systech. I'm careful about that when I think a job might get dangerous, but this one had seemed pretty tame.

Strangely enough, it wasn't the implied threat of the photo that bothered me. It was the sense of intrusion, the idea that this guy had been following me, knew things about me, might know about Molly.

I'd been halfway persuaded by Sheila's theory that the purpose of the photos was to get her to back off from her current policies. But that didn't explain why *I* was getting them. I wasn't a company employee, and I had no role in Systech's office politics. It was a bit farfetched to assume that someone had gone to all this trouble to hassle me in order to distract and scare Sheila.

Unless, of course, that someone knew that I was a private investigator. I looked at the photo again and wondered if I'd slipped up somewhere. Jesse and I hadn't bothered to change our names for this job. It didn't seem necessary. Maybe we'd been wrong.

I called Elaine and Tonia to see if they'd received similar photos. They hadn't. Sheila was out, but I got her secretary to tell me that she'd received a brown envelope with no return address. Now *that* was interesting. The focus had narrowed to Sheila and me.

Whatever was going on, I didn't like the idea of Molly coming home to an empty house. Peter was out of town for the night, so I called my secretary, Amy, and asked her to wait at my place until Molly got there, then take her to one of her friends.

"Why don't I just take her home with me?" Amy said. "We'll hang out and bake cookies." Amy is a twenty-nine year old with the soul of a grandmother. It used to annoy me when she fussed over me, but I've come to enjoy it, and in times like this, it's really useful.

Next I called Jesse and arranged to meet him after work. I didn't want to risk going to our office, so I suggested that he meet me at Peter's.

Peter's office is in what used to be his apartment, on the ground floor of a house owned by a friend from "the good old days." It's several blocks above Haight Street, the geographic center of those same good old days. Today, the Haight still has something of its carnival feel and vestiges of the sixties remain, but there are too many burned-out cases to make it the joyful place it once was.

Peter's house is up the hill, surrounded by much grander Victorians. Once crash pads for alienated kids, these fine old houses have acquired fancy facelifts as the neighborhood has gentrified into a community of families and young professionals. Bugs and buses have been replaced by Volvos and Hondas. It's getting harder to find a parking spot.

I let myself into his apartment. The door opens into the living room, which serves as his office. Peter's office plays Dr. Jekyll to his bedroom's Mr. Hyde. You'd never guess from the tidy desk top that this was a man who thought closets were for stacking case files and chairs for holding clothes.

The place smelled dusty, and the three houseplants that had survived Peter's periodic neglect looked unloved and droopy. I gave them some water, and considered, but only for moment, sweeping up the dust bunnies that were multiplying in the kitchen. Their size and number gave me a new insight into why they're called bunnies.

The fridge contained its usual staples: beer and half-and-half. The doorbell sounded and I pulled out a couple of beers before going to let Jesse in.

I handed him the photos. "Only Sheila and I got this batch," I said.

He studied the one with my picture pasted on it. "Any idea where this was taken?" he asked.

"No. You?"

He shook his head. "What do you think's behind it?" he asked.

"When I look for a connection between Sheila and me, I get two possible scenarios. We're both uppity women who've challenged men. If one of those men has a screw loose, this could be his way of striking back. Scenario two is that this has something to do with whatever Sheila's up to with Kingsley and DeMarco. If they've figured out I'm an investigator, they might assume I'm helping her."

"If we're talking loose screw, any candidates?"

"Maybe. It's a long shot," I said and told him about Scott Jorgensen. "He's clearly into power and domination, and it feels like that's what the photos are about. But the guy really doesn't feel like a loose screw. I can see him getting turned on by those pictures. I can't see him sending them."

Jesse nodded. "I don't like the idea that this guy's following you," he said.

"It doesn't thrill me, either. You think he could be dangerous?"

Jesse sucked on his lower lip the way he does when he's concentrating. "I don't know," he said. "My gut feeling is still no. Even if he does get off on this sort of pictures, it doesn't mean he'd do anything. And if he's using them to scare you, he probably chose them for their shock value. I just don't think there's a connection between pornography and violence." He paused, then added, "But I still think you should be careful."

"I think I should talk with Allen Leggett tomorrow," I said. "He should be told about the misdirected fax and your monitoring of the computer system, as well as the snuff photos. And maybe I can find out something more about what Sheila's up to."

Jesse nodded but whatever he was going to say was cut short

by a sneezing fit. He suffers from allergies. "This place is too dusty for you," I said. "We better get you out of here."

I looked at the photos one last time as I picked them up to leave. They were the work of either a sick mind or a clever and unscrupulous one. I wasn't sure which was worse.

I didn't sleep well again that night. I woke tired and vaguely depressed, and I didn't feel a whole lot better when I reached Systech. I called Allen Leggett's secretary to request an appointment and was told that he could see me immediately. Oh, great, I thought. If I'd known I could get in so quickly, I'd have waited till I'd had at least one cup of coffee.

Leggett was a pencil of a man with a head that seemed a bit large for his body and a prominent Adam's apple. He had pale blue eyes and blond hair so fine it never quite stayed in place. He was soft-spoken, but his voice had a quiet authority. He listened more than he talked, and when he said something, it was worth paying attention to.

In marked contrast to Jerry Keegan and his circle, Leggett dressed simply. Today he wore chinos and a blue Oxford cloth shirt open at the neck.

I told him about the alteration of the saleswoman's fax file and Clark Phillips's incursions into the computer system. He nodded and didn't interrupt. His face was grave. When I paused, he said, "Hold on a minute, I want someone else to hear this." Then he picked up the phone.

"Scott," he said, "I want you to come in for a minute. I'd like your opinion on something."

Oh, great, I thought, just the man I wanted to see.

If my presence bothered Jorgensen, he sure didn't show it. Leggett had me repeat what I'd told him, and it became apparent fairly quickly that Jorgensen was the CEO's adviser as well as his VP of sales. No wonder he'd felt he could get away with hassling me yesterday.

He was polite but cool. I was too. I silently kicked myself for antagonizing the boss's best buddy. Being a smart ass is usually stupid. You'd think I could remember that.

"Sabotage is certainly a possibility," Jorgensen conceded when I finished my report, "but it's also a convenient excuse."

"In a situation like this, it's prudent to assume the worst and take precautions," I said. I explained Jesse's plan to monitor the computer network to catch anyone going for super-user privileges. Leggett nodded approvingly, obviously reassured by a technological solution.

As I talked I watched Jorgensen watch Leggett. As long as the boss was nodding, his VP would be all for the plan. The minute Leggett expressed doubts, Jorgensen would cut my throat.

Not the time to bring up the snuff photos, I decided. Not with Jorgensen just waiting to put me down. I'd have loved to see his reaction, but I didn't want to risk it. I wasn't going to play this game on his home field.

I'd better watch my back, I decided as I walked to my office. With Leggett turning to Jorgensen for counsel, there was no telling what mischief the VP of sales might stir up. If he was the source of the snuff photos, there were layers to the game that I hadn't figured out yet.

I holed up in my office for a while and tried to imagine what Jorgensen might be up to. I didn't get very far. Finally, I did what I always do when I'm stumped. I went to get a cup of coffee.

On the way back I saw a familiar figure standing over the copy machine. It was Frank McFadden. As one of the salesmen who'd been denied a place in the client-server group, he stood to gain if Kingsley or DeMarco were fired or Sheila was demoted. Either move would open up a slot that he might fill. I decided to see what he was up to.

He was copying a long document, and when he realized I was there, he moved to shield it from me.

"Hi, Frank," I said. "Copying the Manhattan phone directory?"

The polished surface he presented the world slipped for only a moment and he looked like a nervous teenager, then it was back in place—the affable smile mirrored in wide-set brown eyes, the interested, sincere expression. "Nah, just the usual stuff," he said, still standing between me and the machine. "You going to figure out a way to save us from this?"

"No one can save us from the mighty copier," I joked. "How did they ever get along without them?"

We joked and bantered. He was an attractive man, and he knew it. He flirted but he wasn't putting much into it. I'd watched him with a young woman who'd just been hired as a secretary, and I knew that I was only getting about twenty percent of the McFadden performance. I was crushed.

"I'm afraid I haven't got everybody straight yet," I said. "I know you're in minicomputer sales. Are you part of the client-server group?"

"No, but I am in minicomputers."

"Oh," I said as if I were surprised. "For some reason I thought you were part of the group that came from KeeGo."

"No, I've been with Systech for years, but I was in Chicago. I transferred to San Francisco about the time the KeeGo deal went through."

"What brought you here?" I asked.

"I was ready for a new challenge. Thought it'd be exciting to work on the client-server products. But they didn't take many of us from Systech into that group. They'll probably expand it later." He smiled as he said it, and if it bothered him that he'd been denied a place in the group, he certainly didn't show it.

"How disappointing to make the move and be left off the team," I said. "Sounds like you were plenty qualified."

"Well, I am," he said, continuing to smile his pleasant smile, "but there were only so many places and Sheila Wainwright has more programming background than I do, so at this point in time, she was a better choice for regional manager."

A better choice for regional manager. Now that was interesting. I'd assumed he was shooting for a place on the team, but he had his eye on the top spot. I hid my surprise and said, "Some of the guys aren't too wild about working for Sheila Wainwright. They're not sure she can handle the new sales campaign."

"Oh, I'm sure she'll do fine," he said. "Sheila's very competent. It's always hard getting started. She'll do fine in time."

He was certainly gracious. Too gracious. First he'd told Tonia that Sheila got the job because Leggett was afraid of the feds, then he'd told another guy that she'd earned the promotion on her back, and now he was telling me she was better qualified. If I'd been asking questions to get straight answers, I'd have quit right then, but I was curious to see what McFadden would have to say about the pranks. "Well, I don't know if it's because you have a bunch of new guys or what," I said, "but I have to tell you, I've worked with lots of companies, and I've never seen anything like some of the crazy stuff that goes on here."

His smile never wavered. "You mean the mice in the drawers?" Well, no, I meant the snuff photos and my stained skirt, but I didn't say that. What I did say was, "That and the other stuff."

"You mustn't judge us by the pranks," he said. "There are just one or maybe two guys who have an attitude problem. Most of the men in this office deplore the pranks."

He said it with the smooth delivery of a politician, and I believed him about as much as I believe most of our elected officials. I was surprised that he'd passed up the opportunity to cast suspicion on the KeeGo salesmen, then he added, "It's just that those guys from Texas are having a hard time settling in."

The copier spit out a final page, purred a second more, then went quiet. McFadden scooped up his papers, still using his body to block my view of them, bid me a cordial but relieved good-bye, and hurried off. I wondered what he was so careful to hide.

As I watched him go I thought of Sheila's allegation that Kingsley or DeMarco had gone through her office. It hadn't made sense that someone might break in and yet not take anything. Not until you realized that for some people at Systech, a copy might be just as good as the original.

Chapter

11

I watched for tails when I left work that afternoon and looked over my shoulder about twenty times more than absolutely necessary. Not that I was scared, just cautious.

Actually, I was in a better mood than I'd been in for days. Peter had called earlier to say that my sister, Marion, wanted Molly to spend the weekend with her and Molly had agreed. Those two can only go about twenty-two hours before Marion starts to inventory her daughter's personality defects or Molly turns up the music and goes sulky, but for tonight Peter and I would have the house to ourselves.

Snuff photos weren't part of my plans for the evening, so I left the latest batch at my office and resolved that for tonight, at least, we wouldn't talk about Systech.

I'd bought some sea bass, a bunch of pencil-thin green beans, some potato-rosemary bread, and a very nice bottle of Chardonnay. It was my turn to cook, but Peter's much better at fixing fish, so he cooked the bass while I set the table and worked on the wine.

"So how are things at Systech?" he asked.

"Not worth talking about when I've got you all to myself," I said.

Peter grinned. "I'd suggest we move right to dessert," he said, "but fish doesn't reheat well." He left the bass untended long enough to give me a slow, very sensuous kiss. I was ready to abandon the bass right there, but Peter takes dinner very seriously.

After a peek at the broiler, he said, "Come on, tell me about it. You don't just get a bunch of snuff photos and decide not to talk about it."

I sighed and told him about the second set of photos. He frowned, but I changed the subject before he could ask all the questions Jesse and I'd already kicked around. I told him instead about what else had been happening at Systech, starting with my encounter with Jorgensen. "I could just strangle that guy," I said. "He's so smug, so damn sure that he can get away with this shit. And the truth is, he can. That's what really infuriates me."

"We all hate feeling powerless," Peter said.

"Yeah, but it's different for you. A woman could look at you the way Jorgensen looked at me, it wouldn't mean anything. When a man does that to a woman, it's a reminder that sex is part of the equation. There's an implied threat."

Peter poked at the fish to see if it was done. "Uh huh," he said, as much to the fish as me. I realized he'd never really understand sexual vulnerability and all the emotions it created. How could he? A man's body was his protection; a woman's is too often a liability.

He looked up and must have read some of my feelings on my face. "Hey, this case is really getting to you, isn't it?"

"I guess so," I said. "I've got to stop letting that happen. I should be concentrating on the prankster, and here I am getting in a feud with Jorgensen. It's stupid." Stupider still to let wounds from almost half a lifetime ago intrude on me now. Something that wasn't a big deal even then. I almost told Peter about my criminology prof, but I couldn't bring myself to do it. So I changed the subject and told him about the alteration of the fax file and Sheila's allegation that someone had sneaked into her office. "Sheila was so sure that someone had been through her things," I said. "She isn't the kind of person to make unfounded accusations. But Jesse's equally sure that the computer-key files couldn't have been altered."

Peter pronounced the sea bass done at that point. I poured more wine and decided it was time to forget about Systech for a while. But I'd aroused Peter's curiosity.

"Is there any other way in?" he asked. "Some way not controlled by the electronic locks?"

"I don't think so," I said. "Unless there are doors that connect to the warehouse."

"What warehouse?"

"The north half of the building is still a warehouse," I said. "They only renovated half of the space for offices. The rest isn't much different than it was fifty years ago. I think they use some of it for their own storage and rent some of it out. I've never been over there."

Peter had finished his sea bass and was eyeing the piece left on my plate. "Oh, no you don't," I said. "You got me talking, now you're going to try and sucker me out of the food I haven't had a chance to eat. Have some more wine."

"Boy, you sure have become distrustful," Peter said. His grin admitted that I'd been right in my suspicions. "Could your prankster have come through the warehouse?"

"I doubt it but it's worth checking," I said as I hastily finished off my meal.

Marion and Molly managed almost thirty-six hours before the fourteen year old gave in to the temptation to tell her mother all about Craig, the would-be biker. They showed up on my doorstep wearing grim, glowering countenances like mother-daughter outfits. I reacted poorly. I laughed.

For my penance I was subjected to a lecture from my sister on the responsibilities of caring for a teenage girl. When I asked Marion if she'd brought a chastity belt, she left in a huff, which was probably the best outcome I could hope for. Molly camped in her room for the rest of the day, building a wall of sound with pulsing rock 'n' roll.

The weekend's entertainment was almost enough to take my mind off the snuff photos. Until I left the house. Then I felt exposed, the casual assumption of anonymity stripped away by the prankster's camera.

I wanted to believe as Jesse did that the photos didn't represent a real danger, and I'd just about succeeded. Until I talked to Tonia Monday morning.

We met in the elevator. She smiled when she greeted me, but the smile didn't light her eyes, and she looked dull and tired. Small wonder, given the snuff photos. She was so anxious to appear tough and confident that I knew she'd never ask for help. All the more reason she might need it.

"You look like you could use a cup of coffee," I said. "I've got a thermos of French roast. Why don't you come up and have some?"

She looked unsure, almost too tired to decide, then agreed. "Sure," she said. "The stuff in the lounge is like battery acid and the guys on the second floor brew theirs to industrial sludge."

When we got to my office, I pulled out my extra mug and poured us each a cup. "You hear anything more from the prankster?" I asked.

She hesitated. I waited. "Yeah," she said in a soft voice. She looked down at her hands. "Saturday I found an envelope on my back porch. It contained pictures of my kitchen and bed-room windows and there was a letter." She stopped and I could tell she was sorry she'd brought up the subject.

"It's okay," I said. "Go on."

"I don't want to talk about what he said, but it was clear he'd been watching my house. And that he knows me from work."

"Watching your house? As in more than once?" I asked.

She nodded. "Yeah. He knew I had two robes, and he described them. Said he liked the black one best because it's shorter and shows more thigh. Then he went on to describe what he'd like to see me wear. It was disgusting."

It was a lot more serious than disgusting. My heart speeded up and my mouth got dry. "Staking out your house goes way beyond a prank, Tonia," I said.

"I feel like such a fool." She jumped up and walked to the window, pretending to look out.

"Whoa, wait a minute," I said. "Being a victim doesn't make you a fool."

"I should have been more careful about keeping my blinds closed," she said. "I'm always careful about the ones on the street, but I've gotten careless about the ones in back. After all, there's no way to see in except from my backyard, and it's not all that easy to get into there."

"So this guy has been sneaking into your backyard." My heart had kicked up a couple of more notches. I didn't like to think of the man who'd sent the snuff photos being in Tonia's backyard.

"Yeah, and getting his jollies watching me parade around half-dressed. God, I feel like such a fool," she said again.

I looked at Tonia with astonishment, then understanding. She had every right to feel outrage or fury, but her anger turned inward against herself. "I don't think you're the one to blame here," I said.

"I should have been more careful."

Ah yes, as if being more careful would have made any difference, as if somehow *her* failure to pull the shade was what caused *him* to sneak into her yard. "It's always the woman's fault," I thought bitterly.

"Have you complained to the company about this?" I asked.

"Absolutely not. And I'm not about to. It's too damn embarrassing."

"Tonia, this is serious," I said. "The guy who sneaked into your yard committed a crime. He could go to jail for that."

"Come on, Catherine," she said, "even if they knew who it was, they're not going to put him in jail for this. They're going to slap him on the wrist and tell him not to do it again, and in the meantime, everybody in the office is going to be snickering and talking about how I'm a closet exhibitionist. I'd spend the next two years listening to jokes about my sexy black robe and God knows what else. Not on your life. I'm not that much of a fool." She got up from the chair and walked quickly to the door. "And I don't want you telling anyone, either, understand?"

"I understand," I said. "It's up to you. But I'd be real careful to lock my doors and windows if I were you."

I called Jesse as soon as Tonia left and told him about Tonia's Peeping Tom. His voice was serious when he answered. "Peepers aren't usually dangerous, but put that with the snuff pictures—looks like our boy might not be playing with a full deck."

"I think it's time for a little informal chat with the experts," I said. "We're in over our heads on this. The police are the ones to tell us if we ought to be worried."

"The only thing you've got to report is a peeper," Jesse pointed out.

"That's why I said 'informal.' And I think we should warn the women." We agreed that it was time for another talk with Allen Leggett.

• • •

A call upstairs confirmed that Leggett was in and he could see me in about thirty minutes. He was probably hoping I had caught the prankster. I wished to hell I had.

It was a long thirty minutes, even with shaving off five at the end and heading upstairs early.

Scott Jorgensen was with Leggett when I arrived. "Scott will sit in with us on this since it affects his people," he informed me. I could see that I was going to get plenty of opportunity to regret my foolish behavior with Jorgensen.

"There's been a change in the pattern of the prankster's activity," I said. I laid out both sets of pictures on the desk. "Several of us got these through interoffice mail."

Leggett looked stunned. He stared at the photos in shock.

"Good lord, is that real?" Jorgensen said. If he was the source of the photos, it was an Oscar-level performance.

"And that's not all," I said. "One of the women told me today that the prankster has been hiding in her backyard and looking in her windows at night."

"Who?" Leggett demanded.

"That's not important," I said. "She doesn't want to report it, and I promised not to identify her, but the point is that the prankster could be moving from annoying to dangerous. Following a woman home from work and spying on her is serious business."

"Come on," Jorgensen said sarcastically. "A guy peeps in a woman's window. It's dumb, but it's hardly a federal offense. I think you're blowing things way out of proportion."

"I'm telling you," I said, working hard to keep the anger out of my voice, "that there's a good chance that your prankster is mentally unstable. A taste for violent pornography may not seem like much to you, but when you add that to the fact that he's following women outside of work, I think it's time to consult the police."

Leggett had looked concerned as I talked, but with the mention of the police, he looked distressed. "The police?" he said. "I don't know."

Jorgensen jumped in. "We've just started marketing a new product. The last thing we need is bad publicity. And over what? A Peeping Tom, a guy who likes dirty pictures. That's exactly the kind of thing we hired *you* to prevent."

"I'm not suggesting filing a report," I said, "but I think it would be prudent to talk with someone in the sex-crimes unit. I also think we should warn the women. I understand your concern about publicity, but I think you have to weigh that against the real possibility that this person could be dangerous."

Leggett, usually so clearly in control, was at sea. He looked to Jorgensen. "What do you think, Scott?"

"I think she's overreacting," he said. "I understand how pictures like those can be disturbing to a woman, especially when her photo's pasted on one, but this is just boys-will-be-boys stuff. If Ms. Sayler feels personally threatened or offended, then we should allow her to withdraw from the case. But I don't think we should get everyone all upset over this foolishness."

Leggett nodded. He was clearly relieved to have Jorgensen handle the sticky personnel issues. "Yes," he said. "Yes, that's reasonable."

"So the decision is yours, Ms. Sayler," Jorgensen said smoothly. "Do you want to continue with the case?"

It was more of a challenge than a question. Take it or leave it. I took it.

The next few days were uneventful. As far as I could tell, there'd been no more snuff photos, no office pranks, and the E-mail messages were tailing off, but the tension was only growing. Sheila was on edge and resisted every attempt I made to talk to her, Tonia jumped a foot if you spoke to her, and

Elaine stayed out of the office as much as possible. I couldn't tell whether they'd gotten threats they weren't telling me about or something else was going on.

Wednesday, I decided to ask Sheila to join me for lunch. Maybe I'd be more successful getting her to open up outside the office. To my surprise, she not only accepted, she seemed in high spirits.

She suggested that we drive to the Delancey Street Café. The café is down near the waterfront, almost beneath the Bay Bridge, in a complex of buildings designed for the Delancey Street Foundation.

Delancey Street is a bootstrap program for drug addicts and alcoholics. It offers help in drying out and employment for those who are successful. You start with a broom and work your way up. And "up" goes all the way to running one of the foundation's flourishing businesses. The government could learn a lot from Delancey Street.

The heat spell hadn't broken and it was marginally cooler near the bay, so we sat outside. There's usually a good breeze down here, but today the air lay ripe and still everywhere. Across the bay a dirty yellow blanket covered Oakland. The East Bay hills were indistinct and smudgy in the background.

We both ordered ice tea and salads. "You seem awfully chipper," I said. "Almost like you might be dining on canary."

Sheila laughed. "I think I've solved a whole bunch of problems," she said. "Our boys from KeeGo may just have outsmarted themselves."

She wouldn't tell me more than that, and I tried every way I knew to worm it out of her. Finally, I changed the subject. "Did you get any more photos?" I asked.

Sheila made a face. "These guys just don't give up," she said. "This time they pasted a photo of my face on one of the disgusting things."

Our lunches arrived looking a whole lot better than the

offerings at Mama's, and Sheila started in on her chicken salad. The photos obviously hadn't affected her appetite.

"So you don't think this guy could be dangerous?" I said.

She shook her head. "Not the way you think," she said. "This isn't about sex. Whoever sent those is trying to intimidate me. They chose those pictures because they were the grossest, scariest stuff they could think of."

"Then why did I get a second set, complete with photo of me?" I asked.

She looked surprised. She frowned and took a bite of bread while she considered it. "I don't know," she said. "Maybe because you stood up to them. They wanted to give you a bad time."

"And why is someone hiding in another woman's backyard and taking pictures of her windows?"

Sheila looked startled. "Whose?" she demanded.

"I promised not to tell."

"It's Tonia, isn't it?" she said. "The bastards, they're really playing hardball."

This time it was my turn to ask who.

"Never mind," she said. "If this is what I think it is, I'll take care of it."

"And what if it isn't?" I said. "What if these guys are really dangerous? I think you should tell me what's going on." But of course she didn't.

It's times like this that being undercover is a major pain. I couldn't press any harder without blowing my cover, and there was absolutely no reason for her to tell Catherine, the telecommunications expert, what Catherine, the investigator, needed to know.

"Don't worry about it," she said. "Guys like this are cowards. They like to scare women; that's how they get their kicks. But they don't have the balls to do anything."

I wasn't so sure. I wished she weren't so sure. "I still think it'd pay to be careful," I said.

Chapter

12

Thursday morning the oppressive heat of the past week finally broke. It was a relief to wake to gray skies and cool air. Peter, Molly, and I actually conversed during breakfast, a rare achievement for three night people.

When I got to the office, my E-mail had only one entry, and it was from Sheila: "I need to see you. 9:30. My office. If I'm not there, wait for me inside."

I looked at my watch. It was 9:45. I hurried down the hall hoping I hadn't missed her.

Sheila's door was closed. I knocked and got no response. Knocked a second time, then opened the door, stepped in, and froze. Sheila's naked body lay sprawled across the top of her desk. One look told me I didn't need to check for a heartbeat.

I felt as if someone were standing on my chest. I couldn't breathe, and then something inside snapped shut, and I could breathe but I couldn't feel. I backed out and shut the door. Then I walked to the nearest desk, picked up the phone and dialed homicide. I hadn't dialed that number in years, not since my divorce from Inspector Dan Walker had become final, but my fingers knew the number. My mind was on autopilot.

"Homicide, Reilly," a deep voice said.

"I'm calling to report a murder," I said. I gave the address and told Reilly to ask for Sheila Wainwright's office, then I hung up before he could ask any questions.

Bob Kingsley had been listening with wide eyes. "A murder?" he said. The area around us was suddenly very quiet. "Don't let anyone go in Sheila's office," I told him. "And don't go in yourself."

He started to ask me a question, but I didn't wait. I walked to the women's room, shut myself in a stall, and threw up everything in my stomach. I leaned against the side of the stall for a few minutes and waited for my head to clear.

I could see and hear just fine, but everything seemed to be happening at a distance. I was in an emotional bell jar; nothing touched me.

"Shock," I thought. "I've been here before."

I didn't have time to stand around and wait for my emotions to catch up with me. Allen Leggett wouldn't want to hear this from the police. He'd told me more than once how much he hated surprises. I rinsed my mouth with water from the sink, and headed for his office.

His secretary was just coming out of his office when I arrived. She tried to block me, but I slid around her and was in the door before she could get further than "You can't . . ."

Leggett was leaning over a complicated set of diagrams that covered his desk. He looked shocked by my intrusion. I closed the door behind me. "Sheila Wainwright is dead," I said. "She was murdered in her office."

Leggett's usually pale face became even paler. "What?"

"Sheila is dead," I repeated. "Someone killed her." I told him what I'd seen in her office.

"Good lord," he said. He looked like he might need to make a quick trip to his private john.

"I've notified the police."

He nodded dully. Just then the buzzer sounded and Jorgensen's voice came over the intercom, "Allen, I need to see you. There's trouble in regional."

"Come," Leggett said to the speaker on the machine.

Jorgensen bustled in and stopped when he saw me. He looked from me to Leggett. "It's true, then," he said.

"Sheila's been murdered," Leggett said quietly. "In her office." The last part was said with so much feeling that I was startled by it. I wondered if the crime was more horrible to him for having been committed in the public space of her office.

I felt a sudden rush of rage as I watched these two shocked boy wonders try to digest the reality of violent death. "I was right," I wanted to shout at them. "If you'd just listened to me . . ." "If you hadn't been so macho, so sure you were right . . ."

"If you hadn't let them bully you . . ." a small voice said. That was the bottom line, of course. I'd bought into Jorgensen's macho game and ignored my own best judgment. I was as responsible for this as they were.

"How do we play this?" Jorgensen asked.

"We don't *play* anything," I said. "We cooperate with the police. We tell them everything that's been going on, and then we listen to them tell us what fools we were not to call them sooner."

Jorgensen looked angry. Leggett just looked sick. "It'll be in the papers, of course," he said.

"Count on it," I said. But it would only be big news because the victim was well-to-do and white and the crime was so bizarre. After all, women got butchered every day. It wasn't as if sexual assault and murder were unusual crimes.

By now, the police would have dispatched a couple of uniforms and notified the coroner's office. I probably wouldn't know the uniforms, but I'd met the medical examiner, Earl Ganz, enough times that he'd recognize me, and whoever caught the case in homicide would almost certainly be a friend of my ex-husband. It might even be Dan himself.

"It might be best if Jesse and I met the cops someplace private," I said. "Unless you want everyone to know we were working undercover for you."

"Were?" said Jorgensen sharply. "You mean you're bailing out when things get tough."

I silently counted to ten, then said as pleasantly as I could manage, "This is a police case now. The police do not welcome the involvement of private citizens in their investigations."

"But you're already working undercover here," Leggett said. "I should think that would be very useful for the investigation."

"You can discuss that with them," I said. "If they agree, I'll be happy to stay on. In the meantime, I'd suggest that you find some way to get Jesse out of the way before a cop recognizes him and blows his cover. I'll wait in the lounge up here. You can tell everyone that I was so upset by discovering the body that you had me lie down there."

I walked to the lounge in the same airless bubble that had closed around me when I found Sheila. Emotion was outside the bubble. I could think but I couldn't feel. I knew it wouldn't last.

Chapter

13

When it can't stand to feel, the mind pops into overdrive. I sat in the lounge and made notes on every aspect of the case, outlined events since I'd arrived at Systech, and made neat lists of suspects and motives. A uniform came in and did a preliminary interview. I described finding Sheila with great precision and no more emotion than I'd feel about a TV movie.

But the mind can't jump through hoops indefinitely. As I waited for the homicide inspector, the airless shell began to crack. The pain started in my chest and grew like a wound. There was a lump the size of a fist in my throat, but I couldn't cry. Or I wouldn't.

My mind replayed the image of Sheila's body splayed across her desk. I saw it in more detail than I'd been aware of at the time. And a lot more clarity than I'd have liked.

Her face, turned toward the door, revealed the horror of the last seconds of her life. She had not died quietly or easily, every muscle of her face recorded terror. Dark, ugly bruises suggested that she'd been struck repeatedly.

I made another trip to the john. There wasn't anything left in my stomach.

I wanted to forget what I'd seen. The cops didn't need my observations; they could make their own. But the images taunted me. Like a rubber ball that pops to the surface whenever you try to force it underwater, they bounced back as quickly as I pushed them away.

And the questions. Questions that kept repeating themselves, even though I didn't want to know the answers.

I've seen men die, once at my own hand. I'd thought Dylan Thomas had it right: "After the first death there is no other." But that isn't so.

I'd known Sheila—known the sound of her laugh, the lively intensity of her gray eyes, the insistent energy of her gestures. I liked her.

I felt her loss like a hole blown right through the middle of my body. The pain was physical. Still I didn't cry. Tears might have relieved some of the pressure, but my body refused to give them up.

I'd have welcomed anything that distracted me from the memory of Sheila's naked, vulnerable body and the terror mask of her face. Even the inevitable chat with the police.

The patrol officer had his report, but the homicide inspector would want the same information, in even greater detail. And that inspector might well be my ex-husband, Dan Walker. I hoped it wouldn't be, for reasons that weren't entirely clear, even to me.

"Catherine?" The voice was familiar, but not, thank God, Dan's. In relief I turned to face Homicide Inspector Jack Connelly. Jack was about five years younger than Dan. He was the newest man in homicide when Dan and I met, so I always thought of him as "the kid." But he'd put on about twenty pounds and his hairline was in full retreat. Still, there was a boyish quality to his face, and he had one of the widest smiles I've ever seen.

"Hi, Jack. I've been working undercover here."

Jack's ample brow compressed into a frown. "And you found the body?"

I nodded.

"I think you'd better tell me why you were hired and what connection it might have to the murder." He sat down across the table from me and pulled out a tape recorder and a pad. I took him through the whole story from Leggett's first call to our meeting after I found Sheila. He jotted down some notes, but mostly he just listened.

When I finished, he shook his head. "Boy, that's about double what I got from everyone else put together. The women bitched about the harassment, but none of them gave me the whole story. Everyone wants the killer caught, but no one's willing to tell us what we need to know."

"Not surprising. The women are embarrassed and frightened by the harassment. They're working hard to make it in a male world and they don't want to admit to vulnerability." I didn't tell him that was the reason I'd let Jorgensen talk me out of calling the sex-crimes unit.

"Plus, sales is an area where competition's the rule, and information can be worth a lot. No one gives away anything without getting something in return. And no one trusts anyone else very far."

"Terrific," Jack said. "Well, they better learn to talk to us or one of *them* might end up like the lady on the desk."

I felt an involuntary shudder at Jack's grim suggestion. "Maybe Jesse and I should stay on here," I said. "It'd give us a chance to pick up information your men might not get."

"Possibly," Jack conceded. "Let me get back to you on that."

I knew what was in his mind. He wanted to see how it'd fly with Dan. "How do you feel about me using your ex-wife as an undercover informant in a murder investigation?" That was sure to be a big hit.

"Can you tell me anything about the murder?" I asked.

Jack hesitated, torn between a cop's natural reticence and his desire to give a little in hope of getting back more. "Rough estimate is that she died sometime early this morning, probably around one or two," he said. "Probable cause, strangulation. She's got heavy bruising on the neck; looks like he may have broken the windpipe. I say 'he' because it looks like a manual strangulation, someone with big hands and a lot of strength. Probably not a woman."

His tone was almost conversational but his eyes never left my face. Cop's eyes. Recording and assessing every reaction. "Bruises on the face, she was knocked around before. Marks on the wrists indicate her hands were tied. And she was moved after she died. Charlie thinks she was killed on the floor and moved to the desk."

I should have asked more, but I couldn't. I realized that I really did not want to know what had happened to Sheila last night. My imagination had too much to work with already.

I told Jack about Jesse. "I don't know where he is," I said, "But I had Leggett warn him to find a place where he wouldn't be recognized by any of the crime-scene guys."

"You two do this often?" Jack asked, only half-joking.

"More often than I'd like. But it's a first for Jesse. We could be real useful here. Think about it."

Jack left and a sense of exhaustion washed over me. It was one o'clock. I had no desire to eat, just to sleep. The light in the room was too bright. I closed my eyes and concentrated on the inside of my skull. I found just what I'd expected, a tiny spot of pain somewhere above my right eye.

It was just a point of sensation, a seed that would grow over the next hours to fill my entire head and send my stomach and whatever was left in it up into my throat. Damn, I thought, a migraine. A fitting response to Sheila's murder.

I dug around in my purse and found the pills I carry for times like this. I swallowed one and headed for Leggett's office.

The CEO's coloring hadn't improved much. He was still pale and looked as if he didn't feel any better than I did. "Will you stay on the case?" he asked. It was more a request than a question.

I started to tell him that that was up to the police, but it wasn't really. He'd hired me to find the prankster and I don't give up on a case until it's closed. "I'll stay," I said.

"I suppose I should send everyone home for the day," he said. "They're not going to get any work done here, and I don't want them talking to customers right now."

Home. What a great idea. But not yet. Shock strips away pieces of the masks we construct for daily life. By tomorrow they'd be repaired. Migraine or no, if I was to get a peek behind the masks, I'd have to do it today.

"I'd like you to wait for a while on that," I said. "Give me an hour or so after the police leave."

Leggett nodded. "Call me when you're through."

The M.E. was already gone and the crime-scene boys left an hour later. I used the time to get a sandwich that I didn't want to eat and had a hard time getting down. Sometimes eating helps with a migraine. Today it didn't.

Jesse found me in the lounge and we swapped information. There wasn't much. "The cops copied the files for the electronic keys," he told me. "They think it'll give them the killer." We'd thought it'd give us the prankster. I hoped they had better luck.

By the time I went downstairs, the pills had blocked most of the pain and some of the nausea, but I still felt as if I were moving through mud and my mind were wrapped in gauze.

The office was unnaturally quiet. People sat at their desks or whispered in groups of two or three. Most of them were still in shock. The ruddiness was gone from Kingsley's complexion, and DeMarco was so pale he was almost blue. Tonia's face was blotchy from crying; Elaine's mascara made dark smudges under her eyes.

Anna Proudfoot looked devastated. Tear tracks stained her face and a mountain of used tissues tumbled off her desk onto the floor. Anna was a motherly woman in her fifties. The matriarch of the office. A benevolent matriarch, quietly efficient and comfortingly serene even in the face of Sheila's driving energy and the sometimes frantic demands of the other salespeople in the minicomputer division. But not today.

I hated to bother Anna, but a question nagged at me, and only she could answer it.

"Are you okay?" I asked. She wasn't, of course, but she nodded. She stared at her pile of tissues. "Who could have done such a thing?" she asked. I shook my head. "Surely no one here," she said.

But of course it was someone here. Someone she knew. Someone she *thought* she knew. And that made it all the worse. Today, the shock of Sheila's death overwhelmed her coworkers. But in time they would adjust to that. What they would not, could not, adjust to was the knowledge that one of them was a killer.

"Anna, didn't you usually talk to Sheila before ten o'clock?" I asked.

"Oh, yes. You know Sheila, she was always early, had fifteen projects started before anyone else had their first cup of coffee."

"But you didn't see her today. Why?"

"Because of the note," she said. Then realizing I had no idea what she meant, she added, "She left a note on my desk, asking me not to disturb her until after her 9:30 meeting with you."

Through the fog of the migraine, alarm bells sounded. "A handwritten note?"

"No, from her printer." Anna looked confused.

"Did she ever do that before?" I asked.

"No. No, she didn't. She usually used voice mail," Anna said. Then her eyes widened in comprehension, and she said softly, "Oh. Oh, you don't think . . ."

But I did think. "What happened to the note?" I asked.

"The police took it."

So the police thought so, too. Though they hadn't mentioned it to me. They must assume, as I did, that the note was from the killer. And that could only mean that he or she had set me up to find Sheila's body.

If I was part of the killer's scenario . . . ? But my mind skidded away every time I got that far. I was still too raw. I could deal with that nasty discovery later.

Chapter

14

It wasn't the migraine that drove me out of Systech two hours later. It was seeing my own pain reflected in the eyes of everyone there. Unexpected death is always a shock, but violent death, homicide, shakes the very foundations of our inner world. It strips away all illusion of safety and taints the sense of loss with fear.

I got home before Peter and Molly, struggled out of my clothes and climbed into bed. It was hours later when the music from the other room woke me. I was a long way from feeling good, but then I doubted that anyone at Systech was feeling good. Except the killer.

It was my night to cook, but Peter had sized up the situation and had Molly chopping vegetables for stir-fry. He wrapped me in his arms and I relaxed into the comfort of his embrace. He stroked my hair. "How you doing?" he asked.

"Miserable," I said. I started to tell him about Sheila but stopped as I realized Molly was right behind me.

"We know about Sheila," Peter said.

"How?"

"Both Jesse and Dan called while you were asleep."

"I listened in on the extension," Molly said, looking more frightened than contrite. "I'm sorry. I was going to hang up, but . . ." She shrugged. Her eyes seemed larger than usual, and her face had lost its teenager-with-attitude expression; she looked like a scared little kid.

"Come here, tiger," I said, motioning to her. "I could use a hug."

She's gotten stingy with her hugs since she hit puberty, but this one was long and tight, with a desperate quality, as if she feared that I'd disappear if she let go. "Hey, it's all right," I said. I wanted to tell her that I wasn't in danger, that things would be okay. But that would have been a lie, and she wouldn't have believed me, anyway.

I held her and thought what a lousy surrogate parent I'd turned out to be. We'd been through a very scary situation when she first ran away from home and now I was plunging into another one. No kid needs that kind of insecurity.

She didn't cry, though it would have been better for her if she had. We get that from the same place, the Brits' damned stiff upper lip. You swallow your tears till you choke.

Molly finally pulled away and went back to chopping vegetables. Peter watched us both, concern written across his face. I collapsed into a chair. "What did Dan say?" I asked.

"That Sheila'd been murdered. They think the killer could focus on you next."

I could imagine the part of the call he wasn't telling me about—Dan warning Peter that I wouldn't back off and asking him to keep an eye on me. It cost Dan a lot to do that. He still resented Peter. But he couldn't resist the desire to protect me from myself, even though he knew that I wouldn't let him get away with it.

"I'd better call Jesse," I said.

I was still groggy from the migraine and the medication, and

I bumped into a chair as I walked to the phone. Peter reached out to steady me, then looked into my eyes as he held me. "You've got a migraine," he said.

"The perfect complement to the perfect day," I said.

"Go back to bed. You can call Jesse tomorrow morning."

Bed sounded real good right now, but I resisted. "I won't sleep tonight if I go back to bed," I said. "I don't feel like calling anyone, but I'd like to just hang out with you two."

"Can I make you some tea?" Peter asked.

"Thanks," I said. He put the kettle on, and Molly turned down the music to a soft murmur in the background.

"So tell me about school," I said to her, trying to pretend that we were just a normal family.

It was a sign of how much Molly wanted to participate in that fantasy that she told us more about school than she'd managed in the entire month before. I drank my tea, Molly talked, and Peter cooked. A warm family scene, but closer really to a play performed for each other's benefit. And Sheila Wainwright's body was at the center of that play as surely as if it had been laid out on the kitchen table, more powerful for the fact that we could not mention it.

I felt better the next morning. Marginally. Until I got a call from my ex-husband. Never a good way to start the day.

Dan is a terrific person; he'd be a good friend if he weren't an ex-husband. Having been married does weird things to a relationship. There's a bit of regret, maybe even guilt, a certain almost parental proprietorship, and more than a bit of frustrated attraction. That would make things messy even if the personal and professional were kept neatly separate. Which they aren't.

"Catherine, are you all right?" he asked in a sharp tone that always annoys me but is really just a sign of concern.

"I'm fine, Dan," I said. "Finding dead bodies isn't my favorite thing, but I'm doing okay. I assume Jack's told you about it."

"Pretty ugly scene," Dan said. "I'm sorry you had to see it."

"It appears that someone set me up to see it," I said.

There was a pause. "What makes you think that?" he asked.

"Come on, Dan, Jack told you about the note. He didn't tell *me,* but I'm sure he told you. You guys expect me to tell you everything I know, then you hold out on something like this. You might tell Connelly that cooperation runs two ways."

"I'm sorry," he said. "Jack wasn't sure how you'd take it. He didn't want to spook you."

"Very kind of him," I said drily. "But what spooks me is knowing there's stuff you guys aren't telling me."

"I know, I know. I told him that this wasn't your first homicide and that you're . . ." He paused, searching for the right word while I wondered exactly what description he'd given Connelly that he didn't want to repeat to me. "Not easy to spook," he finished. "Jack said you were considering continuing at Systech."

"I've told them I'll stay on. I haven't finished my job there, and I may be able to turn up something useful."

"You realize you could be in considerable danger there," he said tightly.

"The thought had occurred to me."

There was a pause, a long pause, while Dan swallowed all the things he wanted to say. "I hope you'll be careful," he said at last. "If you need anything, if you even suspect you might need something, call me, please."

Dan was used to issuing orders. It was hard for him to ask, especially when he couldn't quite keep the need out of his voice.

"I will," I said. "I promise. And I won't do anything careless. Believe me, I have no desire to end up like Sheila Wainwright."

I got him to agree to urge Connelly to be straight with me.

He got me to promise that I'd tell the police everything I learned and that I wouldn't do anything on my own. Neither one of us was going to cooperate as much as the other would have liked.

Jesse and I met for breakfast at a café on Fillmore. He didn't look a lot better than I felt. "You were right," he said as I sat down.

"About?"

"The pictures."

I usually love being right, especially with Jesse. Today I didn't love it. "Twenty-twenty hindsight," I said. "I should have gone with my gut feelings."

"Beating ourselves up won't do much for either of us," he said.

"So what do you think?"

"Best guess: several pranksters, one murderer. Maybe they overlap, maybe not."

"I want to stay on the case," I said. "The cops can't force us off as long as we're working for Leggett."

Jesse nodded. "Motivation?"

"The killer's?" I asked.

"No, yours. Have you asked yourself why you want to stay on this case?"

I had. And I had plenty of reasons, but I knew what Jesse meant. He wanted to know how much of my motivation came from guilt and anger. The answer was plenty. "It's just what you think," I said. "Not lofty, but effective."

"Yeah," he said. "Be nice if one of us could be detached."

"And you can't?"

"After I talked you out of two warnings? Hurts my pride to be wrong twice."

He said it lightly, but I knew it wasn't his pride as much as his sense of self. And it wasn't only about being wrong. Not exactly. "You feeling caught on the wrong side of the gender barrier?" I asked.

He stirred more sugar into his *latte*. "You sensed something and I didn't back you up. At some level I didn't take you seriously. Makes me feel like a jerk," he said. "And I keep wondering if I had backed you up, would we have found a way to stop things before they got this far."

I put my hand on his. "You're not a jerk," I said. "And seeing things differently isn't sexism. Ease up on yourself."

"I'll go back over everything that has to do with the E-mail," he said. "See if there's anything I missed."

"And pick up whatever gossip you can. Maybe people'll talk more freely now. At least those not involved. I've got a call into Connelly to see what the key files showed."

"You think they're going to turn up empty," Jesse said.

"I'd love to have the killer's name, but if someone got in without using a key last week, he could do it again. Or someone else could. There's a hole there someplace. I'm going looking for it."

Chapter

15

I got to Systech just before ten. The office was almost deserted. Anyone who could find an excuse to be somewhere else was gone. The few souls who were left wore long faces and somber colors. It was like a color film that had suddenly gone to black-and-white.

Connelly and his partner, Mike Rico, arrived around ten-fifteen to do another round of interviews. He came to my office first.

He gave me an apologetic grin as I closed the door behind him. "I'm sorry about not telling you about the note. I probably should have done it yesterday, but I figured you were in shock. I didn't want to hit you with *that* right then."

I smiled at him, my first smile that day. I was getting too prickly when I mistook a gesture of kindness for paternalism. "Would you like some coffee?" I asked, indicating my thermos. "The stuff in the lounge is even worse than precinct coffee."

Connelly nodded gratefully. "Yeah, I could use some."

I couldn't find my extra cup so I went to the lounge to get

one. The room was empty and the coffee pot was full. People were really hunkering down.

Connelly took his coffee black. I usually add milk but today the black, bitter brew suited my mood.

"Did the electronic key files show anything?" I asked.

"Zip," he said. "Not a damn thing after the last guy went home at ten. There were a couple of programmers on the second floor, but no one up here."

"And everyone's accounted for, they all left?"

"Yep. And given the way your partner was monitoring the computer, it doesn't seem that anyone could have tampered with those files without him knowing. There has to be another way in."

"The warehouse," I said. "There's a door into the warehouse next to the room with the copy machine."

He nodded. "I know. But it's on an alarm. We tested it last night. The whole warehouse is wired. You open that door a half-inch and the alarm sounds. Same's true of any of the outside doors."

"So there must be another way in."

Connelly took another sip of his coffee and shook his head. "That's the problem. There isn't. It's the damnedest thing. We've been over this building twice. Those are the only two ways in, and the murderer couldn't have used either of them without us knowing."

"But . . ."

"That's not possible. I know," he said with the same apologetic smile. He sort of slouched in the chair and gazed at me with a pleasant, slightly expectant expression.

Someone had to have tampered with either the alarm system or the electronic files. Connelly was too good a cop not to be checking on those possibilities. He must be playing dumb to see what I'd come up with.

It worked. As I considered what he'd told me I got an idea. I reached for the copy of my case files I'd made for him, opened the log and scanned it. "Here's something interesting," I said, passing it to him. "Sheila told me that someone had searched her office last Thursday. She was convinced they'd done it the night before, so I checked the electronic key files. No entries. Just like the night of the murder, also a Wednesday. Makes me wonder if something's different on Wednesdays."

Connelly glanced over the log. "We'll look into it," he said. He turned to the front of the file, and I realized he might be planning to read it now. "Do you have autopsy results yet?" I asked.

He shook his head. "Another day or two." He was still scanning the file.

"But you've got preliminary findings," I said. "I'll help you guys any way I can, but I'll be a lot more useful if I'm not stumbling around in the dark."

"Okay," he said, looking up. "It's pretty clearly a sex killing. You could tell that from the body. There's a voyeuristic quality to the way he put her on the desk and set you up to find her. He propped up the right leg by wedging the foot in the desk drawer so the first thing you see is the exposed genitals."

I realized I'd blocked that from my mind, not wanting to think about it, but the positioning of Sheila's body had had a profound effect on me. It was so exposed and vulnerable.

"That's what's most revealing," Connelly said. "What makes this one different. He didn't just want to kill her. I think he wanted to humiliate her, and probably to terrorize you."

I nodded dully. He was right. I could feel it. I tried to get my mind to engage, to come to grips with what he was telling me. It was like turning the key when the battery's dead.

Connelly was watching me closely. He looked concerned. Probably assumed I was about to go to pieces on him. I shifted my focus from what I couldn't think about to something I could. "Any physical evidence?" I asked.

"Not at this point," he said. "Killer must have worn gloves and wiped surfaces clean. Your fingerprints are the only ones on the doorknob. There are none at all on the desk drawer."

"Real careful," I said. "He must have taken some time cleaning up."

"He had all night," Connelly pointed out. He took a sip of his coffee and was quiet for a minute. "Most of the physical evidence is useless, anyway. If the killer was someone who worked with her, he's been in that office enough times to have his fingerprints all over the place. Even if we found something like a fountain pen, there'd be no way of proving it wasn't dropped in the normal course of a work day."

Outside, a horn blared, brakes squealed, and someone shouted an obscenity. Business as usual. I tapped my pen against my thumb and tried to force my sluggish thoughts forward.

Connelly closed the file I'd given him and put his mug on the edge of my desk. He pulled a notebook from his jacket pocket and flipped it open. "What do you know about Bob Kingsley that isn't in your notes?" he asked.

I put just about everything in my notes. They're a stream-of-consciousness summary of whatever I've seen, heard, or thought that might be relevant to a case. I told Connelly that, but he was looking for "the stuff you filtered out" or "things just at the edge of conscious thought" and he seemed to believe that if he just kept asking, something significant would emerge.

I tried my best. Significance did not emerge. Exhaustion did. We worked our way through every person on the third floor that I knew even slightly, then started on the second. When we got to Clark Phillips, I asked, "Have you questioned him yet? He's the key to the pranksters. I'm fairly sure he's not in this alone."

"We'll be talking to Phillips," he said. It was as if an invisible shield had just slipped down. Connelly was in information-gathering mode; sharing time was over.

"Will you tell me who the other prankster is when you find out?"

He looked at me through the shield. "I'm not sure I can do that," he said.

I nodded. It took some effort not to grind my teeth. "I can understand that," I said, a flat-out lie. "But if you don't tell me, I'll have to blunder around on my own to find out, and that could be disruptive to your efforts."

"I'd hoped you'd want to cooperate," Connelly said, poker face firmly in place.

"I do want to cooperate. I have a job to do, but I also want to stay alive, and knowing who pulled the pranks might help me do that."

Connelly frowned, then seemed to loosen up a bit. "I can't make any promises. We get this guy in interrogation, it's going to be a lot easier to get him to talk if he doesn't think it's going right back to his boss."

"And if I promised that it wouldn't go any further?"

"We'll see," he said. "If I can tell you, I will."

We continued with the crew on the second floor, most of whom I didn't know, then went back over the key players on the third floor. By the time we'd finished the whole roster, I figured my next migraine was only a few minutes away.

Connelly didn't look a lot better than I felt. We sat in silence for a minute and he finished off his coffee. When he spoke, it sounded as if it took an effort. "She wasn't a random victim," he said. "He chose her. He also chose you to find her. The way he set it up so you'd be the first one into the office and the display of the body—that suggests that there was some connection in his mind between you and the victim. Any idea what that might be?"

I paused before I answered. Not that I hadn't spent much of the last twenty-four hours thinking about that very thing. I just hadn't gotten anywhere. "We were both uppity women," I said. "I've certainly been doing everything I could to irritate the office chauvinists, and Sheila tended to push people pretty hard. But that's hardly a reason for murder, and while some of the guys around here are jerks, I can't see them killing anyone."

Connelly nodded. His face was without expression, and his eyes didn't give away a thing.

"I told you yesterday about Sheila's battle with the KeeGo guys. I don't know what she had on them, but there might be a motive there."

Connelly grimaced and shook his head. "No, this isn't about office intrigue. This guy's a nut. A very clever, very careful nut."

He said it with such finality that there wasn't any point in arguing. I had to agree that it certainly felt like a sexual killing. Still, I wondered if someone so clever and so careful might not be clever enough to stage a crime to look much crazier than he was.

Chapter

16

"Remember, very smart and very crazy," Connelly said as he rose from his chair and walked to the door. The man knew a good exit line when he had one.

Smart and crazy are not desirable traits in an adversary, especially not when combined.

And stingy and patronizing were not good traits in an ally. Connelly wasn't anxious to share information, and he hadn't been much interested in what I considered two promising leads. Big surprise.

There must be something he wasn't telling me about how the killer got into Sheila's office. Locked-room murders may be a favorite in mystery novels, but they're not a common feature of police reports. I decided it was time to find out more about Systech's alarm system.

It was a short walk to Allen Leggett's office, but it was like visiting another country when you moved from regional to corporate offices. Physical and psychological distance from the

115

victim had lessened the impact of the murder, and while the people in corporate seemed subdued, they didn't have the shell-shocked blankness of Sheila's coworkers in regional.

Except for Allen Leggett. He was even paler than usual, and the skin under his eyes sagged into pouches. He agreed to see me as soon as I asked for an appointment. On his usually cluttered desk a single sheet of paper was centered on the blotter. I doubted that he was getting much work done.

When he spoke, his voice was flat, an old man's voice, thin and tired. "Any progress?" he asked.

I shook my head. "Not yet. That door at the end of the hall, near the copy machine, it leads into the warehouse, doesn't it?"

Leggett nodded. "Yeah. The cops thought it might have been the way the murderer got in, but it's locked and alarmed. Security would have known the minute anyone touched it."

"Is the alarm on during the day?" I asked.

"No," he said. "It goes on at six when the other alarms are activated."

"So if someone opened it during the day, you wouldn't know."

"No, but they'd have to have a key," Leggett said, "and only a few of us do."

I'd checked the lock. I didn't think you'd need a key. "I'd like to know more about the alarm system," I said.

Leggett hesitated. The first tenet of security is never tell anyone more than they need to know. I guess he finally decided he could trust me, because he nodded and got up to go look for something in a cupboard behind his desk.

"The diagrams are right here," he said. So were about seventy-five other diagrams all rolled up and all looking about the same. It took him a few minutes to find the one he wanted.

He spread it out, and we practically bumped heads as we leaned over it from opposite sides of the desk. The first page showed the ground floor. The building was divided roughly in half, the south side having been renovated and the north left in its original state.

"Someday, we'll need that space to expand," Leggett told me. "That is, if the mayor doesn't decide to stick a stadium on top of us." Systech's building sat right in the middle of the area being jealously eyed by Giants' supporters, who'd promised the team a new stadium and sunny weather forever if only they'd remain in San Francisco. "We need some of the storage space ourselves," Leggett said, "but we can't use it all, so we rent out what we don't need."

"Who do you rent to?"

"A good chunk of the second floor goes to AG Electronics; they store parts, mostly. Another chunk's used by a plumbing-supply firm. The rest is leased to smaller tenants for a variety of stuff. We've even got a bunch of mountain bikes on the first floor. If you want more specifics, you'll have to talk to Vic Carter. He's in charge of the warehouse. I don't pay a lot of attention to that side of things."

"Exactly how does the alarm system work?" I asked.

"It's pretty standard," he said. "Contacts on each of the doors and windows, both internal and external. Any kind of movement sets them off. We never put the warehouse on digital keypad. It's on a separate system, a minicontroller with a digital dialer hooked up to it. The whole thing's on a timer. Closed, that means on, at six at night, open, or off, at eight in the morning."

It was a fairly standard setup, all right—sensors that sent information to an electronic brain, which then told another machine to dial the security company and alert them to call the cops.

"But you can override the timer," I said.

"Sure. We can reset the timer, but we have to let the response center know. We do it for late or early pickups and deliveries."

"Could the timer be altered, for example, to shut the system off at different times, without you knowing it?"

"Yeah, but the response center'd know, and they'd be on the phone to the cops and to Vic. If the system doesn't open or close when it's supposed to, we get a call."

"Where's the minicontroller located?" I asked.

"In a locked closet down the hall."

I asked to see it, and Leggett took me to a closet about twenty yards from his office. The lock on the door was a good deal more secure than the ones on the doors in regional.

The minicontroller was in an eleven-by-fourteen-inch metal box mounted on the wall opposite the door. A second, smaller box that probably contained the dialer was next to it. A set of wires connected the two. A second set of wires ran to a timer.

"Where do you keep the keys?" I asked. If they were like most companies I'd worked with, the keys to the metal boxes would be someplace inside that closet. That made it easy to open the box, a choice of convenience over security.

"They're up there," Leggett said, indicating the ledge of the doorframe.

I opened the box and peered inside. It was what I expected. The printed circuit board looked a lot like the one in my PC, a green rectangular card with silver tracing going to what looked like tiny brightly colored insects. The major difference was that instead of the multifaced plugs for additional cards there was a terminal strip, a row of screws to which wires could be attached. Two of those screws held the tripwires that connected the minicontroller to the dialer. Remove those wires and no matter how many alarms were set off, the information would never reach the response center. You'd have to do it by hand, and it would have to be after the system closed at six and before it opened at eight, but between those hours, anyone with the key to the closet could disable the alarm.

"Who has keys to the closet?" I asked.

Leggett thought for a moment. "Vic Carter, he's the warehouse supervisor; Charlie North, my chief of facilities; me, of course." He thought for a moment more. "I think that's it."

I was disappointed, I'll admit it. I was hoping one of my prime suspects had that key. Things are rarely that simple.

I went back to square one, which in this case was to the third-floor door to the warehouse. The door on the regional sales side of the third floor was at the end of the hall just beyond the room with the copy machine. It was your basic, nondescript door, and it had your basic not-too-secure lock. The same type of lock that was on the office doors.

I took out my credit card and slid it in the door right where the lock was. I know investigators do that all the time on TV, but it's not part of my usual professional repertoire. Do it on the wrong door at the wrong time, and you can go to jail. Not my career goal.

But, this wasn't the wrong door, and even I could open it on the second try, so I did.

It swung open and I peered into the cavernous dimness of the warehouse. It was probably just the emotional baggage of Sheila's murder that made me hesitate to step into the dark, empty space on the other side of the door. The office side seemed suddenly bright and familiar and safe compared to the unfinished, unknown area ahead of me.

Oh, great, I thought, now I've got the willies. Just what I need. Still, I wasn't going to see a lot without a flashlight, so I went back to my office to get the one I carry in my purse. It's not very big, but it gives off a good amount of light for its size. I also picked up a roll of tape to make sure the door didn't lock behind me.

I got the door open on the first try this time, and as I taped the latch bolt in, I wondered if this was what the murderer had done. It would have been easy enough to open the door before five, tape the bolt, sign out with your electronic key, then slip back in through the doors on the first floor before the alarm system was activated at six. Or you could give someone else your key and have them sign you out while you hid on the warehouse side of the door.

Thinking about how a killer might have used the warehouse didn't make it any easier to step through that door and pull it shut behind me. I did it anyway.

Once my eyes adjusted, the warehouse wasn't as dark as I'd thought. Tall windows on the east wall let in slabs of sunlight that illuminated that end and left the area in the middle where I stood in a kind of dusky half-light. Only the west end was so dark that I couldn't make it out clearly.

Much of the space was empty, and with no walls to chop it up, it seemed even larger than the half of the building that had been converted to office space. No carpeting covered the bare plank floor, and its rough surface recorded every scrape and gouge of its long history.

Boxes of paper and other office supplies were piled along the wall near the door where I stood, telling me that someone must use this door fairly regularly to replenish the paper supply in the copying room. I switched on the flashlight. It didn't look like it was going to be a lot of help.

As I crossed the warehouse I could make out what looked like giant cages against the north wall. Walls of chain link fence dropped from ceiling to floor, marking off spaces that were filled with boxes and other goods. One cage was piled high with furniture, another contained a jungle of fake plants. Others were full of unidentified boxes. Each cage had a door secured with a heavy padlock.

The chain link cages varied in size and extended all the way to the dark west wall. My tiny flashlight wasn't much use in exploring that area, but what I could see didn't seem much different from the area at the lighter east end. The major difference was that there were more cages near the windows, probably because the freight elevator was located at that end.

There were also stairways at both ends, and they went all the way to the ground floor.

I spent less than a half hour exploring the third floor of the warehouse, and it was all I could do to stay there that long. My senses were hyper alert, and my system was drenched in adrenaline. I didn't for a minute think there was any danger or I wouldn't have been there, but my body had a mind of its own.

I got back to my office a little before lunch, and Connelly arrived as I was getting ready to go out for a sandwich. I told him what I'd discovered about the warehouse doors and the alarm system. He nodded. That was all. "Were you in Wainwright's office before you found her?" he asked.

"Yes."

"Would you take a look, tell me if anything's changed? I mean if you don't mind going in there."

"Sure," I said, aware of how very much I did not want to go back into Sheila's office.

Yellow crime-scene tape and the M.E.'s seal barred the door. Connelly opened it and held the door for me to enter. The office had been transformed from a place where a human being worked to a crime scene. Smudges of black powder covered the room like measles. Even the smell was different, a mixture of chemical and organic odors.

In a way, the transformation was comforting. The room no longer looked as it had when I found Sheila on the desk. Still the memory of her body assailed me. I stood in the middle of the room and breathed deeply, letting my emotions settle and my attention center.

After the preliminary investigation, Dan often went back to a crime scene and sat quietly in the room, letting it "speak to him," he said. He'd simply take it all in passively, not looking for anything, waiting for his attention to settle on a detail that everyone else had overlooked. I wondered if Jack did that.

Maybe it was easier if you hadn't known the victim. Certainly it was easier if you weren't concentrating all your energy on not bolting out of the room.

"Sheila's secretary, Anna Proudfoot, would know more about what to look for than I do," I said.

"We've had her look," Connelly said. I waited for more, but it didn't come. I guess he'd volunteered all the information his stingy cop's psyche could manage. I could ask Anna later.

I forced myself to look around the room again. It's not easy to assess change in a room full of piles of paper. The papers on Sheila's desk had been knocked to the floor in a jumble with everything else that had been on it. I bent down to look at the papers.

Connelly didn't protest as I looked through the ones on top, taking care not to change their order or position. "These are all code," I said.

"Yeah, computer code. Can you read it?"

I shook my head. "No, but there's no reason for Sheila to have pages of code up here. She was in sales, not development."

Connelly shrugged. I stared at the sheets of symbols and recalled lunch on Wednesday. "Remember what I told you about Sheila's battle with the KeeGo guys?" I said. "I'd bet these pages of code are connected to that."

Connelly looked impatient. "I was more interested in something that didn't belong here, that might have been left by the killer," he said.

I looked around, tried to remember what I might have seen before, but my mind refused to focus. Anything smaller than a rhinoceros on the file cabinet, I probably missed.

Chapter

17

Sheila's family held a memorial service for her on Saturday at Saint Gabriel's in the Sunset district. The church was about three-quarters full, and I recognized a number of faces from Systech. Connelly and Rico were there, too.

Sheila's mother and her sister waited outside the church door as the mourners filed by with condolences. I was struck by the resemblance between the mother and both her daughters. I had the eerie feeling that I was seeing what Sheila would have looked like in twenty-five years. Tears stung my eyes.

I murmured my condolences to Sheila's mother, and she thanked me. I wanted to reach out to her, to offer some kind of comfort. But there wasn't any. Not for a woman burying a daughter who'd died at the hands of a sadistic killer.

The service was followed by a reception in the parish hall. Long tables displayed platters of food, all home cooked, probably assembled by friends of Sheila's mother, and older women in somber dresses poured steaming coffee into paper cups.

Allen Leggett stood by himself at the side of the room, looking as if he'd just buried a daughter. I started toward him and nearly bumped into John DeMarco. I was shocked to see the change in DeMarco. Gone was the snide sneer. His face was a mask of pain and too much emotion held too tightly inside. He held himself stiffly, as if only the force of his will kept him upright.

I followed him to the buffet table where he had stopped to talk with Bob Kingsley.

"I gotta get outa here," he said in a tight voice. "I feel like I'm suffocating."

"Why don't you go on home," Kingsley said. "You've put in your appearance."

"I don't know. I guess I'll stay." DeMarco walked off with his strange sticklike gait.

I moved closer to Kingsley. "I've never seen John like that. He must have been close to Sheila."

Kingsley shook his head. "No, his kid died a couple of years ago. He can't stand funerals."

"This must be awful for him," I said.

"Yeah," he said. Before I could say more, he turned away and went to get a cup of coffee.

I watched the other men with DeMarco. They approached him, chatted for a few minutes, then drifted away. The male ritual of support. Seemed pretty thin to me.

It must be lonely to be a man, I thought, not for the first time. Women wrap their own in expressions of concern and comfort. They encourage each other to talk about their pain, to let it out. DeMarco carried his alone, and it looked like it might well choke him.

Sheila's secretary, Anna, was talking with the dead woman's sister. I approached them and stood near enough that she turned to include me in their conversation. Anna introduced us. The sister's name was Sarah.

"You must be the artist who did the paintings in Sheila's office," I said.

Sarah Wainwright smiled and nodded. "She was my biggest fan," she said. Tears swam in her eyes and threatened to overflow.

"She was very proud of you," I said. The tears spilled over and Anna handed her a tissue.

"I just can't believe it," Sarah said. "I don't understand how it could have happened. She was so happy about the promotion. So excited. How could anyone . . .?"

Anna had pulled out a tissue for herself.

"I keep wondering if she had any warning," I said, using their pain to get to answers that might not come later and feeling a bit like a ghoul for doing it. "Was she afraid of anything or anyone?"

Sarah shook her head. "No, not at all. She was just so excited by her new job."

Anna didn't say anything, but the soft features of her face sharpened slightly and she stared at the floor intently. She knew something. She wouldn't say it in front of Sarah, but she might later.

I needed a longer talk with Sarah than the reception afforded. I asked if she was a professional artist.

"I guess you could say that," she replied. "But the professional part is commercial. I do a lot of freelance stuff to buy paint for the art that doesn't sell."

"I like the paintings in Sheila's office," I said. "I wonder if I might stop by and see more of your work sometime." It was true, I did like her work, though I was afraid that those vibrant colors might be a bit exhausting over time.

Sarah's face lit up like a child's. A rosy flush colored her pale cheeks. "Oh, I'm so glad, that you like the paintings, I mean. Please do come by, anytime." She began rummaging around in her purse and came up with a business card.

"I live in a loft, so work space and home space are the same," she said. "One phone gets both."

I took the card and promised to call her soon.

I spotted Elaine and Tonia across the room and went to join them. Elaine looked drawn; her skin stretched tight over her already sharp features. In contrast there was a soft, doughiness to Tonia. Her face was sallow and puffy, and her voice was uncharacteristically soft when she greeted me.

"We're about to leave," Elaine announced. "Some of us are going to a place nearby for drinks. You want to come?"

"Yeah, I'd like to," I said, and I meant it. Maybe I'd pick up some useful information, probably not. But right now, what I really wanted was the companionship of other women.

I followed Elaine's car to a restaurant about six blocks away. The outside had been designed to look Spanish, but the name was Italian and inside had pictures of Venice and Florence and red checked tablecloths. It was early for dinner, but they were happy to bring us drinks. I guess we looked like we needed them.

There were six of us—Elaine, Tonia, and three women I recognized from regional sales. I sat down next to a young woman with a haircut shorter than most guys. She introduced herself as Allyson, and she sounded like she came from New York. The woman next to her spoke with a Southern accent—not Deep South, maybe Georgia or South Carolina—and had bright red hair. I missed the third woman's name, but she had dark hair and a very wide mouth that barely stretched over prominent teeth.

"I don't think the priest even knew Sheila," the redhead complained. "That was the most generic sermon I've ever heard."

"Somehow I don't think Sheila was big on going to church,"

Elaine said. "She went to Catholic girls' school, and she didn't
have a single good thing to say about it."

The waitress came and took our drink orders, a couple of
white wines and the rest hard stuff. We stumbled along trying
to make conversation and not quite succeeding until the redhead said, "I just can't deal with the fact that someone *we* know
did it."

That was a real showstopper. We all sat in silence, then
Elaine said, "I guess it has to be, doesn't it?" She paused. "I
keep hoping it was a client or some weirdo who broke in, but it
really has to be one of *us*."

"I can't help looking at all the guys and wondering, 'Could
he have done it?'" Tonia said. She wrapped her arms around
herself, though it was far from cold. "I mean, what about Clark
Phillips and all that gross stuff on the E-mail. I know he's
obsessed with sex and he doesn't have much luck with women,
but is that enough to . . .?" She couldn't bring herself to finish
the sentence.

"It makes you look at all guys differently," the woman from
New York said. "I mean, I've been dating this guy with some
pretty kinky ideas. I don't think I want to see him again."

"You think he's connected to Sheila?" I asked.

"Oh, no. No, he's in drugs, pharmaceuticals, I mean. Never
even met Sheila. It just makes you think, 'Could this one turn
out to be a nut?' Who wants to take that kind of chance?"

We all nodded soberly. "That's what I wonder," said Elaine.
"Take John DeMarco. He can get real physical when he's
angry. And he and Bob Kingsley both really hate women."

"I don't think they hate us exactly," said Tonia. "They both
have oversized egos, and they're into putting people down, but
I don't know if that's hate or just poor manners."

"It's hate," Elaine said sharply. "Maybe not for all women
but certainly for the ones who don't know their place. I've seen
plenty of the type. You watch DeMarco's face the next time a

woman speaks back to him. He really hates that. And Kingsley hides it a little better, but he just hates like hell to have a woman question his judgment or tell him what to do."

I nodded, but it wasn't really agreement. I thought of DeMarco and the pain he must be carrying around after losing a child. Maybe what we saw as his hostility to women really had very little to do with us.

"I had an uncle like that," the redhead said. "Used to go on and on quoting scripture, or at least it sounded like scripture. How it was an *abomination*—he used that word a lot—for woman to put herself above man."

"Or on the same footing, I bet," Allyson said. Everyone nodded.

"Yeah, but that's the point. Lots of guys feel like that. But they don't go around killing women," the dark-haired woman said.

Elaine shrugged. "Who knows? And what does it say about Frank McFadden that he only dates younger women?" She turned to Allyson. "I saw him hitting on you, Ally. Did you go out?"

Allyson shook her head. "Not me. I don't date in the office. It's too tough when the relationship breaks up. He was sure persistent, though; and he got real sullen when I wouldn't change my mind."

"Which hardly makes him a murderer," Tonia protested.

"That's the tough part," Elaine said. "Stuff you didn't think twice about, now you wonder, 'What did that mean?'"

The waitress arrived with our drinks and distributed them. "To Sheila," Allyson said, and we all raised our glasses. Some of those glasses were half-empty before they returned to the table.

"Did Sheila ever date anyone in the office?" I asked.

"Never," Elaine said adamantly. "She had a real thing about that. I once dated a guy in development, and she must have told me a hundred times what a dumb idea that was."

"I got that lecture, too," Tonia said. "I started dating a salesman, and you'd have thought I was out picking up guys in bars
to hear Sheila tell it."

"So who were you dating?" Elaine asked.

Tonia colored slightly. "Doesn't matter. He broke it off."

"Did you know that Jerry Keegan hit on Sheila?" the dark-
haired woman asked.

Everyone turned to her in surprise. She nodded and looked
pleased. "I swear it happened. I was waiting when he came
storming out of her office, mad as hell. She looked just as
pleased as she could be. Said he'd been hitting on her and she
told him that wasn't professional behavior." She smiled at the
memory, then froze. "Oh shit, you don't think he could be the
one?"

Chapter

18

I hadn't drunk enough after the memorial service to feel as bad as I did Sunday morning. It wasn't exactly a hangover, didn't feel like a migraine, but it took me almost an hour to get out of bed and two cups of coffee before I spoke to anyone. Peter and Molly stayed out of my way. At some point I got tired of feeling sorry for myself and made a stab at behaving like an adult.

I decided I might feel better if I got out for a walk, so I suggested an excursion to Mount Tam. That got as much enthusiasm as if I'd announced we were going to the dentist. "The 'Niners are playing today," Peter protested.

"And Craig's coming over to help me with my algebra," Molly said.

"Oh," Peter and I said at once, like parents on a bad sitcom.

Molly looked disgusted. "Don't make a big deal out of this," she said.

"Right," I said. "I'm cool."

Molly rolled her eyes.

• • •

Craig arrived dressed all in black—pants, T-shirt, leather jacket with many metal studs, and boots. He had not one earring but four, three in his right ear and one through his nostril. The smile I gave him took a lot of effort.

Molly introduced us, and he responded with a nod and a monosyllabic utterance that might have been a greeting. After an awkward pause, he and Molly disappeared into her room and turned the stereo up to max. Peter grinned. "I know why I used to do that," he said. "I hope that's not why *they*'re doing it."

I groaned. "I'm not ready to deal with this," I said. "Not today, probably not next week, maybe never."

"Makes you feel about a hundred and fifty years old, doesn't it?" Peter said.

It did, and that made me cranky. I took my cranky energy to the refrigerator and threw out everything that looked like it might be growing alien life forms. There wasn't much left when I finished.

I was just about to join Peter for the Forty-niners game when the phone rang. It was Jack Connelly.

"Thought you'd like to know—we've interviewed Phillips, the programmer, three times. He admits to sending the E-mail messages but denies doing anything else. And he won't give us the names of the other pranksters."

"Have you arrested him?'

"For sending raunchy messages on E-mail? Hardly. We don't have proof of anything else."

"I'm sure he knows who pulled the other pranks," I said.

"Yeah, I'm sure he does. But he's not telling us. And there's no way I can force him to. We've leaned on him as heavily as we can, but he's a smart kid. He knows we can't do anything."

"Do you think he could be the killer?"

"Any of them could be the killer. But Phillips is a better-than-average possibility. His messages were equal parts lust and hostility. He has trouble getting together with women. It's possible."

"Did you ask him if he'd been in Sheila's office the Wednesday night before she was killed?" I asked.

"He claims he was never in Sheila's office."

"I checked the lock on the door from the third-floor offices into the warehouse on Friday. You can open it with a credit card, and all you'd have to do would be tape it, then you could come into the offices from the warehouse."

"Except that everyone signed out, so he wasn't hiding in the warehouse, and the warehouse perimeter is on a sensitive alarm system, so he couldn't come back in," Connelly said. "Look, we appreciate your efforts to help, but the way you can do that is by talking to people. Get them to tell you what they won't tell us. We'll take care of catching the killer. That's our job."

It took every shred of self-control I had not to point out that they weren't making much progress on their job. I thanked Connelly for the information on Phillips; he promised that he'd keep the pressure on the programmer, and I got off the phone before I could give in to the temptation to tell him exactly how much I hated being condescended to.

The loud music continued in Molly's room. I considered how to lure them out without appearing the uptight parent. My stomach supplied the answer. Food. I walked down to the local deli and ordered enough food for a small basketball team. With luck, it'd get me through a couple of noncooking dinners, too.

I waited till halftime to announce lunch. Craig accepted the invitation to join us in his low-key, monosyllabic way. The sandwich he made for himself suggested that he hadn't eaten for at least forty-eight hours.

As Peter was making his sandwich he asked me, "So, Catherine, do they have the autopsy report on the murder?"

Now, in most households that's not a question you hear over lunch. And most people over sixteen would find it in poor taste, but it's a real grabber with fifteen year olds.

"Not till Monday," I said, playing along.

Craig turned to Molly to catch her response to our strange conversation. "They're both P.I.s," she said. "Catherine's working on a murder case." She was Ms. Cool and she was obviously enjoying it.

After that, it wasn't too hard to get Craig talking. Peter introduced the subject of motorcycles, and we discovered that there was something Craig was passionate about. He came alive as he described the Honda 600 Hurricane he was saving his money for.

Peter had a Harley at one time, and with that revelation they plunged into serious guy-talk. Molly looked impressed, then bored, and finally maybe a bit jealous. I found it fascinating to watch Craig. As he discussed engine performance I began to see beyond the leather and earrings. It was as if there were a couple of different people inside the same set of skin. Sometimes you could see the boy he'd been, others the man he was becoming.

Molly finally dragged Craig away from the table and back to her room. When he left at four, she looked furious and he looked confused.

"What's the matter?" I asked when she came into the kitchen to get a Coke.

"Jeez, I don't understand what it is with guys," she complained. "Craig doesn't say ten words to me, but Peter mentions the word 'Harley' and he's like Mr. Conversation." She slammed the refrigerator door, took a glass from the cabinet, and slammed that door, too. "What is it with them anyway? Can't they talk about anything but cars and sports?"

"Politics," I said. "Lots of them can talk about politics."

She ignored me. "That stuff's so boring," she complained. "Who cares about Barry Bonds's batting record?"

I cared, but I let it go. "Men don't talk like women do," I said. "I don't know why that is, but they don't, at least not with other men. Maybe they like sports and cars because those are safe things to talk about. They don't have to reveal anything about themselves."

"Maybe they don't have anything to reveal," she grumbled as she poured her Coke. It fizzed up over the top of the glass and ran down the side. "Damn."

I handed her a dishrag to wipe the table.

"I don't know if they're worth the trouble," Molly said.

I laughed. "Oh, they are, or at least some of them are."

By Monday everyone at Systech was trying to get back to a semblance of normalcy, but we were mediocre actors going through the motions with no real feel for the part. People talked too soft or too loud, seemed either a bit manic or depressed.

I spent a lot of time in the employee lounge, watching and listening. No one came up with a confession.

Around eleven I stopped by Anna Proudfoot's desk. I didn't know Anna well enough to ask what I needed to know straight out, but I knew that she was the emotional mother of the sales department, and I figured I could rely on her care-giving instincts.

I allowed myself to look the way I felt. "Pretty quiet today," I said.

She nodded, then seeing my miserable expression asked, "Are you feeling all right, Catherine?"

"Not really," I said. "I can't sleep. I keep seeing Sheila . . . on her desk." It was only a slight exaggeration.

Her face creased into lines of concern. "I'm so sorry," she said. "That must have been awful for you."

I put on my best trying-to-be-brave act, and Anna wrapped me in warmth as comforting as a soft blanket. Finally, I said,

"The police asked me to look at the office to see if there was anything different. I didn't see anything, did you?"

Anna shook her head. "No. It was so hard to go in there after what happened."

I nodded glumly. "I had lunch with her the day before. God, it just doesn't seem possible. She said something I keep trying to remember because it might be important, something about 'taking care of the guys from Keego.' Does that mean anything to you?"

Anna looked uncomfortable. I was sure she knew something.

"I guess I should have told the police," I said. "I worry that maybe it had something to do with her death."

"Oh, I can't imagine that's so," Anna protested. Then she paused and looked thoughtful.

"Somebody here killed her," I said. "The police seem sure of that. If there's a secret, it could be dangerous."

Now Anna looked positively distressed. "I think perhaps you should talk to Tonia," she said. "She knew more about what Sheila was doing. If there were any danger . . ." She left the sentence hanging, unable to finish it.

I called down to programming only to find that Tonia was out for the day. I telephoned her home but got no answer. I told myself that she'd probably gone for a walk or out for lunch or maybe to visit a friend. Still, I worried.

Nothing was happening around the office. Most of the salespeople continued to find excuses to be out in the field, so I decided to call Sarah Wainwright and see if she'd talk to me.

But first I called Allen Leggett. "Has anyone cleaned out Sheila's office?" I asked.

"I don't think so," he said. "The police have unsealed the door, so I guess I can have maintenance do it soon. Is there any sort of policy on this type of thing?"

You're in the wrong business when people ask you that kind

of question, I thought. "I don't think so," I said. "I'll be calling Sheila's sister. Can I tell her I'll help arrange for the return of her paintings and Sheila's other possessions?"

"Oh yes, thank you very much."

"I can't make those arrangements myself, you know," I said because I suspected he'd forgotten that, to maintenance and everyone else at Systech, I was still the phone lady. "You'll need to make them. I want to tell the sister that I'm making them, so I'll have an excuse to talk with her."

"Oh," he said. "Of course. I'm sorry, I seem to have trouble concentrating."

I understood that. Violent death has that effect on lots of people.

I called the number on the card that Sarah Wainwright had given me. She picked up the phone on the second ring.

"Hello, I'm Catherine Sayler," I said. "I worked with Sheila; we talked at the funeral."

"Oh, yes," she said, her voice belying her words. She was either generally spacey or hadn't a clue who I was.

"I asked if I could see your work sometime," I said.

"Oh, of course."

"I noticed that Sheila's things are still in her office. Would you like help in arranging for their return?"

"Oh yes, thank you," she said. "I didn't know what to do, but I'd really like to have the paintings back. For personal reasons, you know."

"I'll make sure that they're handled carefully," I said. "I know that this is a hard time for you, but I wonder if I could stop by and see you for a few minutes."

"Sure," she said. "When?'

"Today or tomorrow?"

"I'll be out tomorrow. Could you come today?" she said.

We settled on three-thirty at her loft.

Chapter

19

Sarah's loft was on South Park, only a few blocks from Systech. The block-long park was designed by a builder who wanted to create an English mews in the middle of the warehouse area of San Francisco. He surrounded a narrow oval of tenacious grass with three-story buildings designed to offer both work and living space. Over the years, age and industrial grime have taken their toll on the buildings, but South Park still keeps its feeling of being from another time and place.

Sarah's building was at the west end of the park. There were seven names taped next to four bells. I rang the one that said "Wainwright/Janowitz."

Sarah answered the door, wearing jeans, an oversized denim shirt, and an old pair of sneakers covered with paint. She was slender like Sheila but less sturdy, willowy almost. Her complexion was paler, but she had the same lively gray eyes.

I expressed my condolences again. She offered me tea. There was no way I could ask what I needed to know unless I told her who I really was, so as she was boiling the water, I fessed up.

"I'm not working on the murder officially," I said. "But I really want to see the police catch Sheila's killer. Will you help me?"

"Of course," she said. "I'll do anything I can. But I've told the police everything I know."

Before I could ask my questions, she had plenty of her own. There weren't many I could answer. When it was finally my turn, she told me what she'd told the police. It wasn't much, either.

"Let's back up," I said. "Just tell me about Sheila. What kind of a person was she?"

"She was wonderful and kind and funny," Sarah began, her eyes filling with tears. She talked for almost an hour, telling stories of her sister, some from childhood, some more recent. The more she talked, the deeper the sense of sadness and waste I felt. I had to fight to keep my focus, not to let myself slide into emotional entropy.

"She never married?" I asked.

"No," Sarah said. "She dated, but not a lot."

"I'm told she never dated in the company," I said.

"Never," Sarah said. She paused and I sensed there was something she wasn't telling me.

"Why did she feel so strongly?" I asked. "Did something happen?"

Sarah nodded. She stopped to find some tissues. She blew her nose and wiped her eyes. "It was a long time ago," she said. "I don't know exactly what happened. She wouldn't talk about it in any detail, but it was her first real job. She'd gone back east and was working for some computer firm, not Systech. Someone else.

"She was dating a guy in the company. They'd been intimate, but after a few months he started acting possessive. She wasn't very self-confident back then, not at all like she was as she got older, but eventually she confronted him. And the bastard attacked her."

"Physically?"

Sarah nodded. There were tears in her eyes. "He raped her," she said. "He called her a slut and a whore and said a lot of awful things, then he said he'd teach her a thing or two, and he raped her."

I felt sick, and when I tried to swallow, there was a lump in my throat that almost choked me. "Oh, shit," I said. Her death was awful enough, but coming after that . . . "Did she go to the police?" I asked.

Sarah shook her head. "She was too ashamed. After all, she'd been dating this guy. She'd slept with him. Do you think the cops would have taken her seriously? This was twelve or thirteen years ago, remember."

"She must have been terrified."

"And humiliated," Sarah said. She paused for a minute, then blew her nose. "She couldn't go back to work and pretend nothing had happened. She quit and moved back here. I don't think she ever told anyone but me what happened."

"No wonder she felt so strongly about not dating in the company," I said.

"She was really afraid of dating at all for a long time. It wasn't just the physical trauma. She didn't trust herself anymore. You can imagine—you think you know a guy and he turns out like that, how can you trust yourself not to make the same mistake again?" Sarah's eyes brimmed over and tears flowed down her cheeks. She wiped them away and blew her nose again, then continued. "For a long time, she just didn't want to take the chance. I think maybe that's why she never married. She just wouldn't risk letting anyone get close."

I nodded. "Did she ever have problems with any of the men at Systech, before the pranks, I mean?"

Sarah thought for a minute. "She liked most of them fine, but she had trouble with her boss once. I don't remember his name, but he put a lot of pressure on her to go out and he hassled her when she wouldn't."

"Was that Scott Jorgensen?" I asked.

She shook her head. "I really don't remember who it was. It was years ago."

"Was there anything recently?" I asked.

She started to shake her head and stopped. "Actually, there was something, I think, but I don't know what it was. It was maybe six months ago, around the time they acquired that other company. She was real upset for a while."

Sarah paused and stared into space as if trying to recall something. Finally, she shook her head and said, "No, I can't remember what she said, but something stirred up all that old shit. I'm pretty sure of that."

It was a quarter to five when I finally left Sarah's loft and headed back for Systech. My stomach was still queasy and the lump pressed hard against my throat. But the shock and sorrow were now mixed with a burning anger.

When I thought of Sheila, I saw a bright, self-assured woman; it was hard to imagine her so humiliated and terrified that she wouldn't report being raped, wouldn't seek vengeance. But her sister was right. She knew it wouldn't do any good. It'd be a hard enough case to make today, impossible back then.

So she'd chosen the path many women choose, silence. And the safety of building a hard shell that keeps men at a safe distance. And still she hadn't been safe.

I needed to stop at Systech to pick up some papers I'd left there. But I sat in the car and let my emotions settle down before I got out. The anger dissipated and the lump in my throat grew smaller, but the heavy sadness in my chest refused to budge.

It was only five, but the office was almost empty.

On the way out I met Bob Kingsley at the elevator. He was uncharacteristically quiet and his usually florid complexion seemed a bit pale.

When we got to the ground floor, he hurried out the front

door and walked off quickly down the street. But when I got to my car, I found him just getting out of the silver BMW parked next to me. His face was bright red.

"Damn car," he said as he slammed the door.

"Problems?" I asked.

"Forty-four thousand dollars, and the piece of shit won't start. I'm meeting a client at six-thirty. No way I can make that now." I made a quick calculation and put duty before pleasure. I might not get a chance like this again. "Where are you going?" I asked. "Maybe I can drop you there."

He shook his head impatiently. "It's down the peninsula, in Cupertino."

"You're in luck," I said. "I have to go to San Jose." I hadn't planned to, of course, but Cupertino's at least an hour's drive at this time of day, and Kingsley would have to find something to talk about in that time.

He seemed surprised by my offer, but after a moment's thought, he said, "Okay, thanks. I'll get my wife to bring me back." He climbed in my car and we headed for the Bayshore Freeway. Cars were already backed up at the on-ramp. If the traffic was like this all the way, we'd have a lot longer than an hour to make conversation.

"This is really very kind of you," Kingsley said as we sat on the on-ramp. "I sure do appreciate it."

"I'm happy to help," I said.

"How's the voice-mail system coming?" he asked, and for the next ten miles we chatted about telecommunications. He had a salesman's gift for gab, and I realized as we rounded "hospital curve" that he could easily make small talk all the way to Cupertino.

When there was a lull in the conversation, I said, "The cops questioned me again this morning. Did they get to you?"

He nodded. "Yeah. Boy, they do go over and over things. What'd they ask you?" He tried to sound casual but couldn't quite pull it off.

"Stuff about Sheila, the pranks, office politics," I said.

"Those dumb pranks." He let his breath out in a hiss of disgust but didn't say more.

A minute later he asked, again in a too-casual voice, "The cops have any suspects?"

I took my eyes off the road long enough to look at him. He wasn't facing me, so I couldn't read his expression. He was talking to the windshield. "Not that they're telling me about," I said. "Are they putting pressure on you?"

"Me? No. Why would they pressure me?"

"I don't know. Maybe because everyone knows you didn't like Sheila."

"I didn't *dis*like her," he protested. "Hell, I didn't even really know her. I didn't like working for her. She probably disliked me more than I disliked her."

I nodded. "Still, it puts you under pressure, I bet."

"You better believe it," he said with feeling. "People look at me like maybe *I* did it. Do you know what that feels like? I mean, how can anyone think I'd do something like that?" He sounded genuinely shocked.

"I mean, I guess I don't win any awards for sensitive male of the year, but I'm a lot better than some guys. I don't put women down, I keep my hands to myself, and I don't make inappropriate advances. And now I catch women looking at me like maybe *I* killed Sheila. Jeez!"

We passed Candlestick Park. To our left, the bay was ruffled with choppy waves. To our right, billows of soft white fog, unusual here in late October, crept over San Bruno Mountain and spilled down its barren gold-brown side toward the green enclave of Brisbane at its base. Traffic was moving at a decent pace by now.

"I don't understand the women at Systech," Kingsley said. "They're always pissed off about something. Right now Elaine Burskin is on my case because I set up a party for some big clients in our box for the Giants-Braves game and didn't include her. How the hell was I supposed to know she likes baseball?"

"I don't know that she does," I said, "but I know she cares about meeting clients."

"This isn't really business," Kingsley said. "And besides you gotta be able to talk sports, even guys who aren't big fans can handle that."

I am a Giants fan, and I can tell you that there are guys who cannot talk intelligently about baseball. It is not a sex-linked characteristic.

"It's just something you women don't understand," he went on. "There's a kind of chemistry when a bunch of guys get together. Having women there spoils it."

"I can understand that," I said. "Same thing's true with women, but you'd be pissed if the major clients were women and Elaine took them to the ballet and left you out."

"Yeah, I suppose I would," he said. "Of course, I would. Good point."

The words were right, but the tone was a bit too smooth and easy. A salesman's tone. The-customer-is-always-right tone. And just as smoothly he switched the conversation onto safer ground, asking me what I thought of caller-line identification.

We were driving through Palo Alto before I had another chance to shift the conversation. "John DeMarco was telling me about the practical jokes you guys used to play at KeeGo," I said. "You must have had quite a time."

"KeeGo was a fun place to work," he said. "Jerry Keegan loves practical jokes. And a bunch of us graduated from UT— University of Texas—together, so we were buddies before we signed on with him. We had a good ole time. Worked hard, played hard."

"Systech must seem a bit dull," I said.

"Well, it's different," he said. "You know, I don't condone those practical jokes, the mice in the drawers and stuff, but that wouldn't have been such a big deal at KeeGo. People here tend to take things too personally."

I wondered how he thought I could not take it personally when someone soaked my chair with red ink, but that was old business. "Maybe," I said. "So you don't think I should have been bothered by the photos of women being tortured and murdered?"

I'd pulled into the slow lane, where traffic was light, so that I could take my eyes off the road to check Kingsley frequently, but a red sports car cut in front of me just then, and I missed seeing his reaction.

"What?" he asked. Again he seemed genuinely surprised.

"Sheila and I and a couple of others got photos of women being tortured and killed. You didn't know?"

"How the hell would I know?" Shock and challenge mixed with fear in his voice. "I sure as hell didn't have anything to do with something like that."

I didn't respond.

"Are you saying you think I sent something like that?" He tried to sound indignant, but the undercurrent of fear was still there. He started to say more, then stopped himself. "No, wait a minute, this is your idea of a joke, right?" he said.

"If those photos were a joke, someone has a very strange sense of humor," I said.

"No, well, of course, there's nothing funny about something like that," he said. "I didn't mean to be insensitive, I just didn't know. It must have been a hell of a shock for you."

The shift from indignation to playfulness to solicitous concern was fascinating to watch. I had no idea which, if any, of the emotions were real and which were a performance calculated to produce a desired effect.

That ability to sense what the other person wants to hear or feel and then to give it to them is the mark of a master salesman.

Or a psychopath.

Chapter

20

The ride back from Cupertino gave me a lot of time to think.

I hadn't learned much from Kingsley. I doubted that I ever would. He and Frank McFadden were masters of evasion, and I suspected that both considered truth a relative concept. Often the most useful thing you learn from someone like that is not to trust them.

Sarah's story haunted me. Sheila's experience must have affected her relationships on the job. My recent experience with Scott Jorgensen was enough to remind me how powerfully emotional baggage can influence you. Would I have picked a fight with the man if the stories about his conduct hadn't stirred old memories? Probably not. And my job would have been easier if I hadn't antagonized him.

Sheila's memories were infinitely more painful than mine. If, as Sarah thought, something around the KeeGo merger had stirred up those memories, it would almost certainly have affected her. Had it interfered with her judgment enough to make her push someone she shouldn't have pushed? Caused her to miss signs that might have warned her?

The more I thought about it, the more anxious I was to talk to Tonia. And the more concerned that I hadn't been able to reach her.

I called as soon as I got home and was relieved to find that she was all right. She planned to be at work the next day and she seemed pleased by my suggestion that we meet for lunch.

I met her in the lobby at noon the next day and we walked to Mama's Café. The sky was gray and overcast; it matched our mood.

We both stared at the menu. Even small decisions seemed to take a lot of energy since Sheila's death. Tonia was obviously having the same problem. "I don't know," she said. "I just don't care enough to choose one thing over the other."

"I know," I said. In the end I ordered soup and a half-sandwich and she asked for the same.

Tonia looked terribly young and vulnerable. Already thin, she had a waiflike quality now. Her dark eyes were sad and her shoulders hunched forward in a slump. She was wearing a forest green long-sleeved shirt with navy slacks; I wondered if she'd consciously chosen such dark colors.

"I can't sleep," she said. "I haven't really slept since . . . you know."

I nodded. "Yeah, I'm having the same problem." Actually, sleep was less the problem than the nightmares that disrupted it. It was getting to the point where I thought insomnia might be a blessing.

"I took yesterday off, thinking maybe I could sleep during the day," Tonia said.

"Did it work?"

"A little, I guess, but then I didn't sleep last night."

"Have you thought of seeing a therapist?" I asked. "It might help. They're trained to help people get through stuff like this." I knew. But I also knew it didn't help with nightmares. Not mine, anyway. Only time did that.

"Yeah, I might do that," she said without enthusiasm.

I tried to help her talk about it, but Tonia wasn't a big talker. The waitress arrived with the soup during one of our silences. While we were eating I decided it was time to get down to business. "Something's bothering me," I said. "The day before she was killed, Sheila told me she had something on the Keego guys, something that was going to get them off her back. I asked Anna about it and she said I should talk to you, that you knew what Sheila was up to."

Tonia froze. She had her soup spoon halfway to her mouth and she simply froze for several seconds, then raised it to her mouth and slowly put it down again. "I don't know a thing," she said.

"Anna thinks you do," I said. "Look, Tonia, this could be important. It could have something to do with Sheila's death."

Tonia shook her head. "No," she said. "And it's company business, Catherine. I just can't talk about it."

"Tonia, you got photos, I got photos, and Sheila got photos. Now Sheila's dead. You and I can't afford to ignore anything."

She didn't respond, just kept eating her soup, raising the spoon rather mechanically from the bowl to her mouth. Finally, she looked at me. "I just don't know what to do," she said.

"Maybe I can help," I offered. "We're in this thing together, you know. If you're worried about me shooting off my mouth, I can promise you that I won't."

She paused and I was getting ready to try a new approach when she said, "I have to talk to someone. I'm having such trouble thinking things through."

"I won't repeat anything," I said.

"Well, you know that Sheila's promotion put her in charge of regional sales for the new client-server applications. She was supposed to oversee the sales program, but she got real interested in the new product.

"I think I told you that she had a tendency to get involved in things that weren't really any of her business, and she wanted to know everything about the product. Well, the more she looked at it, the more she thought there was something wrong.

"Jerry Keegan demonstrated it with Valley Savings. But that's one of our smaller accounts, and Sheila wanted to be sure that it could handle the heavier load and greater demands of a bigger bank, someplace where the transactions ran into the billions.

"She leaned on QA—that's quality assurance—but the guys there who were assigned to the client-server applications were all from KeeGo, and she started to suspect that they were stonewalling."

"So Sheila did a bit of research on her own," I said, remembering the sheets of code I'd seen in her office.

Tonia nodded. "And she asked me to help. It took us a while to find it, but there is a serious problem in one of the applications that handles ATM transactions. I suppose Keegan figured we'd never catch it, because it's only a problem when you get to a really heavy load and most of our customers aren't likely to have that many transactions in a short period of time. He probably thought he'd have figured out how to solve it before anyone realized it existed."

"Or he'd have gotten the majority of his money from Systech, and Leggett would be left holding the bag," I said.

"I've got to tell Allen, but it just didn't seem so important after Sheila's death. And I guess I'm a little scared to just walk in and tell him that his new product has a major bug."

"But he needs to be told," I said, "and so do the police."

"The police?" she almost gasped. "Why do they have to know? I mean you don't think Sheila's death has anything to do with this, do you? I mean, people don't kill each other over something like this."

Something like money, reputation, power. Sure they do. All the time. "I think Jerry Keegan and his associates could be in serious trouble when this comes out. I don't know how the agreements are drawn, but I doubt that much money's changed hands yet. An undisclosed flaw would give Leggett grounds to void the sale and probably claim significant damages."

"But Sheila was killed by a psycho," Tonia protested. "The police said it was a sex killing."

"That's what it looked like," I said. "Doesn't mean that's what it was."

Tonia was looking at me very strangely. I realized too late that I'd stepped out of character. "You're not a consultant," she said. "Who are you?"

I decided it was time for the truth, with Tonia at least. I needed her help, and the charade of being the phone lady wasn't going to get me what I wanted. "No, you're right," I admitted. "I'm an investigator. Allen Leggett hired me to find out who was harassing the women at Systech."

She didn't look shocked. She just nodded. "I thought there was something funny. You seemed so much more interested in the company than other outsiders. But I figured it was because of your skirt, that you wanted to get even. Did Sheila know?"

"No," I said. "She may have wondered why I was so nosy, but she never knew."

"And now you're looking for her killer."

"The police are looking for the killer. I'm just sticking around to see if I can help. Besides, I feel like I have a stake in this."

"You think Keegan killed her because of what she discovered?" Her voice was incredulous. "But he didn't know. No one did except for Sheila and me."

"Someone could have suspected. I'll admit it's a long shot, but the police have to be told."

"Oh God, Allen's going to be so upset. There goes his new expansion plan. A sex killing and a product with a major bug, we're going to look really great in the industry." She stopped suddenly and looked stricken. "I can't believe I'm worrying about our place in the market when this might have something to do with Sheila being killed. Of course, I'll talk to the police."

I considered. I did have a responsibility to Allen Leggett. I was working for Systech, not the city of San Francisco. I owed it to him to tell him what I knew before I took it to the police. "We could talk to Leggett before we go to the cops," I told Tonia.

"Oh, that'd be much better," she said. "I'd like it better anyway."

I preferred talking to Leggett before the police, too. As soon as we got back to Systech I called his office and arranged for Tonia and me to see him, then I called Tonia and asked her to arrive five minutes after I went to his office.

He didn't look any better than he had the day before. Maybe none of us was sleeping very well. When I told him what Tonia had told me, he looked a whole lot worse.

Tonia arrived just as I finished delivering the bad news. She was carrying a stack of printouts, and they spent over an hour going over pages that she had marked. By the time they'd finished, Leggett looked like he'd been the main course at a vampire feast.

"It looks bad," he said. "I'll pull in some guys from QA and spend the evening checking it again, but I think you and Sheila were right. We'll have to put the marketing on hold until we know for sure. We can't sell this thing in the shape it's in. Who knows what else might be wrong with it."

"I guess this explains the pranks," I said.

"You mean they did it to throw us off the track?" Tonia said. "No, I don't think so. The pranks began before Sheila ever suggested we check out the product. The first one was a few days after she was appointed sales manager. It was almost a week later that she asked me to help her check the applications."

Leggett didn't seem to be listening to us. He stared down at the pages of code. "Sheila had pages like this in her office the night she was killed," I said.

"She would have," Tonia said. "We made copies of the parts we thought were suspicious, and she kept them in her office."

"You have to tell the police," I said. "You just can't hold back information in a murder investigation."

Now Leggett looked up. He looked tired and resigned. "Yes, of course, I suppose we'll have to. Then the whole thing will come out, won't it?"

"Not necessarily," I told him. "The police don't publicize everything they learn. I don't see any reason that this should come out unless there's a direct connection with the murder. But they have to be able to investigate it."

"Can you give me an hour or so to decide how I want to handle this?" Leggett asked. "I will tell them, but I need to decide what to do about Keegan."

"It's your call," I said. "I'll help any way I can."

"Thanks," he said. "In the meantime, not a word to anyone about this. I don't want Keegan to know I'm on to him until I'm ready."

Some color had returned to his face, and his voice seemed stronger, his shoulders straighter. I had a feeling that Allen Leggett might actually be looking forward to his confrontation with Jerry Keegan.

An hour later, he called me in again. The transformation was impressive. Gone was any trace of depression or indecisiveness. In its place was a quiet power and intensity that I had only sensed before. I shouldn't have been surprised. Sheila's death had left us all feeling confused and powerless. I'd brought Leggett the cure for those difficult feelings—an enemy who had a face and a problem that had a solution.

"I want a crack at Keegan and his crew before the police question them," he announced. "I think that will be to the cops' advantage, actually. I'll make it clear that one condition of continued employment here is complete cooperation with the investigation."

"I'll see what I can do," I said, "but I doubt that the police will give you the first shot. They'll want to see Keegan's reactions for themselves."

"Then I want to see him the minute they finish with him. He mustn't have time to do anything more than wonder whether he's headed for jail."

I didn't get to be present for either Keegan and company's meeting with Connelly or their session immediately afterward in Leggett's office. I did hear that they looked shocked and nervous when they left the police meeting and that, when Leggett got through with them, they looked like he'd chewed them up and spit them out.

Leggett told me later that he'd simply explained his lawyers' version of the situation and its legal and financial ramifications. "I told Jerry Keegan that if he ever wanted to work as anything more than a janitor in this industry, he'd better find a solution to the problem, and I gave him three months to do it," Leggett said. The way he said it made me almost sorry for Jerry Keegan.

"And I told them all that I wanted to know exactly who was responsible for the pranks. It was just who we suspected—Kingsley, DeMarco, and Phillips. They will be issuing personal apologies to the women they harassed. Do you think the women will consider that sufficient?"

"With all that's happened, I don't think the pranks are such a big deal now, but I'll try to get a sense of how the women feel."

"Good. I'll ask them myself, but you may get a different answer. I want it to be very clear that we won't tolerate this sort of thing. I'd like to keep these guys to work on the problems with the new product, but if I need to fire them I will."

I called Connelly to find out what he'd learned from the interviews with Keegan and the others. I didn't expect him to thank me for discovering what Sheila was up to, but I thought he might at least show some appreciation by being a bit less tight-lipped. I was wrong, of course.

All I got out of him was that he still didn't believe that the motive in the killing had anything to do with Sheila's efforts to expose Keegan's fraud.

Chapter

21

The next set of photographs arrived Wednesday afternoon, a week from the day Sheila was murdered.

I knew what it was the minute I saw the envelope in my inbasket. The same anonymous interoffice envelope with the sender line blank. I didn't even open it. I just dialed Jack Connelly's number.

Jack was out but Rico was there, and he promised to come right over. "Don't handle it; don't open it," he said. I told him not to worry; I wasn't anxious to see what was inside.

Minutes later Tonia appeared at my door, white-faced, holding an identical envelope. She didn't look too far from fainting. I led her into my office and was about to shut the door when Elaine arrived. The hand in which she held the third envelope was shaking. I could hear someone crying down the hall.

Elaine wasn't about to faint, but she looked stunned. I took both envelopes and dumped their contents onto my desk. One was a polaroid photo of Sheila on her desk, the other, a close-up of her face.

I looked down at the images and I was back in Sheila's

office. I saw her, not in the photos but on her desk, her body prepared like a lewd horror exhibit. My heart pounded and I struggled to draw breath into my tightening chest. I was trapped in time, unable to withdraw from the gruesome scene. I closed my eyes to shut it out, but Sheila was still there.

"Catherine, Catherine, are you all right?" Elaine's voice and the pressure of her hand on my arm brought me back into the present. I shook my head to clear it, but my chest still squeezed against my hammering heart. I took several deep breaths and my heart began to slow down, but the flashback had left me drained and feeling slightly ill.

As I got control over my emotions, I became aware of Tonia, who stood white-faced and frozen just behind me. She had begun to cry. There was no sound, but tears streamed down her face.

Elaine wrapped an arm around her and they clung together. "It's so . . . awful," Tonia said.

I tried to make my voice calm and businesslike as I asked Elaine, "Did anyone else get these?"

She nodded. "Allyson did, maybe some others."

I walked out onto the platform. The sounds were different. You could tell something had happened because the usual background office noise had ceased and been replaced by new noises. Anna Proudfoot was sobbing at her desk. Both Frank McFadden and John DeMarco were trying to comfort her. A Polaroid of Sheila lay face up. DeMarco turned it over as I walked up.

"It's a photo, of Sheila," he said hoarsely. "I . . . I . . . had no idea." His face was stiff with shock.

McFadden knelt beside Anna and spoke softly to her. Her shoulders shook with sobs. McFadden looked up, his own eyes damp. "Who the hell could do such a thing?" he asked.

Small knots of people were collecting around the office. Some women refused to show the photos they'd gotten; others handed them to coworkers who gasped in shock. Everyone had known the basic facts of what happened, but none of them had seen Sheila's body.

"He did this, then he took pictures of her," one woman said, her voice mixing shock and anger.

The men were as shocked and upset as the women, but a subtle barrier divided the sexes and each suffered on his or her own side of it. For the women, Sheila's murder was intensely personal. It confronted them with the stuff of their private fears and nightmares. Each envelope was a reminder that the recipient might well be on the killer's list of potential victims.

The men were shut out, not potential victims but potential suspects. They stood around awkwardly, wanting to offer comfort but unsure of how it would be received as the women, knowing that there was a killer in their midst, turned suspicious eyes on men they'd known for years.

No one seemed to know what to do, so it was a good thing that Rico arrived about that time to take charge. He had the women bring him the photos and envelopes, questioned the kid who delivered interoffice mail, then talked to everyone on the floor. The envelopes had appeared outside the mailroom that morning. No one had seen who left them, and they'd been sorted into the morning delivery without anyone giving it a second thought.

Rico picked up my envelope from the desk with a large pair of tweezers and put it in a plastic bag. "The boys at the lab can open it there. I'll tell you what they find."

I had a pretty good idea what they'd find and I didn't think it'd include fingerprints or any other evidence to help them trace the envelope back to the killer.

As he was leaving, Rico said, "Still think this is about business?"

•　•　•

I had to admit that he was right. I didn't want him to be. I wanted the motive to be nice and neat and clean, something I understood, like greed or revenge. I wanted there to be a logical connection between victim and killer. But there was no logic to this crime. It grew from twisted emotions I didn't understand and didn't want to confront.

The image of Sheila's body forced its way into my consciousness again, and just as quickly I pushed it away. I couldn't let myself feel the emotions it brought with it. Most of all, I couldn't admit the one I'd worked so hard to suppress—fear.

I looked at my watch and realized it was lunchtime. Outside there was a mass exodus. No one wanted to stay in the building. The women came together in groups; most of the men wandered off alone. I had no appetite and I wasn't sure my stomach would accept food, but I could certainly use some human contact, so I joined the group at the elevator.

I had lunch with Elaine, Allyson, and three other women from the third floor. It was a somber affair. Conversation was strained, with everyone making an effort to find something to say on topics that no one cared much about. There were some long silences, but no one mentioned the photos or the woman in them.

No one seems to have dessert with lunch anymore, but today was an exception. Maybe because none of us wanted to go back to Systech, maybe because we all needed a good hit of comfort food. As the waiter doled out the dishes a short brunette named Lynne finally broke the silence. "I've been thinking about moving back to Oregon to be closer to my folks. They're getting on. It's hard to be so far from them." She paused. "Now, with *this* I'm going to do it."

"Where in Oregon?" Elaine asked.

"Medford."

"Can you get a job there?" another woman asked.

"Not as good as this, but I'll find something," Lynne answered. "I'm not crazy about living in the city. There's nothing here worth risking your life for."

Each of the women was suddenly very involved in eating her dessert.

Connelly called shortly after I got back. "We opened your envelope," he announced. "You got the same kind of Polaroid, a bit grosser than the others actually, and something extra—a note made from words cut out of a newspaper, with the message, "Enjoy the show last week? You could be the main event.""

I shuddered and felt suddenly cold, but only for a moment. Then I was furious. The bastard was playing with me, playing with all of us, like a cat tormenting a mouse. Only I don't play that kind of game, not as the mouse, anyway.

"Terrific," I said.

"I think you should get out of there," Connelly said. "You've been very helpful, but you've probably gotten all you're going to get. It's time to pull out."

"What about the other women?" I asked. "Should they pull out, too?"

"They'll have to do what they think best. If it was my wife or friend, I'd tell her to take a long vacation and look for a new job. But the point is, you're the one who's got his attention. You're the one he's threatening."

I made a sound that I hoped was noncommittal, and said, "Thanks for the information. And the warning."

"You going to take it, the warning?"

"I don't know. I have to think about it," I said.

Bob Kingsley stopped by my office that afternoon. He looked a good deal less cocky than he had when I first met him. "I've come to apologize," he said. "I was the one who put the red ink on your chair. I'd like to pay whatever it cost to clean or replace the skirt."

I was surprised, not just by the apology but by the tone in which it was offered. He sounded genuinely sorry.

"Apology accepted," I said. "Would you like to sit down? You look awfully tired."

He did look tired. I wasn't making it up. He sank into the chair. "Those photos that you got this morning," he said, then paused. "I suppose I shouldn't have been so surprised. I mean we knew she'd been murdered, maybe raped. But it wasn't really real. . . ."

"And now it is?"

"Something about the pictures, I guess," he said, then paused. I sensed he had more to say and waited for him to find the words.

"The other night when you gave me a ride to Cupertino and you told me about the photos you'd gotten, I was a real jerk. I didn't know. But when I saw that picture of Sheila, I guess I started to understand.

"We didn't mean any harm, not like that. I mean, mostly we were joking around. We were steamed about having a woman for a boss, had a couple too many drinks one night, and came up with that stupid scheme."

Kingsley's speech was delivered to the floor in front of my desk. He didn't seem to be able to make eye contact, but strangely, I believed him, maybe more because he wasn't looking me in the eye.

"I was over in marketing when Karen and Jean got those pictures. They were terrified. Really terrified. And I thought 'What have I done that women could think I'm capable of that?'" He shook his head sadly.

I wondered why he'd chosen me to unburden himself to, then realized it was probably because I was an outsider. Like a seat mate on an airplane, I would leave and he wouldn't have to see me again.

"I don't think Sheila took the pranks personally. She thought you were after her because she was looking for bugs in the new program," I said.

Kingsley looked up in surprise. "I didn't know she knew about that," he said. Then shrugged. "I was afraid maybe she was suspicious. What'd she tell you?"

"She thought you broke into her office a week before she was killed, on a Wednesday night. Did you?" I tried to sound casual, like I was just mildly curious.

Kingsley shook his head. "I didn't. And I didn't hear anything from anyone else. The cops asked me the same thing."

"Then you didn't change a number in one of the women's fax files?" Again, only mild interest.

"No, but I wouldn't be surprised if Johnny did. He and I and Clark Phillips were the ones who pulled the pranks." He looked a bit sheepish. "Leggett knows; everybody'll know soon. I wasn't just apologizing out of the goodness of my heart. Leggett ordered us to."

I didn't pretend surprise. "I always thought it was you guys," I said.

"I wish to hell we'd never have started things," he said with real feeling. "I've been thinking about what you said about the porno photos. I keep wondering if maybe somehow we helped get him started. You know, maybe the pinups or the stuff on the E-mail."

"You certainly provided him a good cover," I said.

"Oh God," Kingsley said. He leaned forward and put his forehead in his hand, then raised his face slowly till his chin rested on the hand and looked at me. He was either truly miserable or one hell of an actor.

Chapter

22

The office was like a ghost town on Thursday, lots of empty desks. Almost all the absentees were female.

The women who did come to work arrived right at nine and left promptly at five. Anxious husbands and boyfriends waited in the lobby to walk them to their cars. During the day they stuck together. For many, even a trip to the copy machine or restroom required a buddy.

A few women like Elaine resisted the herd instinct and continued to function alone, but their bravado didn't hide their tension and you could see them constantly looking over their shoulders. Productivity hovered near zero.

The men were not in a lot better shape than the women. Maybe they picked up on the free-floating tension or maybe they found it hard to concentrate when the person in the next office could be a killer. I know it sure didn't help my concentration any.

Just before lunch I got a call from my ex. It wasn't a big surprise; I knew Connelly'd tell him about the photos. Dan wanted to see me after work; he didn't say why. He didn't have to.

•   •   •

At a quarter to twelve, Tonia called to ask if I'd join her for lunch. Bright sun streamed in my window, so I suggested that we get away from Systech and eat at a little place down by the bay.

As I walked to the elevator I could see groups of women gathering. The employee lounge was empty. The yogurt-in-the-fridge group weren't sticking around today.

We drove down to a little place that caters to the sailboat folk on the Mission Creek Marina. It's a hamburger-and-fries type place with a wood deck on the water. We found a table in the sun.

"What's happening on the second floor?" I asked after we ordered.

"Pretty much the usual," she said. "I was the only one who got a photo, and most of the people didn't know Sheila well, so it's pretty much business as usual. Except for Keegan and his guys."

"I hear Leggett put the fear of God in them."

"Sure looks like it. They've taken over the big conference room at the far end. They're there when I arrive and they're there when I leave."

"You think they'll solve the problem?"

"Who knows? They've got several of our best guys working on it with them. They asked me, but I said no. I just can't work with any of those guys, especially not Clark Phillips. Not after what's happened."

"I can sure understand that," I said.

A sea gull landed on the rail a couple of yards away and eyed us speculatively.

"Tonia," I said, "did Sheila ever mention that she thought someone broke into her office the Wednesday night a week before she was killed?"

"Mention it? She went on and on about it," Tonia said. "She was really pissed! She didn't think they took anything, which was pretty weird, but she was sure they'd been through her papers."

"Not a quick job, given Sheila's papers," I said.

Tonia laughed. "I don't know how she could tell if anything had been disturbed, given the piles of stuff she kept around, but she was really sure."

"Did she have any idea how the person got in?"

Tonia shrugged. "She didn't say. She just told me about a dozen times that someone had been in her office pawing through her papers."

"And you think she was right?"

"Absolutely," Tonia said. "She wouldn't have made such a big deal of it if she weren't totally sure. I know that."

I called Jesse when I got back to the office and told him what Tonia had said. "It's a hell of a coincidence that the break-in and the murder were both on Wednesday nights," I said.

"Not really," Jesse said. "You only got five to choose from. Statistically . . ."

"I don't care about statistically," I interrupted. When a man, any man, starts a sentence with the word *statistically*, you're in for a lecture. I wasn't in the mood. "I think it's more than coincidence."

"You have a hunch," Jesse said. I could hear it in his voice. He had "statistically"; I had a hunch.

"Yes, I have a hunch," I said. My voice said, "You wanta fight about it?"

"Okay," Jesse said, always a quick study. "Hunches are fine. Hunches can be good. So what do we do about this hunch?"

"I think we should stake out the warehouse, see what goes on there after hours."

Jesse groaned audibly. "You can't mean that. I hate surveillance. You hate surveillance. We don't want to do this."

"I think it could be important," I said.

"Then the police should do it. It's their job."

"The police are even less impressed by my hunches than you are," I said. "Don't whine."

"I'm not whining," Jesse said. He hates it when I accuse him of whining. "Let's just say something was going on down here at night. Something involving the killer. That's all the more reason that you shouldn't be hanging around in the middle of the night."

"I'm not going to be standing around on a street corner. I'll be locked in the van, with the cellular phone."

"Why doesn't that reassure me very much?"

"Look, this is the only thing we've got that vaguely resembles a lead. I'm tired of sitting around watching everyone watch everyone else and I'm tired of having a psycho mess with my mind. I need to do something."

Jesse sighed. "Okay. But we can't do surveillance all night and work all day for long."

"How about we do Tuesday, Wednesday, and Thursday?" I suggested.

"Why not just Wednesday? That's the night you think's suspicious." When I didn't respond at once, he said, "Look, there's either something funny about Wednesday night, and that's the only time we need surveillance, or it could be any night, and that means we give up sleeping at home."

Put that way, the choice seemed clear. "Wednesday night it is," I said.

I was glad my meeting with Dan gave me an excuse to leave Systech early. I'd seen more cheerful funeral parlors. Besides, the work at my real office was piling up, and I didn't have the energy to catch up in the evenings. Since Sheila's death, it was all I could do to fix dinner or wash the dishes before collapsing in front of the TV or falling into bed.

I got to my office by two-thirty. The stack of papers waiting for me seemed to grow instead of shrink each time I walked through the door. My assistant, Chris, wanted to go over the cases she'd been handling, and our income/expenditures spreadsheet was a month out of date.

I checked the clock at least fourteen times in the hour before five, and not because I couldn't wait to see Dan. I could wait a long time to have the conversation I knew was coming.

I didn't need anyone to warn me that this case was dangerous. And I didn't need a lecture on just how vicious Sheila's killer could be. I wondered if Connelly had decided I wasn't sufficiently terrified and had asked Dan to whip me into line, or if Dan had been watching over Connelly's shoulder and just couldn't restrain himself any longer.

Amy buzzed me at 4:47 to tell me that Dan was there. I told her to send him in.

He looked terrific. He usually does. It wasn't lack of sexual attraction that made me back out of our marriage. Today he wore chinos and a dark blue cotton shirt with the sleeves rolled up. Either he'd just gotten a haircut or he was wearing his dark curly hair a little shorter than I remembered. It wasn't till he tried to smile and couldn't quite pull it off that I realized how tense he was.

We greeted each other in a strained, too-formal way. I realized he might not be any more enthusiastic about this meeting than I was.

I offered him coffee, and we sat on the couch. Times like this make me sorely regret giving up smoking.

"I guess I might as well cut to the chase," Dan said. "I'm here because I think there are some things you should know about the Wainwright killing."

"Okay," I said.

"Did you know Mike Silva?" he asked. "Works for D.O.J.— California Department of Justice in Sacramento."

"No."

"We've worked together a number of times, become friends of a sort. He does criminal profiling for the state."

Criminal profiling is fascinating stuff, as long as you're reading about it and it doesn't get up close and personal. The field
grew out of the FBI's decision that it would be useful to know
about the psychological background of violent crimes, especially bizarre and repetitive crimes. Agents have interviewed
everyone from Ted Bundy to John Gacy, and they've learned
some fascinating things about the guys who haunt our nightmares.

"Mike was down this week on something else," Dan continued, "so Connelly asked him to take a look at the Wainwright
case. He had some disturbing things to tell us."

I nodded and waited for him to go on.

"Our killer is most probably a white male, late thirties, early
forties. That's emotional age, not chronological. He could be a
mature early thirties or an immature fifties, but he'll 'feel' like
late thirties." I thought of the men at Systech. DeMarco and
Kingsley were chronologically young, but they were also fairly
sophisticated. McFadden was right, chronologically and emotionally. So was Jorgensen. Keegan would fit emotionally;
Leggett was at the older end of the range.

"He's connected to Systech, almost certainly works there,"
Dan continued. "He's into control. Has a high IQ. He's what
we call an organized killer. That means his crimes are carefully
planned and well thought out. He's been preparing for this for
a long time. Probably reads detective magazines and other stuff
that gives him a clear knowledge of police procedure.

"That's why there was no trace evidence. We think he
washed the body after he killed her and before he put her on
the desk, even combed the pubic hair to make sure we
wouldn't find any of his."

I couldn't suppress a shiver at the thought of the killer method-
ically cleaning Sheila's body. Dan was watching me closely. "He's
doing this on purpose," I thought, "just to scare me."

"I get the message, Dan," I said. "This is a nasty guy and he's
dangerous. I knew that already."

Dan's face was impassive, no reaction to my outburst. He was working me the way he worked witnesses and suspects. It infuriated me.

"The guy is a sexual sadist, Catherine," he said quietly. "Do you know what that means?" He didn't wait for an answer. "He didn't wake up last week and think, 'I wonder what it's like to kill somebody.' He's been fantasizing about this for years. Reading violent pornography, tying up his girl friends, getting his kicks by brutalizing women. He's been reading police procedure to figure out how he'd get away with it.

"And now that he's done it, the reality will feed the fantasy. He won't be satisfied, because he can't be satisfied. He'll do it again. And again."

"A serial killer," I said.

Dan nodded. "That's what Mike thinks. This is probably his first killing. He was lucky enough and smart enough not to leave us much to go on. He'll learn by doing, which means he'll be harder to catch each time."

"What makes you so sure that he isn't just a very clever guy who's made it appear that the motive is sexual when it might be something else?"

Dan shook his head. "The whole crime just screams sexual sadist," he said. "The body wasn't bound when you found it, but she'd been tied up before she was killed, and not just a couple of Boy Scout knots. The ligatures were absolutely symmetrical, five rows of perfectly aligned rope at the wrists, the upper arms, the ankles, the knees.

"He didn't need to tie her like that to keep her from getting away. He's into bondage and sadism. He wanted to control her, and he wanted to terrorize her."

I held up my hand. "Enough," I said. "I don't need to know this. You're just telling me to try to scare me off. It won't work. I might get sick and throw up, but I will not quit."

Dan shook his head. He was so tense a little muscle in his jaw jumped. "All right," he said tightly. "But there's one more thing you should know. Mike thinks he screwed up and killed her sooner than he planned. It could have been a lot worse than it was. He won't make that mistake again."

Dan's eyes were fixed on mine as he said that, as if the sheer intensity of his gaze could force the full implications of his words deep into my consciousness. It was all I could do to sit still and hold his gaze. I felt physically ill. My stomach was just below my throat pressing upward, and my body was freezing. But I damn well wasn't going to let him see that.

I waited till I thought I could control my voice and said, "I know you're worried. I don't like this any better than you do, but I can't back out."

"Why?"

I didn't have an answer. I just knew that if I ran this time, I might never stop running. "I can't live my life that way," I said. "And what if I did pull out? That wouldn't keep him from killing again. You said that yourself. Next time maybe it'd be Tonia. And how do I live with that?"

Now it was Dan's turn to be without an answer.

I thought about it a long time after Dan left. If the killer wanted to terrify me, he'd certainly succeeded. Part of me wanted to catch the next plane to someplace on another continent.

But then there were Tonia and Elaine and probably a lot of other women who'd meet a charming stranger and end up like Sheila. Because if Dan was right, the killer wouldn't stay within Systech long enough to get caught. How many women, I wondered, would he kill before he slipped up?

It was a completely untenable situation. I could stay on the case and risk becoming this guy's next victim, a fate I couldn't even stand to think about, or I could walk away and know when the next woman died, she'd taken my place. It made my head hurt just to think about it.

Chapter

23

Friday was like Thursday, maybe a little worse. Lynne turned in her resignation and disappeared. Other women began to consider their options.

I met Elaine in the lounge when I went for my fourth cup of coffee. "I'll bet you're anxious to finish up your job," she said. "You're lucky you can get out of here."

"Are you thinking of quitting?" I asked.

"I can't afford to. Not with the state in recession and everybody cutting back. My creep of an ex-husband hasn't paid child support for six months, but my daughter hasn't given up eating. I need this job."

I noticed that same trapped look in other women that day. Systech had become a prison they couldn't leave and feared they'd never get out of alive.

The weekend was a relief but not enough of one. I discovered Friday afternoon that Peter had to go to Sacramento, then a case I'd thought was closed came unraveled, and a major client wanted me to review suspicious accounts from a division whose profits were unexpectedly low. On top of that, Molly announced at dinner that Craig had suggested she get a nose ring to match his.

I went to aikido Saturday morning. When I got back I could hear voices in the kitchen. Molly and her joined-at-the-hip buddy, Heather, were at the refrigerator again. Heather has a voice that carries. Even her whispers penetrate a closed door.

But today it was Molly who'd turned up the volume. "I don't believe she did that," Molly said. Her voice rang with indignation.

"She told me herself," Heather replied.

"That is so shitty."

"She was afraid she'd flunk the test, and her parents threatened to ground her for the rest of the term if they got another call from her teacher."

"So," Molly fumed. "I spent most of last Saturday studying for that test."

"And Alice spent the afternoon with Karl Morton at the movies," Heather said. "Algebra or Karl—which is the worst?"

The two exploded into giggles.

I walked to the kitchen. They were sitting at the table with a half-eaten bag of Oreos between them. I snagged a cookie. "What's up?" I asked.

That question usually only nets a shrug, but today Molly's anger wanted an audience. "This ditz in algebra got a guy to give her a copy of the test," she said. "And then she got him to figure out the answers for her."

"She got an *A*. Mol got a *B*," Heather informed me. She seemed more amused than angry.

"I just think it was a shitty thing to do," Molly said.

"And I think anyone who's willing to go out with Karl Morton has earned an *A*," Heather replied.

"Karl's this really dorky guy who's a math whiz. He's got a complexion like a pepperoni pizza," Molly said. "Alice has half the lacrosse team drooling over her. I don't know how Karl could ever believe she was really interested in him."

I flashed on McFadden's reference to Sheila "sleeping her way to the top." It infuriated me when men ascribed a woman's success to sex, but it made me even more angry when a woman gave them reason to think that way.

"She's such a whore," Molly steamed. Catching my frown and remembering that I don't like her to use that word, she said defensively, "Well, she is."

Heather's parents were driving up to Sonoma County to buy apples and pumpkins from one of the U-pick farms and had invited Molly to go along. I'd taken her on similar excursions when she was younger, and we both had fond memories of driving through the gray-gold hills and coming home with more pumpkins than she could carve and more apples than either of us could eat. I felt a twinge of envy as I watched the two girls go off chattering at each other in excited anticipation of the day's adventure.

I missed Molly as soon as she was gone. The house felt empty without her loud music, and after the week at Systech, I was jumpy and far too aware of every little noise.

I spent the afternoon going over ledgers with my mind flitting off to the Sonoma hills every twenty minutes. When Molly called at five to ask if she could spend the night at Heather's, I was finally getting a handle on things and had just decided my client had reason to worry.

With the house to myself, I had popcorn for dinner, and by midnight I'd figured out enough to move to the next stage of the investigation. I'd turn it over to my assistant, Chris, on Monday. Too bad. I much preferred a little larceny to the situation at Systech.

• • •

Sunday was looking like a long, lonely day until Jesse called. Claire was out of town on business and he was as much at loose ends as I was. He offered to bring bagels and the Sunday *Times*. I put on coffee.

Jesse took the crossword puzzle and an onion bagel and stretched out on the living room floor. I started with Travel, a subject that had developed a great appeal of late, and a sesame bagel.

To read the *Times* properly takes hours, at least, but we only managed an hour and a half before we were back on the situation at Systech. "I'm not sure why we're still there," Jesse said. "I'm not coming up with anything. Nobody's talking to me. In fact, there's plenty of folks think I might be the killer."

"What?"

"Sure. I'm black and I'm new. I've had several women back away from the elevator when it means they'd be alone in there with me."

He said it matter-of-factly, but I knew it must hurt. He read my expression. "It's okay. You get used to it," he said.

I didn't really believe that, but I let it pass. "Maybe you should split. We could sure use you at the office. Chris really can't handle the rest of the cases alone, and we can't take anything new as long as we're both tied up at Systech."

"But you'd stay?" he asked.

"For now. I want to give it a little longer."

I could tell from his expression he didn't like the idea. "Don't get over protective on me," I said.

He shrugged. "Your call."

Allen Leggett didn't like the idea of Jesse leaving. I pointed out that we'd done the job he hired us for. We'd caught the pranksters. We compromised by agreeing that Jesse would call in sick instead of resigning.

Monday dragged. Tuesday wasn't any better. Wednesday

morning taught me that there are worse things than slow days.

Tonia appeared in my office at ten-thirty. Her face was pale, her eyes seemed unusually large, and her body was tight with tension. She had her hands jammed in the pockets of her olive-green jacket. When she took them out, she couldn't stop them from shaking.

She closed the door behind her, then pulled a photo from her pocket. It was a three-by-five snapshot of the back of a house. Green bushes against the wall, blue-gray paint, dark blue trim. There was a window off to the right, and a figure stood between the curtains, her arms spread. I squinted at the picture; the figure was Tonia; she was pulling the curtains.

I turned the photo over. Printed on the back in crude, almost childlike letters was "I told you not to pull those blinds. You're so sexy in your black robe."

I realized I wasn't breathing. I let my breath out and looked up at Tonia. Her chin quivered and she blinked, like a child about to cry. I got up and put my arm around her. She clung to me then pulled away and collapsed into a chair. "I got it in the morning mail," she said. "Not interoffice, but regular mail."

"Did you save the envelope?" I asked.

"It's down in my office." Her voice was choked and she was on the edge of tears. "It's from *him*. He's been in my backyard again. What am I going to do?"

She looked so small and desperate. I could feel her pain as clearly as if it had been a bleeding wound. I wanted so much to help her, and I knew there was damn little I could do. I hate feeling helpless, and my frustration probably sounded brusque to her.

"Turn the photo over to the police, for starters," I said. "And I think this might be a good time for you to take a vacation. Go away somewhere for a while."

"Where?" she asked, then she lost it and broke down in tears. I put my arm around her shoulders. She leaned against me and sobbed. "I just don't know what to do," she said as she regained control. "I am so scared."

"Do you have relatives you can visit?" I asked. "Where do your parents live?"

"I live with my mom. She's legally blind and her health's terrible. I can't just go someplace and leave her. Besides, I need this job."

"I'm sure Leggett will give you a leave; you could take your mom with you."

"I don't know," she said. "I don't think I could afford it. We're barely making it with her medical bills. I can't afford not to work for long. And I can't leave Systech. I'd lose my medical coverage."

I tried different suggestions. None of them seemed to work, but just discussing what she could do seemed to calm her. Finally, she said, "I'll be okay. I'll get new locks on the doors and an alarm system. Maybe I'll even get a dog. I can't work nights anymore, not here, but I can still do most of the stuff on my computer at home."

I wanted to tell her, "No. Get out of here. Now. Go and don't look back." But I couldn't figure out how to help her do that, so I took the coward's way out and pretended to agree that her precautions would protect her, all the while, hoping desperately that tonight's surveillance would give us the answer we so badly needed.

Chapter

24

I hate surveillance. The boredom, the discomfort, the stiff muscles and eighty other things. Guys can at least drink coffee to stay awake. I can't. I don't drink a thing the whole time, and I'm still uncomfortable by the end of a shift. Anatomy is the best argument I know for a vengeful male god.

It helps to have spent years meditating, but not enough. Surveillance isn't meditation. It's just surveillance. Peter volunteered to come along and entertain me, but that isn't surveillance, either. And getting hot and horny in the back of a van loses its appeal when you pass eighteen.

The van was Jesse's brother's. It smelled of dog and the back where I sat was covered with two inches of hair. Every time I do this, I swear I'm going to buy a van. Then I price the damn things and decide that we don't need one *that* badly. Besides, I have enough trouble finding parking for the Volvo.

I'd parked across from the warehouse next to the fence by the train tracks. That gave me a view of both the front and side, but there was only a quarter moon and the lights across the street were far apart. They dropped pools of yellow light on the tarmac, but they didn't illuminate much beyond a few yards. Most of the warehouse was in dark shadow. The poor visibility meant that I had to keep a close eye on things. A human figure would only be visible within the limited range of the lights. Miss it there, and you'd never notice it in the shadows.

It's not easy to stay alert for hours while the only thing happening is the ticking of the clock. I was trying to remember the fourth verse of "Barbara Allen" when a big truck pulled up at one of the loading bays on the side of the warehouse. I checked my watch. Twelve-thirty. A half hour till Jesse would arrive to relieve me.

I picked up the cellular phone to call him. Static. I dialed. More static. Why the hell does a machine inevitably fail when you need it most?

Three guys climbed out of the truck. One fooled with the warehouse door and disappeared inside. Moments later the larger door to the cargo bay swung open. For the next twenty minutes they carried large cartons from the warehouse and loaded them on the truck. I couldn't tell what was in those cartons, but you don't load legal cargo at twelve-thirty at night.

They finished just before one, climbed back in the truck, pulled onto Townsend, and turned left. I gave them a little over a block before I started the van and pulled out to follow. I wasn't worried about losing them. Tailing a big truck should be easy in the middle of the night.

The truck turned right on Fourth Street. A red light and a Honda Civic with two guys in it stopped me for long enough so the truck was out of sight when I turned the corner. I figured I could still catch it, so I speeded up till I realized that the red lights ahead were the Fourth Street bridge.

The bridge is one of two ancient drawbridges on Mission Creek Marina, a finger of water that runs into China Basin. It crouches like a giant metal monster over the water. I know they raise the bridges once a day, but in all my years in San Francisco, I have never seen that drawbridge raised at night. Never until tonight.

I looked around for a boat, hoping it might pass quickly so they'd lower the bridge. There wasn't one that I could see. And the drawbridge didn't show any sign of lowering. I sat and swore for a couple of minutes, then turned the van around and drove back to the warehouse. It was maddening to think that if the truck had been a minute later or I a minute quicker, I'd have had him.

Jesse was at the warehouse by the time I got back. I gave him a complete, blow-by-blow account of my unsuccessful efforts at following the truck, complete with comments on the fickleness of fate. If the stakes hadn't been so high, the whole thing would have been funny.

We tried to call the cops on his cellular phone and discovered that it didn't work any better than mine did. "Well, our luck's consistent, bad all the way," Jesse said.

"You'll have to find a pay phone to call the cops."

"Don't expect them to rush right down here," he said. "The barn's already empty as far as they're concerned."

"Don't call nine-one-one, call homicide," I suggested. "They'll want to get a look around before people start arriving tomorrow morning."

"Maybe," Jesse said. "But these are the same folks who refused to put surveillance on the warehouse. I wouldn't count on it."

I dug my flashlight out from under the seat. "I'm not. I'm going to take a look myself."

"Whoa, hey, that's not such a great idea."

"Why not? The truck's gone, so are the guys. The door's probably locked, but if it's not, what's wrong with me taking a look?"

"How do you know all the guys are gone?"

"Three guys got off the truck, three guys got back on the truck. I counted."

Jesse wasn't convinced. "How about I take the look, you call the police?"

I'd have given him my evil stare, but it doesn't work well in the dark. "Give it a rest," I said and headed for the door the truck had driven up to.

I didn't really expect the door to be open. It was. It swung inward with a rasping creak. "Maybe you better wait here, while I check," I said. "Then you can call the cops."

It was dark outside, but gray dark; inside the warehouse was black dark. The feeble illumination from the street lights only penetrated a few feet. Beyond that, all was blackness.

My flashlight made a yellow-white oval that moved ahead of me into the darkness. I jumped as the door slammed behind me.

It's damned hard to get a sense of your surroundings when you can only see them in small patches. I shined the light on the space to my right and found the wire wall of a storage area a couple of yards away. It seemed to be filled with crates piled on top of each other. To my right, another wall of wire rose. Grotesque shapes pressed against the metal. For an instant I saw a cage of monstrous beasts, then I realized it was only ornate antique furniture.

I moved forward. The oval of light swept before me. Even though I knew I was alone, it made me uncomfortable to announce so clearly my exact position. Maybe it wasn't the smartest thing to come in here alone.

I was still trying to shake the sense of unease when what felt like half the building landed on my right shoulder. A jolt of pain like fire shot down my arm, and I dropped the light.

The force of the blow knocked me down. I landed on my left side, rolled to my right and came up turning to face the direction of the attack. Even using my left hand to reduce the pressure on my right arm during the roll, it hurt like hell.

I forced myself to keep my breath shallow and hoped that my movements hadn't advertised too clearly where I was.

With the flashlight out, there was only blackness. I stared into it with no more than a general idea of where my attacker might be. I listened for some sound to give him away. A car drove down the street outside, stopped and a door slammed. Muffled voices. But inside the warehouse, silence. He must be waiting just as I was, listening for some sound to tell him where I'd ended up and which direction I'd move next.

Hours seemed to pass and still no sound from my assailant. Had he managed to slip away without me hearing? Could he be moving even now without me knowing?

I forced the clutter of words from my mind and centered myself again. Then I heard the floor creak someplace in front of me and a few seconds later a second creak farther away. I stayed absolutely still and hoped he was backing toward the door. A couple of eternities later, the door opened and a dark silhouette dashed through it toward the street.

I followed, but slowly. At the door, I could hear sounds of a struggle, then Jesse's voice called my name. I made the mistake of reaching for the door with my right hand, and felt a searing pain in my shoulder. I wasn't going to be opening anything with that hand for a while.

Outside, Jesse was on top of a man in dark clothes who lay face down on the sidewalk about five yards from the door.

"Don't move. I'll blow your fuckin' head off," he growled menacingly. He was holding the end of a small metal flashlight against the base of the man's skull. "You all right?" he called to me.

"Yeah," I said though it was only loosely true.

"He ran right into me. I thought you said the warehouse was empty."

"My mistake," I said, looking down at the figure on the ground. It was hard to tell how tall he was, but he seemed about Jesse's size, medium build, dark hair. Just in front of him lay a heavy metal flashlight, probably the thing he'd hit me with.

"Get some rope from the van so we can tie him up," Jesse said. "What's wrong with your arm?"

"Nothing serious," I said. I hoped I was right. The kind of pain I'd felt when I reached for the door isn't a good sign. As long as I didn't move the arm, the pain wasn't too bad. But I knew from experience that there's a natural anesthesia right after an injury. It would wear off soon enough. I hoped it'd hold till we could get this guy tied up and the police on the scene.

There was some clothesline in the back of the van but with no light and only one hand, it took me a while to find it. I brought it back to Jesse. He handed me the flashlight and said gruffly, "You hold the gun on him while I tie him up. If he moves, shoot him." I felt like I was in a B-movie, but Jesse was obviously enjoying the hell out it.

Once he had my attacker tied up, he turned to me. I must not have looked too good.

"Shit! What happened?" he asked.

"He hit me with something," I said. "Probably that flashlight. The guys in the truck are bound to be back before long. Let's gag this one and dump him in the van. I can wait there while you call the cops."

"You going to be okay?" Jesse asked. "You look like you're hurting."

I was, but my main concern was getting out of the way so we wouldn't scare off the guys in the truck if they returned.

We loaded our prisoner into the van, and Jesse made a gag from some cloth we found in the back. "Get some ice if you can," I said as he got out of the van. "I'm going to need it."

"You're going to need a doctor," Jesse said, "but I'll try to find some ice for the short run."

I sat in the front of the van and waited. The pain arrived before the cops did. It hit with searing intensity; my whole shoulder seemed to pulse with it. I thought for a while I was going to throw up.

Leaning back against the seat was out of the question. I struggled to find a better position and discovered that every move inflamed the pain. I ended up sitting crosswise on the seat with my left shoulder against the back. It wasn't comfortable, but it was better.

I'd have liked to question our prisoner, but I couldn't risk taking the gag off in case his buddies came back. He started banging around in the back. "Cut it out," I said sharply. "Or I'll give you a headache to match what you gave me." He quieted immediately.

Time passed. Jesse didn't come, neither did the truck. Or the police. I closed my eyes and tried to breathe into the pain. It took a little of the edge off, maybe. Mostly, it just gave me something to do while I tried not to think and not to throw up.

Finally, I heard a siren. The black-and-white pulled up in front of the warehouse, flashing garish pulses of light. So much for the possibility that the guys in the truck might stumble into their grasp.

Two cops climbed out of the squad car. The one nearest me looked to be about fourteen. I opened the door of the van, and they both ducked behind the car. Oh, great. Now I had to worry about getting shot by San Francisco's finest.

"Don't shoot," I yelled. "I'm on your side. I'll get out slowly, but I can't raise my right arm because it's injured." Injured was a pallid word to describe the throbbing fireball of pain that engulfed my right shoulder and shot down my arm every time I moved. I climbed out clumsily and tried to look nonthreatening.

A blast of light hit me in the eyes as one of the cops turned his flashlight on me. The light slid down my body. Without a sufficiently obvious injury, I still qualified as a suspect, and these guys weren't taking any chances. The light moved back to my face, blinding me while one of the cops approached.

"I'm a private investigator working for the company that owns that building. My partner's the one who called you," I said.

"He reported a robbery in progress," the cop said. He sounded disappointed that they hadn't found a band of bad guys carrying out stereos.

"That's right," I said. "I saw a truck unload something from the warehouse." Before I got any further, a second squad car sped down Townsend, siren blaring and lights flashing. It braked to a stop, then backed up and turned to illuminate the van in its headlights. Just behind it a sedan pulled up, and Jack Connelly climbed out. I was irrationally glad to see him.

He hurried over to me. "What happened?" he demanded.

The pain was beginning to get to me. I leaned against the van. "Have you got some aspirin?" I asked. "And maybe one of those instant ice packs?" I doubted that either would do much good, but they were all I was likely to get until I could get to a doctor.

"Ice pack?" Connelly said to the uniforms. The fourteen year old moved back to his car to check the first-aid kit. The air felt cold on my face. I realized I must be sweating.

The cop was still searching for the first-aid kit when Jesse arrived with a big plastic bag of ice.

"Thank God," I said. "Where'd you find that?"

"Who's open late and uses ice?" he asked with a grin. "Your friendly local bar, of course."

He arranged the bag of ice around my shoulder. It hurt like hell, but that wasn't a new sensation by now. I must have looked almost as wretched as I felt, because everyone was suddenly very nice to me and Connelly insisted on settling me in the front seat of his car before he started asking questions.

I told him the whole story, a couple of times, while a uniform took notes. Jesse was off with another uniform telling his side of the story. The guy in the back of the van wasn't telling any story. When they took the gag off, the only thing he said was that he wanted a lawyer, and he said it like this wasn't the first time he'd used that line.

Chapter
25

The cops offered to call an ambulance, but I talked them into letting Jesse drive me to the hospital. You take an ambulance and you end up at S.F. General, which is beginning to look like a trauma center in a war zone. I preferred Mount Zion. It's only a few blocks from home and likely not to have such a full waiting room.

Riding in a car seems like a very passive experience, unless you have a shoulder that sends shooting flashes of pain at every movement. Then you discover every pothole and bump in the pavement, and every red light means a stop that's never smooth enough. It was a long way to Mount Zion.

There's a sameness to hospital emergency waiting rooms, especially late at night—little cocoons of flourescent light and stale air, populated by tired people with faces wiped blank by shock and exhaustion. There's always a large clock, though for most people in the room time stopped sometime after they walked through the door.

We got through registration and were sent to the triage

nurse. I asked for something to kill the pain and was told I'd have to wait till the doctor examined me. Then they led me to an examining room and Jesse went to call Peter.

When he came back, he was grinning. "You'll never guess what's on the TV in the waiting room," he said. "It's one of those ride-along, real-life shows about a team of paramedics." He chuckled at the irony of it. I suggested that maybe we should have stayed home and watched "Cops."

"Yeah, they probably had an episode with a gutsy but not-too-bright lady who insists on going into a warehouse all alone and gets clobbered by the fourth of three bad guys," Jesse said with an irritating grin.

"Jeez, you *never* give me a break," I said. "You'll be wise-cracking beside my death bed."

"I'd like to put that off for a while, if you don't mind," he said. The laughter was gone from his voice.

We waited, then we waited some more. Peter came before the doctor did.

I don't suffer well, not at all. It makes me testy. I bitched and grumbled; Jesse and Peter bitched and grumbled. I was considering climbing down from the table and hunting down the doctor when a tall guy who looked like a stork in a white coat finally appeared. He had an accent, maybe Scottish. His eyes were red and he looked very tired.

The doctor obviously thought there were too many of us in the room. He shooed Peter and Jesse out, which was just fine with me. It meant I didn't have to worry about putting on a brave front.

"We'll need to take off your jersey," the doctor announced. "It would probably be less painful if we cut it off."

Less painful sounded good. "How about some morphine?" I asked. I tried not to sound like a dope fiend.

"After the exam," he said as he cut my shirt off. There was some swelling, but the shoulder didn't look nearly as bad as it felt. He poked and prodded with a skill that made me suspect he'd been an inquisitor in a previous life. When he tried to move the shoulder, I almost passed out.

He took out something that looked like a crochet needle and poked at my hand and wrist. I could feel it; that seemed to please him. He had me flex my hand and move my arm in different ways, all of them painful. "Checking for sensation and mobility," he said when I gave a particularly wrenching groan. "We'll be done in a minute."

I was done right then, had been for hours. All I wanted was a shot of morphine and my own bed.

I got the morphine, but not the bed, not for several hours. They needed X rays, then someone had to read the X rays, then the ER doc had to call the orthopedist, and none of it happened fast.

But once the morphine kicked in, I didn't mind anymore— not about the waiting or the pain or anything else. I sort of floated above it all. Thank God for drugs.

I floated and drifted until the doctor appeared again with X-ray films in hand.

He called Peter and Jesse in and put the film up on a light box. "She has a fracture of the acromion. That's this bone here," he said, pointing to a bone above the shoulder socket. Peter and Jesse peered at the film. I was willing to take his word for it.

"How serious is it?" Peter asked.

"Well, there's minimal displacement, so she won't need surgery. I'll have to call the orthopedist to see if he wants to come in and check her, but he'll probably have us put her in an immobilizer and make an appointment for her to come back in a couple of days."

"How long will this take to heal?" I asked.

He pursed his lips. "Hard to say exactly," he said, "but a month or so, I should think. The orthopedist can tell you more when he sees you."

"But it will heal? I will be able to use it again?"

"Oh yes, in time. But you'll have to take it easy for a while."

The morphine must have been wearing off, and with it the sense of not caring, for I found that suddenly I cared very much that I'd spend the next month with only one good arm and a psychopath on the loose.

The sky was just beginning to lighten when we finally got out of the emergency room and drove up the hill to home. They'd anchored my arm to a cummerbundlike thing that went around my torso. I felt like a half-wrapped mummy.

We managed to get in and get me settled in bed without waking Molly. Peter lay down beside me, but he didn't undress.

The doctor had given me a couple of tablets of Vicodan and a prescription for more. During the next hours, I discovered that it's a whole lot less effective than morphine. As the morphine wore off, the pain came back like a freight train pulling into its home station; then it just sat there, a dark, powerful presence. Maybe the Vicodan made the freight a little smaller, it sure didn't get it to pull out.

The drugs made my head fuzzy. I couldn't think very clearly, and I was so tired that all I wanted to do was sleep. That was until I actually got to sleep. Then I was assailed by vivid, technicolor horror flicks, starring Sheila, Tonia, and me. I woke with my heart pounding, my body covered with sweat, and the freight train puffing away in my shoulder.

Peter tried to comfort me by holding me, but it's hard to snuggle in body armor. Still, it felt good to lie against his body, comforting, even if it didn't get rid of the train.

Sometime later we heard Molly get up. Peter went out, and I could hear their muffled voices in the kitchen, then her worried face appeared at the door of the bedroom. I wasn't in very good shape to reassure her. "I'm okay," I said. "I'll mend."

"You'll just have to be careful with your hugs for a while," Peter said.

"Did you catch the killer?" Molly asked.

The killer. It was a measure of how out of it I was that I hadn't given much thought to that question. "I don't know," I said.

Molly didn't want to go to school. "You'll need stuff," she argued. "I can help." Beneath her take-charge attitude, I could see the scared kid, and I was sorry for her, but I didn't think it'd do her any good to stay, and I didn't want to have to pretend to be in better shape than I was.

"I'm just going to sleep today, anyway," I told her, hoping it was true. Finally, Peter got her off to school. I managed to wait till she was gone before I started bugging him for the next Vicodan.

We had soup for lunch, and I discovered how hard it is to eat with your left hand. I ended up drinking mine from a cup. Jesse called around one.

"You feel up to talking to him?" Peter asked.

"I guess," I said.

"How do you feel?" Jesse asked.

"Lousy, but I'll live," I said. "What did the police come up with?"

"A storage area full of stolen goods on the third floor, and in the back—stuffed behind some boxes—clothes they think belonged to Sheila Wainwright, a bunch of porno mags, and some glossy photos like the ones you and the other women got. The guy who hit you is stonewalling, but Connelly thinks it's just a matter of time till they convince him that grand theft is a better rap than murder one."

"Do they have anything to tie the storage area to someone at Systech?" I asked.

"Not yet. But the alarm system was off, just as you thought it'd be, and there're only four guys who could have shut it down—Leggett; a guy named Vic Carter, who's in charge of the warehouse; the facilities manager; and get this, your friend Scott Jorgensen."

"Jorgensen?" I said. "Why Jorgensen? He doesn't have anything to do with facilities."

"Not now, but he's a close friend of Leggett's, and back when they were redesigning the building, he was involved. He knows all about the alarm system and at one time he had a key."

I felt as if my brain had turned into cotton wool. I tried to connect Jorgensen, Sheila's murder, and the stolen goods in the warehouse. The freight train puffed away in my shoulder. I couldn't see much through the smoke.

I must have slept some during the day. It was all blurry and diffuse. The freight train was the only thing that was perfectly clear. It got bigger and louder about three hours after the last hit of Vicodan, and that hour before the next dose was long and ugly. Fortunately, when Jesse called around six, I was in hour two, and thus in relatively good shape.

"Your boy with the flashlight just broke," he announced. "Probably he broke a couple of hours ago and the cops just got around to telling us, but here's the scoop.

"He's part of a high-tech theft ring. The stuff in the storage area came from a warehouse down the peninsula and a chip maker in San Jose. They used the Systech warehouse to store stuff till they had a buyer, then they'd move it out for delivery. Our boy claims not to know who the inside man was, but he says there was someone on the inside who made sure that the alarm was off and the coast was clear on Wednesday nights."

I could follow Jesse, but just barely. My mind stumbled along at quarter-speed. I hoped it was just the Vicodan that was making me so slow.

"So the inside man is the killer. Is that what we're assuming?"

"Given what they found in the locker, it sure looks like it. And that almost has to be Leggett or Jorgensen."

"Jorgensen," I said. "It's got to be."

"They're questioning both men now, and they'll go over the electronic-key records to see who stayed late on Wednesdays. That's what I'd do. Hell, that's what I'm going to do."

"But the cops have the records," I said.

"Backups, Catherine, backups. The cops have the records. Systech has the backups. The cops never think to take those."

Backups. They can be real useful in our trade. Lots of folks change or destroy a document but forget all about the backups. That's how the special prosecutor got a bunch of secret memos during Iran-contra. The pols shredded the paper and erased the disks, but they never thought to check for the backups.

"Great idea," I said and yawned.

Chapter

26

Scott Jorgensen broke sometime Saturday. He confessed to being a thief but not a murderer. Actually, he didn't even confess to being a thief, just a helper of thieves. A distinction lost on the district attorney.

Jorgensen claimed that he had been lured into a life of crime by criminals who had taken advantage of the fact that he was a compulsive gambler.

"One of those I-couldn't-help-myself guys," Connelly reported. He'd come by to see how I was doing, which was a bit better than the day before but still on the wrong side of awful. I figured maybe I'd get more out of him since he had every reason to feel guilty. After all, I wouldn't have been in this shape if he'd just agreed to put surveillance on the warehouse. He didn't seem to have made that connection.

"The way he went on about it, this compulsive gambler thing, you'd think it was something you caught like a cold or were born with," Connelly said. "He'll probably claim that it's a disability and Systech can't fire him."

"Yeah, and when he finally confesses to killing Sheila, he'll have a list of reasons that it was her fault," I said.

"He's a piece of work, all right," Connelly said. "He gives a bunch of crooks the keys to his company's warehouse and shuts the alarm off once a week, and then he tells us he didn't mean any harm. And these guys aren't just a bunch of small-time hoods. They're connected."

"Mafia?" I asked.

Connelly shook his head. "No, I don't think so, but I think when we nail it all down, we'll find they're tied in to some pretty big players. And we'll find that Mr. Jorgensen isn't just an innocent fall guy."

"What about the murder?" I asked. I shifted uncomfortably on the sofa. Peter had insisted that I needed to get up. I'd have been happy in bed, but he'd bullied me into letting him "help" me dress, a real trick when you have one arm tied to your body. So here I was with my whole arm buttoned inside one of his shirts, trying to find a comfortable position that didn't make my shoulder scream. Connelly lounged comfortably in an armchair across from me, oblivious to my discomfort.

"He denies it," Connelly said. "Claims he doesn't know a thing about it. Even demanded a polygraph to prove he didn't do it."

"Did you give him one?" I asked.

"We will, but it won't mean much. He'll probably come out clean. The machine doesn't measure truth, it measures how nervous you are. A psychopath who doesn't feel any remorse can slip right through."

I could see Jorgensen with his self-satisfied smile, lying so smoothly the needle didn't even wiggle. "But you've got enough proof to indict him despite that, don't you?" I asked.

Connelly stretched. "Sure. We've got the victim's clothes and the magazines in the storage cage, and while he wasn't the only one who had access, he was the only one who had access to both that and the victim. Plus we found evidence in his office."

"What?" I asked.

"We're not talking about it at this point. I shouldn't even have told you, but we found stuff in his office that connects him to the killing."

"So you've got him," I said, feeling a good deal of relief. "You've really got him."

"I think so. He claims he was framed, but that's what they all say. I don't see how he could weasel out, not with what we've got. And by trial time, we'll have even more. We've just started with this guy."

"What happens now?" I asked.

"He'll be arraigned on Monday, and his lawyer'll ask for bail. With luck, the judge won't grant it."

"Luck?" I said, "You mean there's some chance they could let him out on bail?"

"Sure," Connelly replied. "I hate to tell you, but it happens more often than you'd think, especially for guys like Jorgensen. If he'd kept that stuffed-shirt corporate lawyer he called when we first brought him in, there'd be no problem. That guy didn't know squat about criminal law. But like I said, Jorgensen's no fool; a couple of hours into questioning he figured out the score and called in Grant Matterly, probably the best criminal lawyer in town. If anyone can get him off, Matterly can."

Connelly must have realized from the expression on my face that I took the possibility of Jorgensen's release a good deal more personally than he did. "Oh, look, it's not likely, really," he protested. "And we'll do everything we can to keep him behind bars."

Somehow I was not very reassured.

Connelly's visit wasn't a big pick-me-upper, but it did give me something to think about beside my shoulder. Too bad it wasn't something I wanted to think about.

How ironic that the killer should prove to be the one person
I'd never been able to see clearly. From our first meeting, Jorgensen had been paired in my mind with David Alcott, my
criminology professor from college.

It amazed me that Alcott had such power over me, even
after so many years. He had quite literally changed my life. I'd
planned to get a degree in criminology and find a job in law
enforcement, but to succeed at that I'd have needed his spon-
sorship, and the price for that was way too high. So I'd majored
in history and ended up outside the system.

I'd lost to Alcott, and I don't like to lose. It didn't matter
that I was happier running my own business than I'd ever have
been working for a bureaucracy. What mattered was that I
didn't get to make the choice. And I wasn't going to let anyone
put me in that position ever again.

Sheila hadn't liked to lose any more than I did. I could imagine how Jorgensen's passes must have stirred old memories.
The promotion she wanted so badly had put her under his
thumb again. That must have been hard to take.

In Sheila's position, I'd have wanted an edge, something to
even the power equation. Knowledge can be power, especially
if it's knowledge of secrets. She'd gone after her adversaries
from KeeGo by studying their product till she found its weakness. I wondered if she'd approached Jorgensen the same way.
If she'd discovered that he left late on Wednesday nights and
came in early Thursday mornings, she'd have wanted to know
why.

And once she discovered the warehouse scheme, she would
have had the power. I had no doubt that she'd have enjoyed
using it, or that Jorgensen would have found the situation
intolerable.

The rest of the day passed in four-hour blocks, and Sunday
wasn't much better. It got so I could just about tell time by how

much my shoulder hurt. I was delighted when Tonia called in the afternoon.

She knew that Jorgensen was being questioned, but she hadn't heard that he'd confessed to being part of the theft ring. Now that he was officially in custody, I figured I wasn't giving away any secrets.

"So he's the one who killed Sheila," she said.

"He denies it, but that's what the police think. He had the knowledge of how to get in and no alibi for that night." I didn't tell her what the police had found in the storage cage of stolen goods. "Does it surprise you that it's Jorgensen?" I asked.

"I guess anyone would have surprised me," she said. "I don't know him really, but lots of women complained about him. And the times I was around him I felt sort of intimidated. I was glad I didn't work for him."

Tonia grew more enthusiastic as she absorbed the news that Sheila's killer was no longer free. Her voice rose with excitement. She bubbled on with news from the office, much of it about people I barely knew. "Here's something that'll surprise you," she said. "Bob Kingsley was really upset by what happened to you. I thought maybe he was acting, because he's been so different lately, but I guess he was really sorry."

Kingsley had been different lately. After the day he apologized in my office, he'd stopped by several times to talk. I'd wondered if he was trying to make peace or if he had another motive.

Tonia bubbled on. "I feel so relieved," she said. "I just can't tell you, but then you know. You must be feeling the same way."

I wasn't. Not really. And it wasn't just because my shoulder hurt like hell. But one of us worrying about whether Jorgensen would get out was one more than enough, so I let it pass.

"I'll tell you one thing," she said, "it's a big relief to know it's not someone sitting next to me at work. It's been so weird around the office since the murder. Everyone's like hunkered down. It's hard to talk to someone who might be a killer."

"I know," I said. "This should be a big relief for everyone. As usual, I get to move on just when things get better. I'm going to miss you guys."

"Oh," Tonia said. She sounded surprised. "That's right, I guess you won't be coming back."

"No, the job's done now," I said. "But you've got my number. Give me a call if you need anything." I hoped she wouldn't need anything, but if Jorgensen got out on bail, she might. One more thing to try not to think about.

Neither Peter nor Jesse thought that there was much chance Jorgensen would get out on bail, and the more we talked, the more I agreed. Embezzlers get out on bail, con artists get out, not murderers.

Monday came, I was anxious to hear the results of the arraignment, but I wasn't worried.

Then Jack Connelly called. I could tell from his voice that something was wrong. "I'm sorry," he said. "We did everything we could, but the judge is releasing him on bail."

"Releasing him?" My voice sounded funny, high and a bit shrill. "How can you release him? He's a killer, potentially even a serial killer."

"His lawyer convinced the judge that this was the first time he'd ever been charged with anything worse than a speeding ticket and he has sufficient ties to the community that there's no danger he'll flee."

"Flee? Who cares about flee? What about kill? Didn't you tell me that this guy was likely to kill again? Mike Silva thinks he fits the profile of a serial."

"The D.A. told the judge all that. But Jorgensen is a highly successful businessman with powerful friends. It's like asking the judge to believe that one of his buddies at the club is a serial killer. It's a hard sell."

"So what does he want? Several more dead women to prove that Jorgensen is dangerous? What's it take?"

"Look, I'm sorry. I know how you feel." He didn't know how I felt. *He* didn't have a psychopath sending him lurid photos and suggesting he was next. He had two good arms, and a right hand that could fire a gun. He didn't know how I felt at all.

"I know this is very scary," he said.

I wasn't scared, not now. Now I was furious. Scared would come later.

I took a deep breath and tried to sound calm. "All right," I said. "But I assume you'll have him under surveillance."

"I'm working on it," he said, without much conviction.

"Working on it," I repeated. "Exactly what does that mean?"

"It means that it's damn hard to get surveillance on anyone anymore. You know the story. We're shorthanded. People are blowing each other away like it was Belfast in some parts of this city, and the budget is so tight we're lucky to have toilet paper in the johns. But I am doing my best to convince the bean counters upstairs to do it." He paused. "I just don't want you to count on it."

So Scott Jorgensen was going to be walking around free with no one to stop him if he took it into his head to kill again. And I was going to spend at least a month with a useless right arm. A month of jumping at every little sound, looking over my shoulder, being afraid to go out and afraid to stay home.

I'm not used to fear. I've spent years studying aikido so I didn't have to be afraid. Not that I felt invincible, but at least I knew I had a good shot at protecting myself. The blow from the flashlight had taken that from me.

I wondered how long before I could begin to train again. The arm would be useless for over a month, but I still had my left arm. There are throws you can do with one arm, but I'd need practice to get the balance and timing.

My shoulder was beginning to throb again. I checked my watch. Forty minutes to the next Vicodan. How the hell was I going to get back to aikido when I could barely get through the last hour between pain meds?

Dan called a couple of hours later. He'd heard about Jorgensen's release; he was even less optimistic about surveillance than Connelly had been. "They'll never do it," he said. "They know this thing could drag on for months, maybe even a year. Jorgensen has the money to hire a lawyer to stall."

"Even a month or two would help," I said. "Just until my arm mends."

"Doesn't work that way. Once they put surveillance on, they can't take it off, or if they do, they're liable. Your family could sue the city because, by canceling the surveillance, they'd contributed to your death. City avoids the risk by not approving surveillance."

"Run that by me again," I said. "Are you telling me that if they don't make any effort to protect me and Jorgensen kills me, it's okay? But if they try to protect me and fail, or they try for a while and stop, then they could be sued?"

"You got it. I know it doesn't make sense, but that's what you get when you let lawyers run the country. I think you need to make some plans of your own. I can stop by after work. Why don't you get Jesse and Peter to be there around six."

It was a somber crew around the table that night. Peter had picked up Thai takeout, but no one paid much attention to the food. It sat in its red-and-white paper containers on the kitchen counter forgotten while Dan confirmed what we expected.

"The bottom line is no surveillance—not on him, not on you," Dan said. "You can't fight the bean counters."

"Then we'll have to do it ourselves," Jesse said.

Peter looked thoughtful. "Before we set up surveillance, how sure are we that Jorgensen's the killer?" he asked. "I don't want to end up watching the wrong guy."

Dan looked annoyed. "You buy the story that he was framed?" he asked.

"It's happened," Peter said. We all knew what he meant. A couple of years ago he had been set up for a murder-one charge. It had damn near cost both our lives to prove his innocence.

"The kind of thing that happened to you, Harman, happens once in a blue moon," Dan said. "The evidence is pretty compelling on this one."

"Besides, anyone who knew you knew you didn't kill that woman," I said. "And lots of us who knew Jorgensen think he was perfectly capable of doing it."

"Okay," Peter said. "I've got baggage on this thing. You guys can probably see it clearer." Dan and Jesse nodded, but I was uncomfortably aware that I, too, had baggage. Every encounter with Jorgensen had opened old wounds. I found it impossible to be objective about him.

The phone rang once. I waited for the second ring, but Molly must have picked it up. With Jorgensen free, we'd have to find a way to protect her. I hoped we could do it without sending her back to her mother.

"Surveillance gets expensive," I said. "Remember, while you're watching Jorgensen, there's no cash flow."

"Easiest and cheapest is if you take a nice long vacation, Catherine," Dan said.

Just what I'd suggested to Tonia. And I didn't like the idea any better than she had. Where was I going to go for the months, maybe years, till the trial? And what was I going to live on while I was there?

"You could go visit your parents," Dan suggested.

"Run home to daddy. Great idea," I said grumpily.

"I think you should consider it," Peter said.

"I could keep things running here," Jesse offered. Suddenly I smelled a conspiracy.

"Why do I get the feeling you all want to pack me off to Colorado?" I said.

Their protestations were as good as a full confession. But the ease with which they switched to Plan B suggested that they'd never seriously believed I'd leave town.

"We're back to doing the surveillance ourselves," Peter said. "From now on, one of us is with you at all times."

I groaned. I love them all. I enjoy their company. But not as bodyguards. Not all the time. "Why not watch Jorgensen," I suggested. "That way you'll not only protect me but all the other women who are potential victims. Remember, I'm not the only one he sent pictures to."

"Too risky," Dan said. "We could lose him."

"Too easy to shake a tail," Jesse said. "He goes in someplace with a crowd and more than one exit, he's gone before we know it."

"I can't work that way," I said. "Whose going to hire an investigator who comes with a babysitter?"

"Not a babysitter, a partner," Jesse said.

"We can't do undercover that way," I argued.

"We don't go undercover," Jesse said. "It'll limit the cases we can take, but we're not hurting on the cash flow right now. And besides, you won't be working a full schedule for a while, anyway."

That was the point when I suggested dinner, not because I was hungry but because I needed time to think and a way to distract them from their crazy scheme. Peter dumped the Thai dishes into big bowls, and everyone helped themselves.

I realized too late the weakness in my strategy. It's damn hard to convince people you can take care of yourself if you have to ask them to help feed you. I soldiered on, hoping no one noticed how much of the food ended up in my lap.

"Catherine's got a point," Jesse said, putting down his chopsticks. "I think we should put some surveillance on Jorgensen. Be good to let the man know we're watching him."

"Real obvious surveillance," Peter said. "Right in his face."

"I can't be part of that," Dan said. "But as long as you don't openly harass him, there's no reason you can't do it."

"But not always too obvious," I said. "Better that sometimes he thinks he's open, and after an hour or so, you let him see you. That way he's never sure. Just because he doesn't see you doesn't mean you're not there."

They all nodded. Peter took a second helping of Lemon Grass Prawns. "But we still stay with you, and Molly, too," he said. "At least for the first of couple of weeks till that shoulder's on the mend."

Chapter

27

Two weeks is long enough for an injury to begin to heal, long enough to get tired of never being alone, but not long enough to learn to live with fear.

The bruise on my shoulder mellowed from the blue black of grape jelly to purple, blue, green, yellow, and many unattractive shades between. My upper arm and the right side of my chest looked as if they'd been done in body paint. The worst discomfort subsided, but I still couldn't move the arm without setting off sirens of pain.

I learned to get most of my food to my mouth with my left hand and to dress myself, though it always took a long time and I usually ended up looking like a bag lady. The orthopedist had said that the immobilizer could come off in ten days to two weeks. I couldn't shower till it was off, so it was a long two weeks, and I felt thoroughly scuzzy by the time he finally released me.

Fall was over, even in California. The days were shorter and the hours of darkness longer. I usually enjoy this time when the movement of the seasons is so noticeable, but this year it depressed me. I found myself staring out the window, watching the light fade and dreading the walk home from my office in the dark.

It's funny that we feel safer when it's light out; you can die in the light just as easily as in the dark. But the dark is scarier. I wonder if that fear is coded in our genes from back when we first climbed down from the trees.

Business was down almost thirty percent because there were a lot of cases we couldn't take, and Jesse was spending a lot of time playing watchdog for me or Molly. Peter's business was hit even harder. He didn't talk much about it, but I knew he was turning down cases.

Molly was doing amazingly well under the circumstances. Her social life was pretty much on hold since we couldn't risk leaving her unguarded and most fourteen year olds don't enjoy having an adult trailing around behind them. At first her friends thought it was cool that she needed a bodyguard, but that only lasted about a week.

Craig, of the nose ring, was infuriated that we didn't consider him enough protection. "She'll be with *me*," he said in a tone that made me suspect that he watched old gangster movies. Clearly, having Peter along put a crimp in his style.

It maddened me that Jorgensen was free while Molly and I were under constant guard. He'd proven to be nearly impossible to watch because he went sailing almost every other day, and once his boat left the marina, we couldn't be sure where he was. Consequently, from the time he'd been released from jail, I'd spent every moment with either Jesse, Peter, or Dan no more than a few feet away. After two weeks, it was wearing thin. For all of us.

The phone rang at one o'clock Thursday morning. I reached for it with dread. Calls in the night rarely bring good news. I picked up the receiver and said hello. There was silence, then the sound of someone breathing into the phone. I hung up. "Oh, cute, a breather," I thought.

Then it hit me. "Oh, shit."

The next call was ten minutes later. Peter took it. The caller hung up.

There wasn't much point in calling the police in the middle of the night. Neither Connelly nor Dan would be on duty, and no one else would put on a trace just for a breather. We unplugged the phone.

The calls continued over the next few days. Connelly put a trap trace on my phone, and Ma Bell supplied him with the numbers for all incoming and outgoing calls. The breathers were all from pay phones. The closest we got to nailing Jorgensen was three calls made from a bar near the marina where he kept his boat.

"Not enough," Connelly said. "Even if you could prove he was there at the time they were made, we'd still need someone who saw him actually place a call. I'm sorry."

Not as sorry as I was.

"You could get an unlisted number," he suggested.

"That would solve the little problem, not the big one," I said. "The calls are just the beginning. He's starting again."

Connelly nodded gravely. "I won't tell you not to worry," he said. "I've told the patrols to pay extra attention to your house, and the officer on Jorgensen's beat parks in front of his place whenever he has a chance, but there's nothing more I can do."

Peter, Jesse, and Dan snapped into hyper-protect mode. They'd have dipped me in amber and stored me in a bank vault if they'd had their way. It got so I took long showers just to have a few minutes alone.

Life was definitely too grim, so I invited Jesse and his girl-friend, Claire, over to play poker Saturday night. Claire begged off, but Jesse came anyway. "Couldn't pass up the chance to take your money," he said.

"I hope you can afford that overconfidence," Peter said as he shuffled. It wasn't much of a threat in a game played with dimes and quarters.

Jesse was hot, or maybe it was just that Peter and I were having trouble concentrating. I tried to care about the game, but it was hard just to manage the play one-handed.

"God, I hate the waiting," Peter said as he dealt the cards.

"Sonuvabitch's got us exactly where he wants us," Jesse said. He gazed at his cards, then returned two to Peter. "He's free to wander around and all we can do is wait till he makes his move and hope we get him in time."

"I wish the bastard would just fall off his boat and drown," I said.

"It's enough to make you believe in vigilante justice," Peter said. He and Jesse looked up from their cards at the same time. It wasn't hard to tell what they were thinking.

"An accident," Jesse said. "Maybe a boating accident."

"Hey," I said. "Not funny. It's still murder even when the victim's a killer."

"You could say it's self-defense. We know he's going to kill again. We know you're the likely victim. Why wait and give him the chance?" Peter asked.

"Are you serious?" I asked.

"I don't know," Peter said. "I do know that if it's a choice between letting him kill you or me killing him, it'd be an easy call."

"Well, that's not the choice," I said. "I may look like an invalid, but I'm not going to be this way for long. We'll worry about how to handle Jorgensen when I've got the use of this arm back. Till then no more talk about accidents. It's bad enough that he's turned us into pawns in his game; he's not going to make us into murderers."

• • •

Aikido was my one release from the tension of being a human target. As soon as I could, I went back to the dojo. At first, I heeded the orthopedist's admonition to stay off the mat for six to eight weeks. It was a perfectly reasonable prescription for anyone who didn't have a psychotic killer to worry about. But in my house every time the phone rang I was reminded of my vulnerability, and soon it became intolerable.

I had to do something, and the only thing I could do was begin to reclaim my ability to defend myself. I had to find out exactly what I could still do with one good arm. My friend Joel had suffered a serious shoulder separation a couple of years ago and had trained with one arm for four months. He offered to help me when I was ready. Almost three weeks after my injury, I took him up on it.

The chief instructor gave us permission to practice at the dojo before the evening class. I wore the immobilizer and hoped it would protect me from any risky moves.

We started with shoulder grabs on my good shoulder, and I practiced using my body to counter. After trying several techniques, I decided that until I had some use of my arm, my best defense would be *atemi waza*, techniques where you move out of the line of attack, then step back in quickly, using your body to strike the opponent.

Atemi waza require precise timing. If you move in too fast, you get hit. Too slow and you miss hitting your attacker. My timing was awful. On top of that, having one arm strapped to my body threw my balance off.

After thirty minutes of practice, my balance and timing were marginally better. I wondered how much time it would take to master the technique. And whether I had that long.

My sister, Marion, and her husband, Leonard, wanted Molly home for the Thanksgiving weekend, and they invited Peter and me to join the family celebration. That was their mistake, mine was agreeing to come. Marion and I are so mismatched and have so little in common that I spent my childhood suspecting that one of us must have been switched at birth. Now, after thirty minutes together I'm sure of it.

Molly's half-sister, Stacy, gets us through a lot since she's a natural ham and does her three-year-old best to entertain us. We're crazy about her, and that's about the only thing we all agree on. Molly hates the little froufrou dresses Marion puts on the kid. Today it took her less than an hour to teach Stacy how to climb a tree.

The dress was ruined. Marion was pissed. Molly was unrepentant. And Stacy was so thrilled by her new skill that she tried it out four more times.

Dinner table conversation is always tough. Politics is out. We never like the same movies. Marion finds my work distasteful; I find Leonard's boring. Marion handled her discomfort by sniping at Molly, who rolled her eyes at me and sulked. Leonard tried to distract us with a long dissertation on the shortcomings of the tax system.

Peter and I offered to do the dishes, but Marion dispatched the men to the living room and the women to the kitchen. My shoulder was well-enough healed that I could handle drying dishes, but I still couldn't lift my arm to put things in the cupboard. After a while, Marion noticed that I kept handing them to Molly.

"Is something wrong with your arm, Catherine?" she asked.

"I hurt it a couple of weeks ago," I said casually. "It's still not completely healed."

Marion didn't ask what happened. If it had anything to do with my work, she didn't want to know. "Do you have a frozen shoulder?" she asked instead. "My friend Hannah injured her shoulder and it froze. She couldn't raise her arm."

"No," I said, rather more forcefully than I'd intended. But the voice inside said, "Oh, shit." I'd been trying to ignore the fact that while the pain was pretty well gone, my mobility was not returning. I couldn't lift my arm any higher this week than I could last.

Marion has an instinctive ability to go for the jugular. She wouldn't let up. "Maybe you should get it checked," she suggested. "Hannah didn't realize what was wrong until she went to the doctor. He sent her to a physical therapist who had her do a bunch of exercises. It only took a few months to get better."

A few months! I wanted to scream at her that I didn't have a few months, but I kept my mouth shut. Molly came to the rescue by asking her mother what was happening at the Junior League. Since Molly hates all things Junior League, I knew I owed her one.

On the drive home I forced myself to face up to the fact that my shoulder didn't seem to be healing properly. Ignoring it wasn't going to make it better.

The thought that my relative helplessness might continue for weeks, maybe months, tied my stomach in a knot. I'd been able to tolerate this passivity because I believed that it wouldn't last much longer. But if my shoulder really was frozen, I'd need a new plan.

Chapter

28

It cost me two hours in the orthopedist's waiting room to be told exactly what I didn't want to hear. Yes, the shoulder was frozen; no, he didn't know why it had happened; no, he couldn't tell me how quickly it would recover.

I asked one too many questions and got the hysterical-woman treatment: a stern admonition to calm down and just do as I was told. "This isn't a big deal," the doctor said, "These things heal, they're not permanent or life-threatening. You'll be fine."

A lot he knew.

I chucked the referral to the physical therapist and called my friend Gil Kelly, who does Feldenkrais body work. Moishe Feldenkrais was an Israeli who put together his knowledge from science and judo to teach himself to walk again after an accident from which doctors told him he would never recover. He not only recovered, he figured out enough about how the brain organizes body movement to found a new approach to physical training and rehabilitation.

Gil made time to see me after work. He had me move my arm different ways, then he moved it others. The look on his face wasn't encouraging.

"Yep, it's frozen," he said. "You can see for yourself. Your mobility is real limited. It's going to take work to get it back. I can free up the shoulder some today, and show you exercises to help. It just takes time."

He worked on the shoulder for almost an hour and at the end of that time, I could move it a bit more freely. Then he showed me a bunch of exercises. "Don't slack off on this," he warned. "You have to do them every day."

"I will do those exercises as though my life depended on it," I promised.

I went home and poured myself a good stiff drink. When I poured a second, slightly stiffer drink, Peter commented, "I don't think alcohol defrosts a shoulder."

The calls continued. They came at all hours. Sometimes there was heavy breathing, sometimes a low chuckle, sometimes just silence. I tried not answering, letting the machine pick up the calls, but it didn't help. I still tensed each time the phone rang, and I hated listening to the tape so much that I gave up on it after a couple of days.

It's amazing how something small like a ringing phone can disrupt your life. He didn't call constantly; some nights he didn't call at all, but all the time that I was home, no matter what I was doing, I was waiting for the next call. And every call tightened the knot of tension in the back of my neck.

My phone manners suffered considerably. I worked hard not to snarl when I picked up the phone, but I didn't get close to warm and friendly. Friends stopped calling unless they really needed to talk to me. So I was particularly pleased one night to hear Tonia's voice instead of Jorgensen's obscene breathing.

"How are you doing?" I asked.

"Fine," she said, but her tone didn't match the words.

"Is something wrong?" I asked.

There was a pause, then, "Well, probably not, but I've been getting these weird phone calls. Someone calls, then hangs up; sometimes he breathes real heavy or laughs. That's the really weird thing, when he laughs. I figure it's kids, but I thought maybe I should check with you, since you work with this kind of thing."

I felt a hollowness in my stomach. "How long has this been going on?" I asked.

"About a week and a half."

The time matched with the calls I'd been getting. I told her about my calls and gave her Connelly's number. "Do you have a family member or friend who could stay with you and your mother for a while?" I asked.

"I have a cousin; he's only nineteen. He goes to S.F. State. Maybe I could get him to come for a while." Her voice sounded near tears.

"Why don't you come over and we can talk," I suggested. I could hear the gratitude and relief when she said she'd be over as soon as she could.

I hated the way Jorgensen's calls made me feel, but I hated even more knowing what they must be doing to Tonia. Your skin thickens over the years, especially in a business like mine. But a kid like Tonia doesn't have those defenses. I hoped like hell that she'd get through this without too many scars.

While I waited for her I tried to think of something I could do to help. I drew a blank.

She looked better than I expected when she arrived, and she was working so hard to hide her vulnerability that I figured the last thing she wanted was sympathy. So we just talked, and it seemed to make her feel better. Less alone, maybe. I went over the precautions she should take and got her to agree to ask her cousin to move in. I could see her confidence begin to return. Until she asked how long the cousin would need to stay, and found I didn't have an answer.

It's a fine line between awareness and obsession. I skated along it, never sure which side I was on. The newspapers seemed suddenly full of stories about women who'd been shot by ex-husbands or stalked by men who were obsessed with them.

There was an article on a woman who'd been stalked by a guy for ten years. Ten years! He'd become obsessed with her and every once in a while he showed up and hung around outside her house, followed her, confronted her in the supermarket. The police didn't think he was dangerous. I was amazed she hadn't bought a shotgun and blown him away.

I did my exercises twice as often as I was supposed to, and I kept working out with Joel at the dojo. We found ways to adapt techniques, and my timing and balance improved, but I was still a long way from being able to defend myself. And none of my improvement made Tonia any safer.

The more I thought about Tonia, the less tolerable my sense of powerlessness became. A couple of days after I talked with her, I called Connelly. "Dan said you were working with a profiler from Sacramento," I said.

"Mike Silva," Connelly said. "He's a good man."

"I'd like to talk to him."

"I don't think there's anything he can tell you that you don't already know," Connelly said.

"Maybe not, but I want to talk to him, anyway. I need to understand what's going on. I don't know if it'll help any, but I'd really like to talk with him."

Connelly didn't answer at once. "He can withhold anything

you guys consider sensitive," I said. "I'm not asking that kind of stuff, anyway. Mostly, I just want to understand what makes a guy like Jorgensen tick."

"I guess it's okay," Connelly said. "He was down here yesterday. I'll check to see if he stayed over. If not, he's probably back in Sacramento."

"I don't mind the drive," I said.

Mike Silva was still in town and, with some encouragement from Connelly, agreed to see me. He offered to stop by my office on his way back to Sacramento that afternoon.

He arrived around three. He was about medium height, on the thin side, with dark curly hair and a broad smile that seemed more appropriate to a playground director than to a man who spent his days contemplating the dark side of the human psyche.

I offered him a seat on the couch and a cup of coffee.

"Do you have decaf?" he asked. "I've already had too much coffee today. Another cup and I won't sleep for a week."

"Decaf, it is," I said and asked Amy to bring it in. McGee, the office cat, was stretched out on the couch. He gave Silva a long, skeptical look. The profiler must have thought it was an invitation and reached over to pet McGee, but the uncooperative tom stood up stiffly and jumped to the floor.

"I don't know that I can help you much," Silva said, sitting back and crossing one long leg over the other. "Most of my work is helping police identify potential suspects. You already know who the killer is."

"Did he fit your profile?" I asked.

"He was the right age. His wife claims he never tried to tie her up. Could be she's ashamed, could be he didn't, but I'd bet he tied someone up. She admits he was out a lot, probably had other women.

"One clue is the way the women in the office felt. You know, the way he was into control, the stuff he pulled with you. That fits. The need to control, dominate, humiliate. He'd been doing that in subtle and not-so-subtle ways for years."

"Any idea what pushed him over the edge? Why he killed Sheila?"

"Why he killed her is 'cause he's been dreaming of doing it for years. Why he did it now, I don't know. Something could have changed in his own life, or something in the environment. Or maybe he was like a time bomb and the fuse ran out. Who knows?"

Something changed. If Sheila discovered the warehouse scheme, that could have done it. Or it could have been me getting in his face. Or the whole charged atmosphere created by the hostility of the men from KeeGo and the pranks they pulled. We'd probably never know.

"You know about the calls?" I asked.

He nodded.

"Any idea what they mean? Is he working himself up to kill again?"

Silva looked uncomfortable. "It's possible," he said.

I thought it was more than possible, and I sensed he did, too. "Look," I said, "this isn't going to work if you think of me as the potential victim. I need to be able to ask hard questions and get straight answers. Can you deal with me as if I were someone hired to protect the victim?"

Silva grinned. "Well, I can try." He uncrossed his legs and leaned forward with his elbows on his thighs. "Yeah, he's almost certainly fantasizing about killing again. That's what the calls are about. They're foreplay. For him, murder's the main event."

Just what I wanted to hear. I asked another question I probably wouldn't like the answer to. "There are two of us he's calling, me and a young friend of Sheila's who's a programmer at Systech. I assume we're both potential victims. Have you any way of knowing who he'll go after first?"

Silva considered the question. He put his hands together and began turning the wedding band on his finger. "No way to know, but the fact that he set you up to find his first victim makes me think it could be you. 'Course, he could set you up to find this girl. Or her to find you."

My stomach pressed upward, making me mildly nauseous. I continued. "Any guess on how soon?" I asked. "I mean, is he likely to play with us for a long time?"

Silva shook his head. "I can't help you on that," he said. "Wish to hell I could, but there's no way to know."

"That's what I was afraid of," I said.

At that point McGee decided Silva was worthy of his attention and jumped back onto the couch. Silva ignored him.

"If we don't know when he'll strike, is there some way we could goad or lure him into coming after me?" I asked. "Can we set him up?"

Silva considered the question. His hand continued to turn the band. "Be real hard, and very risky. I wouldn't recommend it."

"But there is a way?"

He grimaced and sort of shrugged. "He's a voyeur, likes to look, likes to think of you looking. You could play into his fantasy, leave your blinds up, walk around in sexy lingerie. Maybe even pretend . . ."

The expression on my face must have stopped him. At the thought of performing for Scott Jorgensen I lost my cool, detached facade. "I don't think I could do that," I said.

Now Silva looked uncomfortable again. I struggled to get back to our previous tone. "What if we set things up so it looked like I was alone? Could we draw him into making an attempt?"

He considered it. "Possibly," he said. "But it's iffy. First, the setup'd have to be extremely subtle, nothing obvious. This guy's smart, and smart guys are more likely to spot a trap than someone who's room temperature. For example, you'd think he'd love to have you go visit this other woman he's been calling. Give him two for the price of one. But he wouldn't go for that. It's too obvious.

"Then there's the issue of timing. He's deep into fantasy and part of what gives him his kicks is terrorizing his victims. The calls could be just the beginning. He may have a whole complicated scenario. Moving sooner than he planned would mean giving that up.

"Also, he's into control. He may want to pick his time. And he's into playing with us, the cops, showing us he's smarter than we are. He wants to get you, but I suspect he'll have a real complicated plan, just like he did for Sheila Wainwright."

"So you don't think a trap would work."

"It's a real long shot," he said. "I know that's not what you want to hear. I wish I thought we could flush him out, but I'm not optimistic."

So we were back to square one, waiting while Scott Jorgensen played his twisted game.

Chapter

29

Molly had started lobbying for a Christmas tree on December first; we managed to put her off until the twelfth. Christmas brings out the kid in me, and the pagan. I love the evergreen, covered with bright lights and colored balls, standing in the middle of the room like a glowing shrine.

But this year I felt the darkness of winter as I never had before, and all the colored lights and bright decorations couldn't turn my mind from the constant threat of Scott Jorgensen. It made me furious that his ominous presence should dampen the pleasure of having Molly with me for the Christmas holidays. After all that she and Peter and I had been through, we needed some holiday cheer.

As we set out for Sonoma to find our tree I tried to forget all about Scott Jorgensen. I succeeded about half the time and actually managed to enjoy tramping through the man-made forest of the Christmas tree farm in search of the perfect tree. Molly did too until she realized that we were going to kill the perfect tree.

"But we can't kill it," she said, as the farmer produced a saw.

"I don't see any other way to get it home," I said.

"Besides, you have to kill it," Peter, the archdruid, said. "It's a sacrifice. It has to die."

Molly stared at him in amazement. "All this shit about living Christmas trees is a way of trying to pretend that things don't die," he continued. "What do you think this season is all about—the solstice, Christmas, Chanukah—they're all about death and rebirth. So the tree has to die."

The farmer stood by with a look that said he'd heard it all, and Molly liked the idea of a pagan sacrifice enough to accept the cutting of the tree, but all the talk of death chilled me and I shivered in the bright winter sunlight.

We strapped our tree to the roof of the Volvo and joined the fleet of tree hunters on their way south. The road from Sonoma looked like Birnam wood on its way to Dunsinane.

We pulled up in front of the house at four, and I went ahead to open the door while Molly and Peter struggled with the tree. Almost as soon as I entered, I sensed that something was wrong. Nothing looked any different, but something had changed. I backed out of the house.

"Peter," I said in as calm a voice as I could manage. "Could you come here for a minute?" I didn't fool anyone. They both froze, then Peter said, "Molly, get in the car and wait for us, please. And lock the doors." For once, Molly did as she was told without question.

"I think someone's been in the house," I said.

Peter stepped in front of me and walked into the entry hall. He could sense it, too. There was something subtly different. I tried to place it and realized that the house smelled different. "Do you smell anything?" I asked Peter.

He sniffed a couple of times. "Cologne, maybe?" he said. "But I don't know what."

I knew what it was, not the brand, but where I'd smelled it. "It's Scott Jorgensen," I said. "It's the kind of cologne he wears."

We moved carefully through the house with Peter in front of me. In the kitchen, the back door stood slightly ajar.

"I know I locked it," I said. "I'm sure of it."

"Let's check the bedroom," Peter said. He led the way.

The smell was stronger in the bedroom, much stronger. The sweet artificial scent filled the room like a presence. It made me want to gag.

In the middle of the bed lay a pair of women's panties. They weren't mine. I had a pretty good idea whose they were. I backed out of the room and struggled to draw breath into my tightening chest.

Having my flat invaded by Jorgensen was only the first violation. Then I had to stand by while Connelly had a forensics team go over everything. The panties were carefully picked up with tongs and placed in a plastic evidence bag. Surfaces were dusted with black powder. It was like being back at Systech again.

"Anything missing?" Connelly asked.

I nodded dully. I'd forced myself to go through my drawers. I couldn't be sure what was missing and what was hiding behind the dryer, but as far as I could tell, he'd taken a couple of pairs of panties, a bra, and two teddies that Peter had bought me. The thought of him pawing through my things gave me chills.

"The cologne's especially strong on the panties," Connelly said. "He also poured it on the bed."

"Looks like he splashed it on the wall and carpet over here," called a technician on his hands and knees behind my dresser. "It's in the closet, too."

"Almost like a dog marking his territory," Connelly said. "This guy's a class-A weirdo."

• • •

I realized as the crime-scene guys were finishing up that I hadn't seen my cat, Touchstone. I got a horrible, sick feeling in my stomach. "These guys go after animals, don't they?" I asked Connelly.

"Lots of them have a history of torturing small animals when they were kids," he said.

I'd sent Molly to Amy's with Peter to keep her away from the macabre circus at home. Now I hurried into her room. The forensics team hadn't gone over it, since there was no smell of cologne, and with most of her belongings in piles on the floor, it would have been impossible to tell if they'd been disturbed.

From the doorway I could see two glass aquariums on the bookshelf across the room. One should hold Reepecheep, Molly's gray mouse. The other was home to the one-eyed snake that Touchstone had brought me as a present almost a year ago. Both looked empty. A wave of apprehension hit my already-queasy stomach as I stepped over and around the piles to get to the aquariums.

I peered into Reepecheep's cage. He was nowhere to be seen. Fighting against my growing sense of dread, I reminded myself that he often burrows into the shavings that cover the bottom of his cage. I poked into them carefully, starting at one end and working my way to the other. I was so tense that when the little guy popped out of the shavings, I jumped and let out a yelp. I wanted to hold and stroke him, but mice don't go for that mushy stuff. He made a dash for his wheel and began running like mad.

Next I checked on the snake. He'd disappeared into the shavings and begun hibernating several weeks earlier. I carefully scraped the shavings away. He looked dead, but he didn't look injured. I poked him gently and he moved. I covered him up and gave a sigh of relief.

When I returned to the bedroom, Connelly asked, "Something wrong?"

"I don't know," I said. "But my cat is missing."

"Shit," he said.

A young technician was standing nearby. "Cats are pretty cagey," he said, trying to sound encouraging. "They're real good at scoping out a situation and hiding out."

I hoped he was right.

None of us was in any mood to put up the Christmas tree that night. It ended up in a pail of water out in the backyard. I didn't mention to Molly that Touchstone was missing, but she noticed his absence almost as soon as she got home.

"Where is he?" she asked anxiously.

"The back door was open," I said. "He probably ran out and is catting around outside."

"He doesn't miss dinner," Molly said.

"But he does sponge off the neighbors," I pointed out. My argument didn't reassure either of us, but we both pretended to believe it.

We went out for pizza because none of us could stand staying in the house. I seethed every time I thought of how long it would take to get the stench of Jorgensen's cologne out of my bedroom. With every day he seemed to intrude further into my life. I stayed angry because it protected me from the much more painful feelings that engulfed me each time Touchstone came into my mind.

There was good news when we got home. The pudgy tom was at the back door howling piteously. He fussed and made his usual nuisance of himself while I fixed his dinner, but we were all so glad to see him that he got a double helping.

I wasn't about to let Jorgensen drive me out of my home, but after an hour in the flat, I had to admit that the ever-present odor of his cologne was making me crazy.

"Why don't we move into my place," Peter suggested. "He

won't know where you are, and you can let this place air out. In fact, we might just decide to stay there till the trial is over."

It was a great idea. And when I realized how relieved I felt, I knew how heavily the burden of the last weeks had worn on me. We loaded the two aquariums, my computer disks, a few clothes, and Touchstone into the car and headed for Peter's.

Once the three, or six, of us arrived there, we realized that Peter's place was less than ideal. It has only one bedroom, and the junk he dumped in there had been multiplying since he moved in with me.

We spent most of Sunday cleaning and moving furniture to try to create a space that Molly could call her own. Peter made several trips back to my flat to pick up stuff we needed. By the third trip, he was making jokes about hiring a moving van. Returning from the fourth, he arrived with the Christmas tree strapped to the top of the car.

"Couldn't leave this where Jorgensen could use it for one of his weird games," Peter said. "It's a real trick to make sure you're not being followed when you've got a tree tied to the top of your car."

I worried that when Jorgensen discovered I'd disappeared he might turn his attention to Tonia, so I called and told her what had happened. She wasn't as worried as I'd expected. Her cousin, who lived with four other guys in a tiny apartment, was delighted by her offer of rent-free accommodations with free meals thrown in. He was prepared to stay indefinitely.

I gave her Peter's number and told her to call if anything suspicious or scary happened. I also called Connelly to let him know where I'd be.

That evening we rented a movie and made popcorn. It was the first night in a month that I'd really been able to relax.

• • •

Connelly called the next day to tell me that the panties on my bed were not Sheila Wainwright's. "Too bad," he said. "If he'd left evidence clearly linking the break-in to the murder, we could lock him up for the duration. The bastard's smart, gotta give him credit."

Credit was not what I wanted to give Scott Jorgensen. "What about the stalking law?" I said. "Can't you get him under that?"

"I could if we could prove it was him. But we don't have anything tangible. You know it was him. I know it was him. But that's not enough for a judge."

"He's playing with us," I said in frustration.

"Sure he is. That's part of what this is all about. Showing us all how smart he is, how he can run circles around us. But that's also his weakness; it's what's going to keep him pulling stunts until he outsmarts himself."

I felt like a mouse being asked to be patient while the cat perfected his technique. The stakes were too high for patience. Peter's suggestion of an "accident" played at the back of my mind. I shoved it away and hoped I wouldn't regret it.

Tonia called Tuesday just as we were sitting down to dinner. Her voice was tight with tension, but her tone was apologetic.

"I'm sorry to bother you. I know it's probably nothing, but when I went out in my backyard tonight I found a dead bird right in the middle of the porch."

I paused to consider it and she hurried on, "It's probably nothing. I'm probably overreacting. It could be a coincidence. I mean, I don't know if *he* left it."

"Don't apologize, Tonia," I said. "You've got plenty of reason to worry, and I'm glad you called. What kind of bird is it? A pet bird or a wild one?"

"It's just a brown bird."

Probably wild. Good so far.

"Could you tell from looking if it was killed by a cat or some other animal?"

"No," she said. "I didn't turn it over. But it wasn't chewed up if that's what you mean."

"What did you do with the bird?"

"I left it there," she said.

"Good," I said. "It might be nothing, but I'm going to call a police officer to check on it. So just leave it there."

Connelly didn't dismiss the dead bird, either, even when lab results showed it had died of natural causes. "Just cause he didn't kill it, doesn't mean he didn't put it there," he said.

By Thursday, I was feeling a strange restlessness. Maybe it was just living away from home. Maybe it was driving miles out of my way to make sure no one was following when I went to Peter's. Or maybe it was the dead mouse I found on Peter's back porch.

He claimed he found mice all the time. The neighborhood cats prefer hunting to eating their prey. It was probably true. Just as it was quite likely that Tonia's dead bird had nothing to do with Scott Jorgensen. But we couldn't know that.

With a madman on the loose, there were no accidents any more. And no coincidences.

Chapter

30

The mouse and bird might have been happenstance, but the dead flowers were not. They were delivered by a skinny guy with pink hair wearing a messenger uniform.

The punk messenger rang the doorbell at six on Thursday night. Peter had gone to the store, so I answered the door, and he thrust a large bouquet of dead flowers toward me. "Surprise," he said. "Someone is thinking of you."

I stared at him in horror. He giggled nervously. I felt a desperate urge to turn and flee. To slam the door and pretend he wasn't there.

"Hey, don't freak out," he said. "It's a joke."

"No," I said, as calmly as I could. "It's not a joke, and I think you'd better come in and tell me who told you to bring those flowers."

"Look, lady," he said, "I just work here. I'm hired to deliver flowers, so I deliver flowers. If you can't take a joke . . ."

I interrupted him. "The man who sent those flowers is a killer," I said, "and the police will want to talk to you."

That got his attention. Now it was his turn to get pale.

He was sputtering protests as I spotted Peter coming up the block.

Peter's presence made the messenger more cooperative. The offer of a beer got him inside and willing to talk. He was actually one of three owners of Poison Poseys. They'd gotten the idea while still in college when one of them was stood up by a particularly bitchy sorority girl. "We raided the garden at her house and made this big bouquet, then we let it dry and when it was all droopy and turning brown, we got a friend to deliver it. Everyone thought it was a hoot, and a couple of weeks later a buddy asked us to do one for him. Word got around; we were in business.

"We get a lot a business from jilted suitors, wives whose ex's alimony checks bounce. . . . I've delivered at least four bouquets to the IRS, one to a meter maid, a couple to the mayor."

"Can you trace this order?" I asked.

"Sure, there's bound to be an invoice, but if they asked to be anonymous, I can't tell you who they are."

"But you could tell the police," I said.

He didn't look pleased by the idea. "Yeah, I guess I'd have to. But, look, maybe we won't have to. Can I use your phone?"

He called the office. There was a long wait while one guy asked the other and they sorted through paper. Our guy nodded and said, "Uh huh," a couple of times but didn't write anything down. When he hung up, he shook his head.

"No luck," he said. "The order was a walk-in and he paid in cash."

"Does anyone remember what he looked like?"

A second call confirmed that no one did, not specifically, but the guy who took the order thought maybe this was the order from a kid who had obviously been hired to deliver it.

"The kid didn't seem to know much," pink hair said. "He was about sixteen, and when my buddy asked him something about the order, he just shrugged. Of course, we don't even know for sure if it was this order."

I was sure, but once again, that didn't matter. What mattered was that Jorgensen had tracked me down again.

"How the devil did he find us?" I asked Peter as soon as the messenger left.

Peter considered it. His face was grim. "I don't see how he could have followed us without one of us noticing," he said. "He doesn't exactly blend into a crowd. That means someone else is working with him, someone good enough to tail us when you and I were being extra careful."

"Not an amateur," I said.

"Not likely. Didn't Connelly say Jorgensen was connected? Looks like he's recruited a friend to help him out."

"I thought serials worked alone," I said.

Peter shook his head. "Usually they do. But that guy killing girls in L.A. had a buddy along. More likely Jorgensen just called in a favor and asked someone to find you. Either way, it's not good."

Now we were both grim. It was bad enough to have Jorgensen to deal with, but at least I knew him by sight. The idea that he had an accomplice was much worse.

I sent Molly to Dan's for the night, and Jesse came over to Peter's after dinner. It looked more like a wake than a meeting.

"What good is surveillance of Jorgensen if he can use an intermediary?" I asked.

"Won't stop the harassment. Might prevent something worse," Jesse said.

"I know someone who could take care of this," Peter said.

"The surveillance?" I asked, but I knew from his tone that wasn't what he meant.

"Hey, man," Jesse said in a warning tone.

"You think he's just playing games, that it'll be enough for him to mess with our minds? How long before the calls and the stunts aren't enough, before he wants more? The big thrill?" Peter asked. His voice was hard. He turned to me. "And maybe you won't even be the target. Maybe he'll go after Tonia first. After all, she's easier."

My mouth was dry. He wasn't saying anything I hadn't thought, but the emotion behind it came from a place I hadn't reached yet.

"Yeah, but murder? I don't know," Jesse said.

"I can't," I said. "I just can't. If he came after me, or after Tonia, I could kill him if I had to, but I can't sit here around the kitchen table and plot his death."

"You don't have to have anything to do with it," Peter said. "I know people or people who know people."

"It'd have to look like an accident," Jesse said. "Maybe a boating accident. All you'd have to do was get into the marina and hide in his boat. He sails at least three times a week, more if the weather's good. You'd hide, and once he was out on the bay, well, a blow on the head and a tragic accident. No one would cry too hard."

"No," I said. "I won't do it, and I won't have it done in my name. I mean it."

They both looked at me. I think they were surprised by the strength of my emotion. I wondered if it would please Scott Jorgensen to know that he'd driven us to consider murder. It was power of a kind, the ability to make someone so desperate that they'd violate their own values.

I hated him, and I'd have happily seen him dead, but I also knew that actions have consequences. If we killed him or hired someone else to do it for us, we'd never, any of us, be the same again.

There was no point staying at Peter's now that Jorgensen knew where we were, so we decided to move back to larger quarters.

The next day I got a cleaning service out to my apartment, ordered a new mattress, and called an alarm company to install a system on every door and window. It was a top-of-the-line system, and it cost me plenty. I hoped I wasn't broke by the time the legal system finally got around to dealing with Jorgensen.

We moved back in Saturday morning. It was one of those glorious December days that makes San Franciscans unbearably smug and tempts Easterners to load up their cars and head west. The sky was a deep blue and the sun was working hard to convince us all that spring was here. There'd been enough rain this year to tease us with the possibility that the drought was over and to carpet the ground with lush, green rain grass.

None of us wanted to be trapped moving stuff back to my flat. We wanted to hike on Mount Tam or ride over to the beach. What we got was an hour off for lunch, which we spent at the marina lying on the grass and watching a parade of sun-dazed San Franciscans pretend it was summer.

A half-dozen kites, not one of them shaped like a diamond, swam in the air above us, a circle of people practiced the slow motion ballet of t'ai chi nearby, and children dashed and shrieked all around us. Even the earnest joggers had smiles on their faces.

The bay was dotted with sailboats. One of them was probably Scott Jorgensen's. *He* could enjoy the day. He was calling the shots. I could imagine him lounging on his boat with a can of beer, smugly savoring his success in tracking me down and plotting his next bit of nastiness. I'm not sure which I hated more, his efforts to terrorize me or the loss of control over my own life. But I know I hated that man, deeply and intensely.

Sunday was another gorgeous day and Molly, Peter, and I were determined to enjoy it properly. Peter always starts a day like this by studying the weather reports for his hometown back in Massachusetts and announcing gleefully how cold it is. It's probably his way of dealing with some vestigial homesickness, reassuring himself that he made the right decision when he moved west.

The ritual weather reading was followed by the Sunday morning cooking project. He and Molly had been trying for weeks to duplicate exactly the raspberry cornmeal pancakes they found at a restaurant in Mill Valley. This morning they'd decided to try buttermilk.

The phone rang and rather than turn down the rock music that formed the soundtrack for life in our house, I took the call in the bedroom. It was Jack Connelly.

"I don't know if this is bad news or good news," he said. "But Scott Jorgensen never came home last night."

I felt numb, like a lab rat that's been shocked one too many times. "He's gone underground," I said. "I don't see how that can be good news."

"He disappeared while he was sailing, so there's a chance that he fell overboard and drowned," Connelly said. A boating accident! My breath caught and a chill swept through my body.

Connelly went on to speculate on where the "accident" had occurred. "His boat ran aground near the Berkeley pier, probably drifted over from someplace around Angel Island. The Coast Guard's searching for the body, and we're not calling it either way yet, but everyone's a winner if he turns up as a floater. It'd save the state some money and all of you a lot of hassle."

I thanked Connelly for calling, and hoped he couldn't hear in my voice the tangle of emotions I was feeling.

Molly and Peter were tasting the first fruits of their labor. Molly was sure the pancakes needed more sugar; Peter was teasing her and arguing for more buttermilk. I watched him and wondered if I really knew him.

I'd thought a lot about our discussion that Jorgensen might

be the victim of an "accident." Spent time wondering if maybe I was wrong to reject the idea. And I knew that if Molly were threatened, my answer would probably be different. If I felt it was okay to kill to protect her, how could I condemn Peter for feeling the same way about me?

But I did. Consistency doesn't count for a hill of beans up against emotion.

"Peter, can I talk to you?" I said, trying to keep my voice neutral. From the way they both looked at me, it was obvious I hadn't succeeded.

He put down his fork and hurried across the room. I led the way into the bedroom and closed the door, but as I opened my mouth to ask him, I realized I couldn't find the words. How do you ask your lover if he's a killer? Finally, I said, "It appears Scott Jorgensen may have had a boating accident last night."

Peter stared at me. "Did they find a body?" he asked.

"No. Not yet."

"Damn," he said. "He's set this up; he's gone to ground. I'd bet on it."

The strength of his reaction gave me a rush of relief. Before I had a chance to think, I blurted out, "Then you didn't have anything to do with it."

Peter looked surprised, then comprehension dawned and he said, "Ah, you're worried that I arranged this."

"It's exactly what you suggested the other night," I said.

"And you said no. That was the end of it, though I have to tell you that if he's gone to ground, we may all be real sorry we didn't take care of him when we had the chance."

"Did you talk to anyone who might have thought you wanted him dead? Someone who might have decided to do you a favor?" I asked.

Peter shook his head. "It's not a subject you discuss in casual company," he said. "No, I didn't have anything to do with this, and I don't think he's dead."

"Could Jesse?" I asked.

"Kill Jorgensen?" Peter was incredulous, but he considered it. "I guess we should ask. But I don't think so. I don't really believe that any of us could kill that easily. It's one thing to talk about it, another to give the order."

"So if the accident didn't have anything to do with us, you think it was staged by him?"

"Definitely. I should have seen it coming. We were on his tail, made it real inconvenient. He could use his buddies to track you down, but I suspect he wants to do this stuff himself. Now there are no constraints. He doesn't have to worry about implicating himself because he doesn't plan to stand trial."

I had a sick feeling in my stomach. I sank down on the bed, then found I couldn't sit still and had to get up and move. "What now?" I asked.

Peter shook his head. His face was grave. "It's back to never leaving you alone," he said. "I know you hate it but it's the only way."

"What about Molly?"

"Same for her."

I considered. There was only a week of school left before vacation. If we watched her carefully, we could get through that. Then I could send her home to Marion. But vacation was only two weeks long, and I had no idea what we'd do after that.

Jesse was as surprised by Jorgensen's disappearance as we were. I was afraid he'd be angry that I considered the possibility that he'd been involved. He wasn't, and his reaction told me that each of us had entertained in one way or another, the idea that the time might come when we'd take matters into our own hands.

Connelly called each day to give me an update, but there was never much to report. They hadn't found the body, but they hadn't found evidence of foul play or that the accident was staged. I didn't really believe Jorgensen had fallen overboard, but the longer we waited, the more I could let myself hope that maybe, just maybe, that trickster Fate had done us a good turn.

We put the tree up and decorated it. We played Christmas carols and made cookies. We shopped for presents. But none of it reached beneath the surface for me. I felt like an actor in a play, and I knew it was the same for Peter. Molly was much better at living in the moment. She could rise above the tension that had become as real as air in our house. Christmas still had magic for her.

Thursday, Peter walked me home from work. The phone was ringing as we came in the door and I rushed to pick it up, hoping for news from Connelly.

There was silence when I said hello, then a click, and an almost-familiar female voice. I realized with horror that it must be Sheila's.

"Please," she pleaded, her voice low, just above a whisper, "please don't hurt me."

Chapter

31

I almost dropped the phone. I managed to get it back on the cradle without hearing more. Then I took several deep breaths, and called Jack Connelly at his home.

"He's got a tape of Sheila the night he killed her," I told him. "He played it over the phone. She was begging him not to hurt her."

"Jesus H. Christ," he said. "What a twisted bastard! Polaroids, audiotapes, he's probably got video as well. What's on the tape?"

"I don't know. I hung up. All I heard was Sheila saying, 'Please don't hurt me.'"

"You're sure it was Sheila?"

"Fairly sure."

"We've still got the trap trace on your phone. At least we'll know if he's still around here. You got the equipment to tape your calls?" he asked.

"Yes."

"Set it up. If he calls again, just put the phone down on the desk and let the machine record whatever's on the tape. You don't have to listen, but be sure to record it."

• • •

The phone rang about forty minutes later. I had the recorder set up, and I let Peter get the call. When he came back to bed, his face was grim. "Don't listen to the tape," he said. "You don't want to hear it."

He'd unplugged the telephone, so there were no more calls that night, but that didn't mean I got much sleep.

In a strange way, the call was a relief. I hadn't really believed that Jorgensen was gone. It was easier to know for sure, even if the news was bad.

The news got worse when Tonia called, nearly hysterical, after hearing the tape of Sheila's voice the next day. "I can't believe this," she moaned, "it's so twisted. It's like living in a nightmare. I've got these pains in my stomach; I'm sure I'm getting an ulcer."

I tried to calm her, but I didn't have any comfort to offer. "You've got to get away," I said. "Take a vacation with your mother. I'll ask Leggett to give you time off if you want. I can lend you money."

"I don't know," she said. "I couldn't go for more than a couple of weeks, then what would I do? I think it'd be harder to come back than never to go."

"Is your cousin still there?" I asked.

"Yeah, most the time. And the guys at Systech have been really great about this. One of them always picks me up in the morning and another brings me home. Bob organized it. And Frank comes over lots of nights just to make sure I'm okay."

"Kingsley and McFadden?" I asked. "Who would have thought."

"They're really great. I know some women still don't trust Bob after the pranks, but he's really trying to get his act together. You know he went to an all-boys Catholic high school and straight from there into a fraternity. He really never had a girl who was a friend. I just think he doesn't know how to relate to women as people."

"Sounds like you've taken him on as a project."

She laughed. "Well, sort of, I guess. Anyway, we talk a lot. I think he's a nice guy."

"And Frank McFadden?" I asked.

"We're sort of going out. Elaine's pissed because she says he only dates younger women, but he says age has nothing to do with it. Anyway, it's nice to have someone looking out for me."

"That's for sure," I said.

"So see, that's part of why I don't want to just leave. I mean now I have these guys taking care of me, if I go off for a couple of weeks, maybe when I come back, they'll think I don't need them anymore."

I wasn't sure it was a good idea to rely too much on either Bob Kingsley or Frank McFadden. They were a bit too smooth and she was a bit too trusting, but if she wouldn't leave town, I didn't have a better alternative to offer her.

I suggested that she get an unlisted number to put a stop to the calls, and made one more attempt to get her to leave town. She agreed to the unlisted phone, but not to leaving. I knew it was a mistake at the time. I should have argued harder.

I'd arranged to take Molly to Palo Alto on Saturday afternoon. School would be out, and my sister, Marion, wanted her daughter to spend the whole vacation with her. Marion has a weird Hallmark-card-type memory that substitutes reruns of "Father Knows Best" for any real-life experience that gets messy. She was thinking of baking cookies; Molly was packing her most outrageous outfits, all of them black, and most involving lots of metal and chains.

"Where did you get this stuff?" I asked.

"I borrowed most of it," she said with a wicked smile. "Don't you think the kids in Paly'll love it?"

"You know I'm not going to let you do this," I said. "Just as a matter of self-preservation, I'm not sending you home looking like a cheerleader for the Marquis de Sade."

"Who?" Molly asked.

"Never mind," I said. "Leather out, jeans and T-shirts in."

We argued a bit, but she knew she was going to lose. "I'm not staying down there for a whole two weeks," she said. "I'd go nuts."

"We'll take that one day at a time," I said. "You can call if things get dicey." Truth was I knew I'd miss her, but I wanted her safe more than I wanted her with me. "With things the way they are here; there's a good chance I won't be able to let you come back, so you'd better make your peace with Marion for now."

Molly made a face and grumbled. She didn't take the black leather out of her bag, but she added enough regular clothes to get her through the visit. I suspected she might find it a great relief to get out of a house where all of life was organized around the threat of violent death. I hoped she'd want to return when this nightmare was over.

The mail arrived at one and included a box addressed to Molly. The return address was a shop on Haight Street. "Hey, looks like you got a present," I called as I brought it to her.

"Wow, who's it from?"

"I don't know," I said.

She peered at the shop name. "Oh, wow, this is so weird. Can I open it now?"

"Shouldn't you wait for Christmas?"

She considered that idea for about two seconds. "No, 'cause I won't be here to thank them, and besides I need to know who sent it so I can get them a gift."

She was so excited. "What the hell," I thought, "I'm not going to get the fun of watching her open presents on Christmas morning, I might as well let her have this one here."

It took some effort to get through the cardboard and tape of the outer box. Inside was another box wrapped in red. The paper on that one came off easily. When she opened the box, there was a moment of silence, then a nervous laugh. "Gol, my friends are so weird. I wonder which one came up with this idea." She handed me the box.

Inside was the skeleton of a human hand.

My entire body went cold. I knew without examining it that it was real, and I knew that the "gift" wasn't from any of her friends.

Peter and I had a hasty conference in the kitchen. "This is my fault," I said. "I should have gotten her out of this house the minute the calls started."

"We talked about it. It just didn't seem like that big a risk, since he was so focused on you."

"But he was also after Tonia. I should have seen this coming."

"It's hard to see what you don't want to see," Peter said. "We both wanted her with us. The issue is what we do now."

"Palo Alto's too close," I said. "She can't go there. He could find her too easily."

"Casey?" Peter asked. Casey was a friend in Idaho who'd taken Molly in once before when things got too dangerous here.

"Possibly," I said. "But I don't even like the idea of Marion being this close." An image of Marion, naked and violated like Sheila, sprang to my mind. I pushed it away, but I could feel my heart pound and my stomach rise to my throat.

Jorgensen was that crazy. And that evil. He might just decide to twist the screw one more time, with one more victim, this time much closer to me. With the photos and audiotape, he'd turned me into his audience. I couldn't risk a repeat performance.

• • •

I'd taken advantage of Marion's lack of interest in my work to keep her unaware of the aftermath of the Systech case. I knew I should tell her, but I also knew she wouldn't let Molly stay with me if she knew I was the target of a serial killer. That made what I had to tell her all the harder.

She didn't take it well. I didn't expect her to. I didn't object when she yelled at me for being irresponsible and putting Molly in danger. It was true. It took a while for her to get the point of why she and her family had to get out of town. When it finally sank in, she stopped yelling and became very serious.

"You mean that this Jorgensen could come after me or the baby?" she said.

"Or Molly," I said. "Any or all of you. He's very crazy."

"And he's after you, right?."

"I'm afraid so," I said, "I'm really sorry to have gotten you into this." I meant it more than I could tell her.

"Come to Denver with us," she said.

"What?"

"Come to Denver. Get out of there now. You're not super-woman, you know. Even with your black belt, you could still get hurt. And what about your arm? Catherine, you have to get out of there."

I was so amazed I didn't have anything to say. After years of bitching at me about one thing or another, Marion was honest-ly, seriously concerned about me. I felt irrationally happy. Then I remembered why she was worried.

Part of me wanted to go with her. To get on a plane and go home to our parents' house and celebrate Christmas with peo-ple I loved around me. But I knew I couldn't. I couldn't risk Jorgensen following me or the possibility that with me gone he'd switch his focus to Tonia.

I'd made my decision months ago, when I chose to stay on the case at Systech. The reasons weren't any different now than then. I'd still rather risk dying at Jorgensen's hands to living with the knowledge that other women had died in my place.

• • •

Jesse handled the arrangements for getting Marion and her family out of town. He got them a flight leaving the next day and took everyone to the San Jose Airport by a suitably round-about way. I longed to go to the airport with them, or at least to meet them to say good-bye, but I didn't want to risk it.

How ironic that it had taken the threats of a psycho to bring me closer to my sister. He'd brought a certain brutal clarity to my life, I thought. It appalled me to realize that it had taken the possibility that one of us could end up sliced and diced to make Marion and me put aside our petty complaints and rec-ognize how much we cared for each other.

Dan offered to take Molly to San Jose to meet Marion. She clung to me when we had to say good-bye. It tore my heart to feel her pain. She was much too young to even know that things like this could happen, not to mention that she could be involved in them.

The flat was painfully empty after she left. The brightly deco-rated tree and the evergreen wreath over the fireplace stood as silent reminders of the holiday that Jorgensen had stolen from us. That night for the first time I didn't plug in the lights on the tree.

I got a call from my dad just after nine. "What's going on?" he asked. I should have known I couldn't fool him.

How do you tell your father you're being stalked by a serial killer? Or maybe not a serial, maybe just a killer who's fixated on you. I stumbled around trying not to lie and not to make it sound as really awful as it was.

"Come stay with us," he said. "There's room. You can bring Peter." That last was a real concession from a man who's never accepted my divorce from Dan.

I tried to explain. I didn't do a very good job, but it didn't matter. There wasn't any explanation good enough to make my dad accept the fact that I was staying.

"All right, I'll come there," he said. "I'll get a flight tomorrow morning."

"Dad," I said, struggling to avoid the tone I'd used all during adolescence. "No. I sent Molly and Marion to Colorado so that you could protect them. You have to stay with them."

"And who's going to protect you?"

"Peter, Dan, and Jesse," I said. "The three of them are keeping me under tighter surveillance than you use on a state's witness."

I knew it would comfort him to have Dan involved. Peter and Jesse were amateurs in his book, but Dan was a pro. Another cop. That was the only argument that kept him from hopping on the next plane to San Francisco. But even as he professed confidence in Dan, I could hear the shadow of fear in his voice. Jorgensen's awful, spoiling touch would poison my parents' holidays along with my own.

Chapter

32

With Molly gone, there was no longer any need to keep up the pretense of a normal life. Breakfast was a silent and somber affair. I was ready to go to work an hour before Peter was ready to escort me, and it drove me nuts to wait for him. By the time we got out of the house, he looked like he was babysitting the client from hell.

Work was the one place I could act as though nothing had changed. I had to turn down a number of cases I'd have liked to have taken, but the ones I worked on got my full attention. I must have been putting on a pretty good act. My clients were pleased.

Monday was a good day, workwise. We cleared a produce buyer of taking kickbacks and caught a not-too-clever accountant who was cooking the books, and I took on an interesting case from a Chinese import firm. I was actually finished at five, though I'd have happily hung around the office for another couple of hours, but Jesse wanted to go home and wouldn't let me stay alone.

He waited with me until Peter got there. I tried to shoo him off, but he wouldn't go. I was feeling more and more like a delicate object that large men handed from one to the other. I like men. A lot. I especially like these men, but spending twenty-four hours a day with them was definitely too much.

We sat around and had a beer and I told them about the Chinese import firm. We used to enjoy shoptalk, but we hadn't done much of that since Jorgensen became our major concern.

Maybe we'd lost the knack for it. I could sense Peter's attention wandering. "I think he's getting ready to do something," he said. No one needed to ask who.

"You want him to do something," I said. "At least I want him to do something. The waiting is killing me."

Jesse nodded. "You were probably right about taking care of him while we could," he said to Peter.

Peter shrugged. I knew he agreed with Jesse.

"Claire's parents are going to be visiting after Christmas," Jesse said. "I was going to take a couple of days to drive up the coast with them, but I think I'd better cancel that."

Peter and I exchanged looks. Jesse and Claire have been working their way toward commitment for almost a year. I wondered if her parents' visit signaled that things were finally getting serious.

"No, go on," Peter said. "You need a break. I'll take off a few days, maybe even convince Catherine to go away somewhere."

Jesse looked uncertain. "Do it," I said. "Maybe we'll all take a vacation."

"If you're sure . . ." he said. He didn't look happy about it. I waited for him to tell us more about Claire's parents' visit, but he's like Molly, you've got to catch him when he feels like talking or you don't get much.

I start my morning with the *Chronicle*. Tuesday was no different. I opened the front door, then jumped back as I realized there was something on the knob. The something was a pair of black panties. I recognized them as one of the ones Jorgensen had stolen from my drawer.

I didn't want to touch them, but I also didn't want to leave them on my front door handle, so I got a plastic sack and put them in it. They reeked of Jorgensen's cologne.

I worked to stay calm, at least on the outside, but on the inside I was seething. He was playing with me again. The panties were his way of saying, "I can get this close. I can walk up on your porch anytime I want."

We went out for dinner that night, and when we got back, Peter buried himself in a book. He was probably as oppressed by our enforced togetherness as I was.

The house seemed unnaturally quiet without Molly. For all my complaints about loud music, I missed the muffled heavy base beat that had become the background sound track at home. Its absence was a further reminder of Jorgensen's violent intrusion into every aspect of my life.

I missed Molly. I wanted her back. I wanted my life back.

It had been a couple of days since I checked on Reepecheep, Molly's gray mouse. He's an easy critter to care for—water in his bottle and food in his dish, a clean cage when the mousy smell begins to build up, an easy boarder to satisfy.

The door to Molly's room was slightly ajar and my stomach tightened as I tried to remember if I'd closed it tight the last time I was in there. Peter'd checked the house when he came home; surely he'd have looked in.

I pushed the door fully open but didn't step through. Then I spotted the culprit and relaxed. Next to Reepecheep's cage, with his nose almost touching the glass, was Touchstone. He wore the same expression of absorbed expectancy that he puts on for the birds outside the kitchen window.

I shooed the cat away and dropped a handful of mouse pellets into Reepecheep's bowl. His tiny gray nose poked out of the cardboard toilet paper roll where he hides when anyone gets too close. As I made sure the lid was secure I felt a certain fellow feeling with the little guy. He carefully emerged from his hiding place and checked out the mouse pellets, then headed for his wheel, where he spends hours running in place as it turns. The cat loves to watch this performance. I wondered if Reepecheep felt about his spectator the way I felt about Jorgensen. No wonder he ran so hard.

Thursday morning was Christmas Eve.

"I've got a surprise for you," Peter said at breakfast.

"Oh good, an early present," I said, though in truth I had not a shred of Christmas spirit in my body.

"Pack your hiking duds and a nice dress. We are going away for Christmas."

Away. That sounded good. Very good. "Might I ask where?"

"You can ask, I won't tell. But you'll need warm outdoor clothes and a nice dress for dinner. Two dresses if you like. One for tonight, one for tomorrow. That's all I'm going to tell you."

The prospect of getting out of town lifted my spirits considerably, and I was in a better mood than I'd been for many weeks when we climbed into the car that afternoon. I realized later that I'd been so excited I hadn't checked to make sure we weren't being followed. I hoped Peter had been more careful, but I couldn't bring myself to ask.

We drove north across the Golden Gate Bridge through Marin County. Heavy dark clouds sailed in from the west; their shadows trailing over the land. The hills were a lush, young green, softly fuzzy with new grass. Vivaldi played on the radio, a fitting sound track for the drive.

When Peter turned west, I knew we were headed for the

coast. The drive along the Russian River through Guerneville is one of my favorites. His, too. He put on a tape of *Workingman's Dead* and we sang along.

We reached the ocean at Jenner before sunset. By now the sky was dark with clouds and a heavy fog bank sat offshore, ready to sweep inland. We raced it as we drove north, until Peter pulled off on a dirt road with a wooden sign advertising The Sea Wind Inn.

The inn was a rustic wooden structure set on the bluff over the ocean, and the fog was rapidly closing in on it. The wind whipped our hair and clothes as we hurried to the entrance. Inside, a fire blazed in a huge stone fireplace and great panes of glass framed the view to the west. The fog had reached us, and it pressed against the windows like a murky gray liquid, giving the room the feeling of a giant fishbowl.

Our room had a fireplace, a balcony, and a bottle of chilled Chardonnay. We lit the fire and started on the wine but got distracted, maybe because I was taking Peter's clothes off.

It was dark when we woke up. Peter opted for the first shower and I poured another glass of wine. But with him gone the room was suddenly too warm, too small. I pulled on my jeans and sweater, slipped my feet into my shoes, then opened the sliding glass door and stepped out onto the balcony. Cold wind struck me in the face and cut through my clothes. Somewhere, far below, I could hear the surf.

I stood in the wind for a few minutes, feeling the damp sea air on my skin. I should have been cold, but I was only dimly aware of the chill; instead I felt exhilarated, alive in a way I hadn't been for months.

The longer I stood in the wind, the more restless I became. To go back into the closed room or down into the dining room full of people seemed unbearable. I needed to be alone, really alone. I stepped back into the room and was relieved to hear the water still running in the shower. I scribbled a quick note to Peter, grabbed my jacket and my flashlight, and fled.

At the bottom of the stairs I turned left away from the lobby and headed down a hall that led to a side entrance. Outside the glass door, pole lamps dropped cones of yellow light on a grassy area. Fog swept by in wispy sheets.

I stepped outside and into the wind and the wildness of the night. Down here I could no longer hear the sea; instead the wind roared in the trees. It struck me full force as I walked onto the grass, away from the protection of the building.

I knew it was crazy to be out here alone. I couldn't be sure we hadn't been followed. But I simply didn't care anymore. I crossed the grass and headed for the path beyond.

The path led along the bluff above the ocean, then down the steep gully to the beach. It was narrow, in places wild grasses and stunted, twisted brush almost swallowed it. The fog swirled through the beam of my flashlight, creating a moving presence in front of me.

The trail was steep and switched back sharply on itself at several points. Beneath me I could hear the surf. My foot slipped on loose rocks; I scrambled to stay upright. A fall on my bad shoulder could cost me a month's hard work.

The sound of the waves grew louder. They crashed against the rocks, but between the fog and the wind I couldn't be sure exactly where the sound was coming from. If someone were behind me on the trail, I probably wouldn't hear him.

The path grew steeper, and it was all I could do to keep my footing, but the surf was loud enough that the beach couldn't be far off. When the strong, briny smell of the sea filled my nostrils, I knew I was getting close.

I slid on a particularly steep section of trail and suddenly I was on sand. I'd reached the beach. I shut off my flashlight and walked toward the water, the sound of wind and waves filling my ears.

As I got closer I could distinguish the white foam of breaking waves against the blackness of sea and sky. A splash of white appeared, then shot out in a horizontal line, only to fade like the trail of a shooting star, followed by another unfolding line, and another.

The wind whistled around me, and I shivered inside my jacket. My ears, nose, and hands felt numb, but I preferred the cold in this wild place to the warmth of the lodge. The crash of the waves was both exciting and comforting.

I sank down on the sand. It was then that I heard what might have been the crash of brush behind me. I turned but couldn't see a thing. I considered switching the light on, but that would simply give away my position. So I waited and listened to the sound of my heart compete with the crash of waves.

Time stretched as I faced the trail and listened for every sound that might betray movement. I thought I heard loose rocks sliding, but I couldn't be sure. The wind seemed to grow louder, then it subsided for a few seconds, and I heard footsteps on the trail.

I was standing on open beach. I had no idea what was around me. There were rocks somewhere, but how close I had no idea. I moved sideways away from the trail. The sand cushioned my steps. It would do the same for my pursuer.

There were no more sounds from the trail. Had he reached the beach? I tried to tell myself that my follower might be simply another guest of the lodge enjoying an adventuresome Christmas Eve walk. But a guest would have used a flashlight. The person following me did not want to be seen.

I waited. Still no sound but wind and surf. Then a beam of light swept the sand in front of me. I backed away but not fast enough. The next sweep caught me at the knees. The light stopped and moved up my body, then past me to one side and back again to the other.

"Catherine." It was Peter's voice. Relief flooded through me and made my knees week.

He ran toward me, the light still in my eyes and grabbed me so tight that he hurt my shoulder. He crushed me against his chest, and I could feel his heart and hear him gulp in air. I had to stifle the impulse to fight against him.

I was gasping for breath by the time he loosened his grip. I pulled back a bit and he tightened his grip on my shoulders, making me wince. "What the hell do you think you were doing," he shouted. "This is the craziest, stupidest stunt. . . . What if he'd followed us? Or found out where we were going? How the hell . . . ?"

"You're hurting my shoulder," I shouted.

"I ought to break your neck," he yelled back, not loosening his grip.

"Peter, let go," I shouted.

"Did you want to get killed?" He was still shouting, and he hadn't loosened his grip in the least. I felt a quick stab of fear. He was so angry he wasn't aware of how hard he was holding me. I'd never seen him like this before.

I didn't want to throw him, and I couldn't risk doing nothing, so I let myself go limp in his arms. Left supporting the full weight of my body, he was pulled off balance and we both went down on the sand.

I rolled free of him. He didn't grab for me again. I switched my light on. He was in front of me and his face was twisted in pain. Now I moved toward him and wrapped him in my arms. As I held him I realized he was crying.

We clung to each other for a long time. I realized that the salt on my face was from my own tears. By the time we got to our feet we were both spent. We climbed the path to the lodge in silence.

Back in the room we sat in front of the fire for a long time. Peter had retreated behind a wall of silence. Finally, I said, "I'm sorry. Sorry I scared you, sorry for all I've put you through."

He looked up slowly. He looked older and more tired than I'd ever seen him. "I know you hate having me always watching you. But how could you go off like that? Didn't you think what could happen?"

"I don't know," I said. "I just know I was suffocating. I had to get out."

"You couldn't wait for me?"

"I couldn't wait for anybody. I know it doesn't make any sense. This whole thing is making me crazy. I think maybe it's making you a little crazy, too."

He nodded. "A lot crazy. When I got out of the shower and found your note . . . And then when your light went out on the beach. I thought for sure he'd gotten you."

"I'm sorry," I said. "I didn't mean to scare you." I could imagine how he must have felt, knew how I'd have felt in his place, and it made me guilty as hell. "He's really got us, hasn't he? We can't go on like this."

"We don't have much choice," Peter said.

Christmas Day was sunny and bright, a postcard kind of day. We got up early for a walk and went down to the beach. Though we walked the same path, nothing about it was familiar. It was almost as if the wild night before weren't real. But the hangover from it was, and the bright sun wasn't enough to lighten our dark mood.

The sea was different, too. Calmer. Now the surf rose and broke rhythmically, its foam hissing as it ran up onto the sand. Waves broke on the rocks down the beach and sent foam flying into the air where it hung for just an instant before falling back into the sea.

We sat and watched the ocean, and its healing power began to work, on me at least. Next to me, Peter sneezed and blew his nose. I realized that my nighttime walk had drawn him straight from a shower out into the cold wind. The perfect set up for a major cold. If we managed to survive as a couple, we'd laugh about it someday. But not soon.

Chapter

33

We stayed at the Sea Wind till Sunday and managed to patch things up. We took long walks by the ocean, spent lazy afternoons in our room, and rediscovered what it was that we enjoyed about each other. A sort of second honeymoon for the unmarried.

But as soon as we pulled up at the house on Sunday night, we were reminded of all we'd left behind. The evergreen wreath on our door had been replaced by one made from black crepe.

I tore it down and threw it in the trash, not even saving it for the cops. There wasn't anything they could do, anyway.

Peter maintains that sex heals and stress makes you sick. His theory was reinforced when his cold mushroomed into major nastiness less than twenty-four hours after we got home. Not a runny-nose-and-sneezes cold but headache, chills, sore throat, and a cough that kept both of us awake most of the night. The hardest part for me was playing the gracious nurse, because it was, after all, my fault.

By the second day we were both sure it was flu rather than a cold. I wanted him to go to the doctor, but Y chromosomes do not visit doctors for anything less than life-threatening conditions. So he stayed in bed and made us both miserable.

Jesse was ready to cancel his trip with Claire's parents, but I headed him off by getting Dan to promise to escort me to and from the office. I wasn't about to give Jesse an excuse to weasel out on the trip.

Dan suggested dinner Wednesday night as he drove me home. "Harman won't mind," he said.

Like hell, he wouldn't, I thought. Peter would regard it as a gross defection, especially given the genesis of his cold. I had penance to do; I understood that.

Peter looked marginally better when I got home, but he was still weak and he had a fever. He was bored and cranky. I felt really virtuous for not holding a pillow over his face.

The phone rang around eight-thirty. It was Tonia. "How are you?" I asked.

"I'm okay, I guess." Her voice said she wasn't. Not really. "Uh, could you come over? I'd like to talk. If you're free, I mean."

"I'm sort of tied up here," I said. "Peter has the flu. Why don't you come here?"

"I can't leave my mom tonight," she said.

I considered. Peter was in no shape to go with me, and I doubted that I could reach Dan. On the other hand, it probably wasn't a great idea to go over to Tonia's alone.

I thought of what Mike Silva had said about the difficulty of luring Jorgensen to act. Going to Tonia's alone was so obvious a setup that he'd smell a trap. Ironically, my most dangerous move was probably my safest. "Okay," I said. "I'll come over."

"Oh, thank you," Tonia said. The relief was evident in her voice.

Peter wanted to go along, of course. I was adamant. "You'd just make Tonia and her mother sick," I said. "And you'd get sicker yourself."

"It's too risky for you to go alone," he said.

"Actually, according to Mike Silva, that's probably the safest thing I could do." I explained what Silva had said about Jorgensen avoiding traps.

Peter wasn't convinced. He tried to argue, but in an argument a man who can barely walk to the kitchen is at a distinct disadvantage. Especially when talking brings on a coughing fit. I got him some water and left for Tonia's.

I parked right in front, and I have to admit it, I was jumpy as I walked to the front door. And grateful that she answered quickly.

The strain of the last months was taking its toll. Tonia looked tense and jittery when she opened the door. Too tense. There was something wrong.

"Come in," she said, stepping back. Behind her stood Frank McFadden wearing his perpetual smile and holding a gun.

It took a few seconds for me to take it all in, do the necessary calculations, and come up with the extremely unpleasant realization of just how wrong I'd been about this case.

"So glad you could join us," McFadden said. "Please do come in."

I didn't have a lot of choice. Confusion slows down reaction time, and I'd already lost the vital first seconds figuring out what was going on.

McFadden backed up and motioned us to follow. Tonia had a deer-in-the-headlights blankness to her, and she moved with a stiff, mechanical quality. She was clearly a victim rather than an accomplice, but that wasn't much comfort, since she didn't look like she'd do me any good in a showdown.

"Tonia," I said, hoping to break through to her. "Are you okay?"

She burst into tears. "I'm sorry, Catherine. I didn't mean . . .
he made me. He said he'd kill my mother." Her eyes begged
for forgiveness. I knew he'd kill her mother, anyway, and she
must, too, but she couldn't let herself accept it.

"Sit," McFadden said. I made a quick survey and chose a
straight chair with a caned seat, one I could get up from quickly if I had the chance. I should have been terrified, but I wasn't.
Instead I felt a strange detachment. I'd spent so much time
thinking about Scott Jorgensen. All that emotion hadn't yet
transferred to Frank McFadden.

"So it was you all along," I said. "It wasn't Jorgensen at all."

"Oh, the warehouse scheme was Scott's. And it was Scott
who so conveniently turned off the alarm. But the rest was
mine." He looked incredibly pleased with himself.

"And I'd have to guess that he's probably at the bottom of
the bay someplace."

McFadden nodded. "Fish food," he said. "It all worked out
even better than I had planned. I thought I'd have to disappear
after I killed you, but now I can stay. It's been such fun watching you all scurry around to stay ahead of a dead man."

The perpetual smile was broader, almost a leer. The gun
looked real, and he had a silencer on it, which meant he
wouldn't have to worry about the sound of a shot alerting the
neighbors. Still, I knew he wouldn't use the gun unless I forced
him to. That wasn't his fantasy. And he wouldn't move fast. I
could probably play for time.

This was Mr. Show-and-Tell; keeping him talking shouldn't
be too big a problem. "What did you do to Sheila?" I asked.

"Oh, you'll find out soon enough. I'll show you." The smile
became nastier.

"But why Sheila? Just because she got a promotion you
wanted?"

"Oh no. Not because of the promotion," he said. "You see,
Sheila and I go way back. Back to her first job, in fact. When

she was a spunky little programmer like little Tonia here. Only Sheila was a bitch even then."

I remembered what Sheila's sister had told me, how she'd been seduced and later raped by a coworker. The story had made me furious; now it gave me a sick feeling. "You and Sheila dated?" I asked.

"Oh yes. And she was just as sweet as honey for the first month or so. You women are so good at that, at making a man believe you think he's the greatest thing alive." Anger crept into his voice and twisted his smile. "She acted real proper, but she was a slut. A few nice words, and she hopped right into bed. Just like you, Tonia."

Tonia began to cry harder. She buried her head in her hands as if to blot out the ugly words. McFadden turned his attention back to me.

"She couldn't get enough of me," he bragged. "So grateful and anxious to please. But then she changed. Oh, she still liked the sex, but she started talking back, contradicting me, arguing. She'd do it at work, too, argue with me right in front of other people. So I had to teach her a lesson. Put her in her place."

"You raped her," I said.

"I showed her who was boss."

"And she quit her job and left town," I said, taking up the story.

"They always did."

"There were others?" I asked, then I thought, of course there were. There had to be.

"You're all the same," he said. "You smile and flatter, but underneath you're just playing games. Well, two can play those games, you know."

He rambled on, cataloging the evils of women. I pretended to listen, but I was thinking of all the young women he'd dated, then attacked. He was nice-looking, could be charming. They'd fall for him, flatter him, and act submissive the way they assumed a woman should; then at some point they'd begin to assert their own personalities. They'd want a turn in the relationship, and he'd show them who was boss.

I could hear Tonia weeping softly. My heart went out to her.

McFadden's voice was rising. His litany of complaints was stoking the deep anger that burned inside. I tried to distract him. "But then you transferred to the San Francisco office, and Sheila was already there," I said. "And this time she was the boss."

"The bitch," he said. "She hated me. She was a ball-buster, just like you. She made my life hell."

It must have been sweet revenge for Sheila to have McFadden in that position. I had no doubt that she'd twisted the screw whenever she got the chance.

"She gave me the worst accounts," he said. "And she didn't miss a chance to put me down or humiliate me. She'd call me into her office and tell me what I could and couldn't do. She was on me every minute."

I didn't remember Sheila being particularly hard on McFadden, but reality probably didn't count for a lot with him. He was too deep in his fantasy world. "She gave you orders?" I asked.

"She watched me like a hawk. Every time I smiled at a woman, she warned me off."

I was beginning to get the picture. "And with Tonia?"

"I figured she wouldn't know what was going on down on the second floor, but little Tonia and Sheila were buddies. The bitch called me in and read me the riot act, said she'd get me fired if I so much as smiled at Tonia again."

"So you killed her," I said.

"I did what a lot of guys wanted to do," he said. "They all acted shocked and sad, but they'd have loved to be the one to do it."

That little piece of projection caught me by surprise. I must have let my incredulity show.

"And they felt the same way about you," he said. The smile broadened. "Figured what you two needed was a good fuck."

I could hear DeMarco or Kingsley say that—locker-room talk, male-bonding machismo. To a psycho like McFadden, it was confirmation of his own twisted fantasies.

He was getting warmed up now. An ugly excitement grew in his voice as he began to describe exactly what he'd done to Sheila. I couldn't afford to listen, just as I couldn't afford to think of what he had in mind for me. Instead I checked out the room. With a weak right arm, I'd need to control the situation. To set up the attack. The gun and Tonia being there complicated things. But knowing what he was planning made some things easier.

He was into control, liked to tie women up. He was working his way toward that. I needed to take him out before he got there.

There was nothing I could do as long as he was across the room. I needed to draw him to me, to pull him into range.

I could play into his fantasy—weep and beg, dissolve into hysterics so completely that he'd have to slap me to regain control. Or I could play counter. I could challenge him, goad him to rage so strong that he'd want to strike me.

Hysterics was risky. For months I'd fought against the very emotions that such a performance would require. It was too close to reality to take the chance.

That left rage.

Chapter

34

"You're a real piece of work, McFadden," I said. "Raping young girls, killing Sheila. A real tough guy." I put every bit of contempt that I felt into the words.

McFadden seemed taken aback.

"I'll bet you were one of those wimpy little boys who loved to beat up younger kids."

He reddened. As I expected, he hated being put down, especially by someone who was supposed to be terrified. But he still wasn't moving. I pushed harder.

"They say men who like big guns have small dicks. Does your gun make you feel powerful?"

"Bitch," he snarled. "I'll make you so sorry. I'll . . ."

"You'll what? Shoot me? Hit me with your big gun? I'm terrified."

He jumped up and charged at me. His face was almost purple. He kept the gun pointed at the center of my chest as he raised his other hand to hit me.

I threw myself to the side and slammed my left palm against his gun hand, knocking it away from me to the right. My fingers curled around his hand just below the thumb, and my own thumb dug into the middle of the back of his hand. I stood and put the full force of my body against the wrist as I twisted it back on itself and dumped him on his head.

I kept hold of the hand and pulled the gun from it, then stepped away from him.

"Don't move," I said. "Not even a little bit." It didn't look as though I needed to warn him, he was too dazed and shaken by the fall to be much trouble.

Tonia came to life at that point. "My mother," she cried. "He locked her in the closet. Oh God, I hope she's all right."

She ran out of the room and I could hear voices a minute or so later, then weeping. Tonia came back eventually, "I told her not to come in here," she said. "She was pretty scared, but I think she'll be all right."

McFadden was holding his wrist and moaning. He looked pretty out of it, but I wasn't about to take any chances with him. On the floor beside his chair was a large paper sack. I figured he'd have brought rope with him, so I checked it.

I was right. He had brought rope. And other things.

I handed Tonia the gun, showing her how to hold it with her finger on the trigger, using her left hand to support her right. "Hold this on him," I said. "I'll tie him up."

She took the gun and kept it pointed at his chest. "Are you okay?" I asked.

"Yes," she said, never taking her eyes off of him. "Yes, I'm okay."

I turned away to get the rope and there was a popping sound. I spun around to see Tonia, eyes wide, holding the gun, and McFadden on his face on the floor.

"He moved. Oh God, he moved, and I . . . Is he dead?"

I didn't know, and I wasn't going to risk turning him over. He might not be as seriously injured as he looked. "Call nine-one-one," I said.

"He cut the phone line."

"Go next door, then." I tried to keep my voice calm. "And come right back here afterward. Understand?"

She handed me the gun and ran for the door. I watched McFadden. A dark circle of blood was already spreading beneath him. He was probably bleeding to death.

I might have been able to stop it, but I couldn't bring myself to touch him. It wasn't that I wanted to kill him. I just didn't want to touch him.

I wondered about Tonia. Had McFadden really moved? Or had her own emotions gotten the better of her? It didn't really matter. I'd go over the story with her, make sure it went down as self-defense. Because even if he hadn't moved, that's what it was.

He was dead by the time the medics got there. They told me that the bullet had hit an artery, and there wasn't anything I could have done to save him. I was glad to hear it, though it didn't change the fact that I hadn't tried.

Tonia and I told our story to the police about a dozen times. Even the uniforms were sympathetic. If they had any question about the veracity of our story, they never showed it.

Dan was on call, so he was the one who caught the case. He was so coolly professional you'd never have guessed we'd once been married. But as soon as we were alone in the kitchen, he gave me hell for coming to Tonia's alone.

"And suppose you or Peter had been with me," I said. "What do you think would have happened? He'd have shot you. That's what he was planning to do. You'd be dead, and I'd have been in the same mess I was in, anyway."

That didn't slow him down much, though there was no doubt in my mind that it was exactly the way it would have gone down. And I doubted that I could have kept such a clear head with Dan or Peter bleeding to death on the floor.

"Just this once couldn't you give me credit for pulling something off?" I said. "Do you always have to yell at me?"

He started to say something, then he stopped. "Okay," he said. "You done good. I'm glad you pulled it off."

I gave him a big hug. It lasted a bit too long, and we were both a little red-faced when I pulled away.

He cleared his throat and gave me a big smile. He seemed suddenly very pleased about something. "And anyway, I'm sure that Harman and Jesse will have plenty to say when they hear about this," he said.

I groaned. He was right, of course. First, my lover would yell at me, then my partner would yell at me, and probably my father would finish the job. I gave Dan a big smile that confused the hell out of him.

It was nice to be loved by four good men.